Nobody's Son

Also by Sean Stewart

Nobody's Son

SEAN STEWART

Magic Carpet Books
Harcourt, Inc.
San Diego   New York   London

First Magic Carpet Books edition 2000
First published by Maxwell Macmillan Canada 1993

Magic Carpet Books is a registered trademark of Harcourt, Inc.

Library of Congress Cataloging-in-Publication Data
Stewart, Sean.
Nobody's son/Sean Stewart.
p.   cm.
"Magic Carpet Books."
Summary: After breaking a curse that has troubled the kingdom
for years, Shielder's Mark is rewarded with the hand of a
princess only to find married life to be as difficult as any
magical foe he's ever faced.
[1. Fantasy.]   I. Title.
PZ7.S84987No   2000
[Fic]—dc21   99-54324
ISBN 0-15-202259-7

HGFEDCBA
Printed in the United States of America

For Kay, Christine, Cait
—mother, wife, daughter—
this book about fathers and husbands and sons

Nobody's
Son

The Red Keep

Memories haunted the Ghostwood, brittle as the twigs that splintered like tiny bones under Mark's boots. Sifting through drooping cedar boughs, the old wind muttered of things that waited in darkness without hope. To every question the Ghostwood had but one answer, made from sorrow, and loneliness, and time.

Shielder's Mark followed a stream into the Forest, whistling a cheery tune and thinking, *God, what a bloody dismal place. Only an idiot would come here on purpose. An idiot with ambition*, he corrected himself wryly. *An idiot who means to collect on the King's promise to grant one wish—any wish—to the man who breaks the Ghostwood's spell. Just because practically every hero since Duke Aron has failed to survive the Wood, that's no reason to be scared.* "That's a reason to bloody panic," Mark growled to himself.

Sure, they were heroes: but could they shear a sheep, or shoe a horse, or mend a fence with a loop of haywire? No doubt a village handyjack has a thousand tricks that would put those famous duelists and adventurers to shame.

Right.

Somehow, this had all seemed a good deal less stupid before Mark had actually entered the Ghostwood.

From time to time the Forest's desolation would run into his limbs like water, and he would have to stop, and spit a long carpenter's spit. *You've nowt to go back to, last and least of heroes*, he would remind himself. *So you might as well go on.*

All his life Mark had longed to seek his greatness in the Ghostwood. His father had abandoned him when he was only a boy. When his mother died, early in the spring of his twenty-first year, he left his home and set out for the haunted Forest. He left his hammer to the cooper, his spare clothes to the miller's son, his mother's grave to the grass and the rain.

He tried to leave his childhood too, but that came after him. Dreaming of fame to come, Mark never looked back; never saw his childhood following behind, cool and dark and vague as a shadow.

It was a hard scramble following the stream into the Ghostwood. After hours of sloshing through eddies and jumping from rock to rock in the channel, Mark suddenly stopped, heart pounding, and stared at a boot cradled in the grasp of a willow root. It had been a proud boot once, fit to grace a gentleman.

Little now remained but tattered pieces of tooled leather, spotted here and there with rust where once a button or a buckle gleamed. *Must have tumbled downward from the Red Keep and gotten snagged.*

Shite.

At the sight of something which had once touched human life, the vague dread of the Ghostwood hardened into panic in Mark's chest. *Probably came off some poor bastard who went to break the spell. Nails to nuts that's you in two days, my friend.*

O god.

O god.

Well don't just stand there staring, you silly bugger. Get on, get on with it!

He spat and scrambled on without looking back.

When some hours later he saw the second boot, wedged between two rocks and half-buried under dead leaves, he felt a different, deeper kind of dread, the kind you feel when faced with the impossible. The second boot was the mate of the first, no question: but it was whole. Worn, but whole.

How the hell! T'other one's been through a hundred years, but this. . . . A buckle, only slightly tarnished, clinked against Mark's sword blade as he brushed away the coverlet of leaves. He'd never heard a lonelier sound. *My god,* he thought: *T'awd stories are true!* Two boots, one old, one young. *You're walking back through time, lad. Back through time!*

He swore and leapt away. He couldn't pretend this was normal any more. He bolted forward, splashing wildly through the stream, jumping from rock to rock or floundering through the freezing water until exhaustion finally drowned his fear. Then he slowed, trudging forward into the Forest's dark heart, feeling himself dwindle like a match falling into a well endlessly deep. For the first time in his life he wished he believed in God.

Hours passed as he hacked his way through ranks of pine boughs. *Bastard way to treat good steel,* he thought ruefully. He wiped off his sword as best he could, but the blade was still sticky with pine-sap when he gave up and stuck it back into its sheath.

And then, a little miracle: a path began to grow from nowhere, a hollow tunnel through the Wood. *Well, that's the worst behind you,* he thought.

And with every step, the shadow of his past streamed out longer and darker at his back.

The stories said there was a Tower at the centre of the Wood, guarded by terrors. Mark had brought his sword, and a set of iron climbing spikes: he figured he had a damn sight better chance of scaling the Tower wall than he had of battling past guardians that had proved too awful for any of the great heroes to defeat.

He walked for a long time while the dirt path got broader and cleaner. Gloomy cedars drooped around him, and chambers of pine, quiet and dusty as cathedrals; as full of death and long silence. At length these gave way to other trees, elms and poplars and muttering oaks. As he travelled back through time, white paving stones erupted from the earth and knit themselves together into a road. But the better the path became, the harder Mark found the walking. He strode through years drifted like withered leaves, rustling around his ankles, his knees, his hips: wading with every step through uncounted empty days. At last he could think of nothing but grief, age, death, abandonment, hollowness, desolation.

"Shite!" *The King can pay a Keep for this: nowt less.*

Think! Think about summat. . . . Twenty servants, then, the King can give you; a stable too, and canty livery. Summat smart, as a man would feel proud to wear. Blue and silver maybe: but soldierlike, not just flashy.

How long had he been walking in the Wood?

One day?

Three?

Five?

It was twilight now, but he couldn't remember when last he'd seen the sun.

The path was paved with flagstones of white marble, gleaming under a ghostly grey tunnel made by an aisle of oaks. Farther on, an orchard of cherry trees whispered with the breeze, their tops a foam of pink blossom.

And beyond that, above a wide moat, stood the haunted

Keep and its Tower, built of red granite. *The Tower*. Mark shivered with wonder. *Tales around that spire like red wool wound around a spindle. Break the spell here and be famous for life. Forever! Shielder's Mark, greatest of champions. Father of a proud line.*

Firelight winked close by, fierce as lightning to Mark's nervous eyes. He smelt smoke on the air, and something else, like foul stew.

There: there it was again, another yellow crack in the dusk, in the shadows by the road, perhaps twenty paces from where he stood. He peered into the darkness. At a place where the low limb of an oak thrust out level with the ground, someone had made a crude shelter, stacking cedar boughs to make a ramshackle lean-to.

Company in the Ghostwood! A warm fire, friendly stories, a meal and someone to share the dark watches of the night!

Mark trotted forward, faltered, stopped. *A fire? Here?* "Only madmen come here," he said to himself. "And ambitious idiots." He tugged out his sword. Where pine-sap had stained the blade it was tufted with sheep's-wool from his fleece-lined sheath.

Shite. Now don't you look ridiculous. He hovered, torn between caution and hunger, loneliness and plain fear.

Balls, boy. If you can't handle a blink of fire, how d'you think ye'll manage the Red Keep, eh? Shielder's Mark, hero of legend. Specialty: running away from things. You aren't standing here for caution's sake. You're soft as lead and yellow as goat's piss. What will you do, mama's boy? Wait for the sun because you daren't cross candlelight?

His fingers tightened around the pommel of his sword and he started forward.

High overhead the oaks whispered, swaying and lamenting, *all gone, all gone*. Around the Red Tower, memories crowded thick as moths around a candle flame.

A huge black squirrel, the size of a big cat, padded from the lean-to and hunkered back on its haunches, looking Mark over. Its black eyes gleamed like polished pebbles. A moment later, an old woman followed it. "Well an' well! Come, Shade: look at what jetsam the dark hath stranded on our shore."

Mark blinked. "Best o' the night to you, awd Mother," he said uncertainly.

"I did not crack for tha to flower from my nut," the old woman said tartly. "Am no man's mother now, boy."

O lord. The old woman's accent was thick as cream and queer as a lead nail. Mark wasn't sure what she'd said, but he got the idea he wasn't supposed to call her Mother.

Easy enough. He looked at the old crone and suppressed a shudder. She was short and thin-boned as a squirrel herself; her black eyes glittered in her pinched face. Once her dress had been rich and proud with braid, but now it was tatters of coal-coloured cloth; her long grey hair was wrapped in a rag of satin.

She was mantled in a fine man's cloak, twice her size, closed with three mismatched clasps. She wore a broad-headed signet ring on each thumb, one marked with the impress of a star, the other with a swan. A crude wooden charm dangled from her neck, hanging from a thread of cedar bark. At her hip hung a duster made from squirrel-tails.

"Art tha moon-mad or mazed, to stand gawping at my door?" the old woman demanded. "Come in, come, boy: I'll have you for dinner."

Mark gulped. "Dinner in me, were that, or me in dinner?"

The old woman cackled and reached out to fluff him with her squirrel-tail duster. "She were not such a scathesome

hag as *that!*" She smiled with small yellow teeth and held
out an acorn. "Oak-egg?"

Thrown by the old woman's firelight, Mark's shadow
trembled behind him like a frightened boy as he hastily
shook his head. Many times had he taken his mother's pigs
into the wood and knocked down acorns to fatten them for
All Hallows. He had no wish to be fattened for the slaughter
himself. A score of witchtales flooded back to him.

He found his hand on his dagger hilt; then slowly took it
off. *Heroes don't stab mad awd women,* he told himself
sternly. *At least, not without a good reason.*

"What's tha clept, boy?"

Mark blinked. "Er, what was that?"

The old woman pursed her thin lips and spat in annoyance. "John? Jack? Ven? Perse? Bill? What's tha clept?"

"Oh!" The light dawned. "Uh, Shielder's Mark. Mark.
And you?"

The old woman sighed. "No easy telling, boy: no easy
tale. I buried my name under a bush and ne'er could find it
more. 'Tis better so, in sooth," she whispered. "Names as
mine are better underground." Her loneliness pierced Mark
like a spear; it seemed as if all the Ghostwood lingered in
her withered frame, everything lost and alone.

Moodily the old woman shook her head. "Tha must clepe
me Husk, as Shade does," she said, nodding at the huge
black squirrel. She flicked her duster at Mark's sword.
"Tha'lt be going to try thy luck at Red Keep."

He nodded.

Husk glanced back at the Tower, her eyes mazy with
hatred and old longing. "Well an' well. I've some speaking
as tha might need to hear, if ye'll be going yonder. But 'tis
my fancy to ask all the fine stallions to take a small fence
afore I give 'em oats—dost tha follow?"

Mark spat, a long working man's spit. "I have to pass a test before ye'll tell me about the Red Keep.—Right?"

"Aye."

"What happens if I don't take it?"

A crinkle of sly crow-footed eyes. "Nought, nought. 'Tis ony if ye care what sooth an old hag might speak, who's waned beneath yonder Tower for a moon's age."

Mark grunted. "Well, set me the task, and I'll do my best."

The old woman hissed, pleased. At her feet, Shade studied Mark with glittering black eyes. "See tha yon oak tree?" the old crone asked. "Each dark I watch the Scarlet Tower gore the dying moon, sitha, but now that oak hath swole and blocked my seeing; stars wiggle fishwise in its twig-nets. If tha were to move that oak-tree from my way, I'd thank tha."

Mark took a long, careful look. The oak in Husk's way must have been sixty years old at least, tall and smooth-limbed and strong.

He had a tinderbox to work with, a lead pencil and a sturdy knife, a hank of string and a twist of haywire that he kept always in his pocket. "An I had a magic sword I could fell it with a single stroke," he murmured.

"Oh aye. Fhilip Four-fingers went that way."

Mark shot the old woman a glance. "You really saw him?"

"All, my chick, all of them."

Mark grunted. "If I were giant I could pull the damn tree over."

"Sir Veramos did; caught splinters in his eyes and never saw the sun again."

Mark studied the oak up close, thoughtfully fingering his tinderbox.

"No fire," the old woman called, as if reading his

thoughts. "Too easy for it to run thruff the trees and gobble up my orchard."

Scratch the tinderbox. A long coil of rope filled half Mark's pack, along with his climbing spikes. Maybe he could use the rope to saw through the oak? Or ring it with spikes and then, and then. . . . *Shite.*

Mark spat reflectively. "An I had spade, I'd dig away at base until the bloody thing fell ower on its own."

Husk nodded. "Aye. Tine Silverhand took it so. Brought a pick for to mole beneath the Red Keep's walls."

"But I don't have a bloody pick," Mark growled. Oh, he was stupid, he was stupid. He'd spent all his life smithing himself into a blade with a single purpose, to storm the Red Keep. Was he to blunt against the first piece of wood that got in his way?

Steady on. Your temper was never your best friend, Shielder's Mark. There's a way through. There's a way through, if only you can see it.

A sharp eye cuts neater than a mail fist.

You've no magic sword, no giant's arm, no pack of tools; so you'd better use your brain. If you don't know the answer then change the question. That's your manner, Shielder's Mark. If the snake's head is slick then grab its tail. . . . Ah!

Aaaaaah. T'awd woman gives the test to every passing Hero: but the tree's still here!

Quickly Mark peered into the twilight. Sure enough, not ten paces away he saw a stump littered with woodchips.

Grinning, Mark ambled back to the old woman. "Grand news, awd Husk! You'll have a fine sight o' moon tonight." He bowed as best he knew how, reached down, and picked up the cedar branch that made the left half of her doorway.

Because of course Husk had to set the test up new for

each hero. There had to be some way *she* could solve the puzzle. And that was to move the hut, not the tree!

Well pleased with his own cleverness, Mark started rebuilding Husk's hovel against the limb of a different oak. *By the Devil's scratchy drawers, you'll make a hero yet, Shielder Mark!*

The old woman cackled too, and ruffled his hair with her bony fingers. "Mayhap tha'lt stay a stranger to worm guts for a little, boy, an' a little yet."

She asked him in, after he'd dug a new firepit and remade her walls. Her hovel swarmed with squirrels. Two crouching squirrels in the middle of the tiny room stared greedily up at five dead fish, blind and stinking, that swung on strings tied to the oak branch that served as a roof-beam. The great black squirrel, Shade, eyed Mark coolly from between Husk's legs.

From the roof-beam Husk had also hung a score of medallions like the one she wore around her neck: chips of wood carved with a crude pattern, a snake eating its own tail. In the corner of the hut were baskets lashed from willow-wands, filled with acorns, sloes, and goosegrass. Husk nursed a reeking stew in a small black pot above the fire; the pot might once have been a knight's helm.

Mark thought uneasily of Husk's borrowed cloak, its three different brooches, her pair of mismatched signet rings. "What happened to the men who didn't pass your test?"

Husk stroked Shade tenderly on the flank. "Why we et them, Shielder's Mark. If a gallant fails an old crone's test, I wis he weren't likely to conquer the Keep! And waste's a sin, tha knows."

Mark gulped. Beside him, the pot that might have been a helmet slurped and burbled to itself. The old woman's eyes glinted over the squirrels that seethed around her. "Dinner, dinner, dinner," she muttered. She squinted at squirrels by the grate, in the thatch, slumbering by her skinny thighs. "We know a wench as failed her mistress, eh, Henrietta?" she murmured, staring at a plump brown squirrel that backed nervously toward the doorway. Husk crept slowly after, crab-stiff and softly crooning. "Thine furry thighs so glossy, eh? Thy cheek so silk. Enspelled by thy own face in the pond, is it? Stuffed with thy own prettiness like a tick full to bursting. Tha'lt be sorry now, won't tha lass?"

"Please!—Let me help," Mark said quickly. O god: Henrietta stew. "I've cheese in my pack, and bread, and a bit of smoked pig." Come to think of it, he'd feel safer eating his own food anyway. "I can't pay much for my dinner, milady. Take this and make my heart easy."

Husk looked him over as he rummaged in his pack. "A smooth tongue in a rough face, i' sooth!" Her curtsey as she spoke was deep and strangely graceful; an echo from some gentler life.

Mark sighed with relief. *Shielder's Mark: squirrel-saver. The legend begins.*

Old Husk smiled at him her haggish benediction. "A forest-full of gentles have I known, most with more good i' their faces and less in their hearts. But art tha not cloddish, i' sooth?"

"Er, what?"

"Base! Churlish! Low!"

"Oh. Am I common?—As dirt," Mark said with a grin.

"Not yet too fine to break bread with a toothless mazed old bitch, eh? Not like Serimus nor Flavian nor Stargad the Shrewd. Him I remember, crouched like a silk-swaddled toad afore my lintel thruff the whole night, and then sidles by at noon."

"You—you met Stargad? But that must have been halfway back to grandfather days!"

Husk plucked Mark's knife from his belt and began shaving slices of pig into the stewpot. "Time, tha knows: time's foxy in the Wood. They all come by here, this Kingdom's heroes: brave-braided all, with their medals bouncing to heartdrums' beat." She grinned at Mark. "Where are thy ribbands and favours, boy? What hast tha done that harpers sing? Cracked a kingdom? Drank dragon-blood?"

"Uh, not exactly," Mark admitted.

"Climbed a mountain's sun-spiring snowpeak?"

"I don't think so."

"Arm-wrestled oliphaunt?"

"No."

"Diced with the Devil on a throw of bones?"

Mark shook his head. "Not as such."

Husk glared at him. "Were ye nought then but breathing? Dost tha come armoured in air and girt with hoping?"

"That's me." Mark fished a hank of haywire from his pocket to fiddle with, unable to meet Husk's eyes. *T'awd bitch is right. How can you expect to win where all the real heroes lost?*

Shade jumped up to Husk's shoulder. Crone and creature gazed at Mark without enthusiasm. "Shade, Shade, Shade," Husk muttered. She cut up the last of the smoked pig. "An hundred hundred nights and weeks and years I've waned beneath yonder Tower, boy. My weft is ravelled and ony warp's left. But still I know the Red Keep is perilous; spell-webbed, fear-fangled. Old nuts rot and nothing green grows up from them: magic has withered since grandfather days. You come with no spell sheaf, no flight of impossibles. Many mighty men that were flesh and fearless i' th' sun are clay now: their soul-pots cracked and ground to dust." Stroking Shade, Husk met his eyes. "What can tha do that they could not?"

How many times had Mark asked himself the same question? "Maybe I can't. Maybe I'll die." He twisted the haywire between his fingers, then stuffed it abruptly back in his pocket. "I go because I must. This is what has been given to me. This is my only gift. I am no general, no lover, no wizard nor duelist, no hero nor thief. I am only Shielder's Mark, who waited all his life to go to the Ghostwood, and went."

Mark fell silent. The stewpot bubbled above the small yellow fire. Beside his boot, squirrel-pups mewled at their dozing mother's side. Shade's tail swished across Husk's face and the old woman sneezed. Then she laughed. "Better to go with fate than wisdom. Odds be, tha'lt die with a shriek in thy throat, but perhaps not. Still, tha must be shrewd!" She dumped a ladle-full of stew into a wooden bowl. "Bend ear a while, and hear an old owl's screeching."

"Gladly," Mark said. "Tell me about Stargad!" The favourite stories of Mark's boyhood had been about Stargad. Not so much the later triumphs, but the early days, learning bladework under his uncle's stern, fair eye. Earning at last the famous sword that perished with him in the Ghostwood. "Did he have Sweetness? Did it sing, like the old stories say?"

"Not singing, exactly: more whizzling, windsome: reed-hollow. Witched the ear and made the heart drunk with a cider oozed from emptiness."

Mark glanced down at the sword belted at his hip. An excellent blade, won on a bet from a travelling duelist. But what was it, compared to Invincible, or Scalpel, or Sweetness?

A name, Mark thought for the thousandth time. He needed a name for his sword. Protector? Valiant? Victor? But who wanted to be less valiant than his weapon? He imagined introducing himself: "Shielder's Mark, good sir! And this is . . . *Victor!*"—Baring his scabbard with a swirl of cloak.

Folk would think you mad.

He tried to get Husk to tell him of the Red Keep, but she would only warn him not to stay longer than a day, then ask him of the outside world, for she was parched with a thirst only his tales of farm-hands and dull everyday chores could slake.

Once she started up and touched his cheek, frowning. "Tha'rt like . . . I cannot filch it back to mind," she murmured. "Did thy father come thruff the Ghostwood, once upon a time?"

Sudden tightness clenched at Mark's heart. "My dad were too great a coward to stick by his wife and child; I doubt he came here," Mark said coldly.

The crone glanced at him with interest. "Aye . . . there's a coal that's not yet embered," she cackled. "But this is the Ghostwood, Shielder's Mark. Here thy shadow throws *tha*: feet run not to the light ahead, but from the dark behind." She barked again with laughter lean and tough as wire. "Well an' well, little clod: I did not mean to hurt tha." She laid a brittle hand on his arm. "A candle this night was, to an old hag drownt in shadows, Shielder's Mark. I have summat for tha, if tha'lt take it." From around her neck she took one of her wooden charms, pressing it into Mark's hands with her dry old fingers. "No longer do I understand the meaning in this wyrm," she said, tracing the pattern of the serpent with her fingers. "Mayhap 'twill serve tha for a luckpiece."

"You honour me," Mark said soberly. He lifted the loop of cedar bark and placed it around his neck. The charm he tucked beneath his shirt.

"Tha shalt come to the Tower soon, to the one black night in the heart of hell." Wearily Husk pointed to a place by the fire. "Lay thy head down, boy. Mayhap a sleep by my fire will do tha more good than any charm I give tha."

All traces of Husk's mad gaiety had fled. Mark felt cold and lonely and very small, not a hero at all: *A young bloody fool, pissing away his last living day with a pack of squirrels and a motherly madwoman.*

Once more Husk stared at him with strange, frustrated almost-recognition. "Cloud of blossoms, such thinkings are," she muttered. "The nightwind blows them all apart."

Under Shade's cool gaze Mark laid his pallet beside the embering fire and laid down his head. Squirrels squeaked and scratched around him. Far into his dreams their rustles followed him, and the sound of tiny claws.

He woke suddenly, gasping with fright, though he could not remember what had scared him. The fire was out. Husk and her squirrels were gone. He felt her talisman against his breastbone, a disc of carven cedar-wood beneath his shirt.

What could it mean? Who was the old woman draped in cloaks she had stolen from murdered heroes? Would her charm really prove lucky? He'd never believed in that sort of rubbish before: such old-wives' babble offended his common sense. *But then what use is common sense in this cursed Wood, that God has framed with a crooked hand?*

God or Duke Aron anyway. How did the awd bugger lay the ghosts to end the Time of Troubles? You'd think he might have left instructions for the rest of us luckless bastards.

He wondered uneasily if he would ever return to the time he knew. *Maybe t'other heroes got this far too: handled the quest and all, turned heels an' left the Ghostwood, only to find themselves—when? A world of winters gone, maybe;*

their kin nowt but a swirl of dust in the corners of an awd Keep.

He shuddered, then spat. *No fear, lad. You've no kin to worrit about you,* he thought grimly.

At least this was his hour: the dark before dawn. He'd lived years in this hour, teaching himself swordplay. Feinting, dodging, thrusting, cut and jump back, stumbling over molehills too small to see by moonlight, feeling his sweat turn cold as the dew on the stubbled fields. In this hour, while the rest of the village slept, he had hammered himself into the man who could dare the Red Keep.

And now the Keep was before him, a granite giant hunkered on the hillside beyond the moat. Around him stood a grove of cherry trees, their gnarled branches poxed with pale blossoms.

The moat itself was thirty paces wide and clotted with drifting petals. A clammy, sour-sweet odour rose from it. *Couldn't be a drawbridge to cross a pool that wide; must be a floating bridge, built in sections like the one down below the Mill at home. Pulled up on t'other side each night, no doubt.* By the light of the bright, thin moon he saw a white marble path leading from the water's edge to a small door in the Red Keep's outer wall.

Mark squatted and reached a finger toward the black water, but a sick dread came over him and he snatched back his hand. Something was waiting there, under the drifting blossoms. *That time they dredged Mad Tom up from the millpond, his patch-pockets full of stones.*

Water spilling from his slack mouth like a tipped canteen.

Mark shuddered and wiped his hands off on his pants. He swore softly to himself. This place was wrong, wrong as summer snow. *God, a manor seemed enow, before you came here, didn't it? But to walk through this horrible Wood is worth a barony at least. Two score servants, a stable and a*

pack of hounds with a sweet-toned bitch to lead the chase.
"All right," he whispered. "What's sowed is grown: now
comes the reaping." He would have to cross the moat, get
through the outer walls, scale the Tower, and—well, he
didn't know what would happen then. He would deal with
the Tower when the time came.

Strength on craft, craft on strength, he reminded himself.
*And if you're fighting fear? Jump in: water's cawdest before
you dive. Don't let the fear blunt you like a lead axe.*

Well and right. He could do that. Many a time he'd held
his fear like a frog caught in his clenched fist and refused to
let it loose. He was a master at controlling his own
weaknesses.

First he had to get across the water. He groped in his pack
until he found a sweet, withered apple and tossed it into the
moat. It fell with a thick plop. A moment later, a swell
heaved up the drifting cherry blossoms and rolled oozily
onto shore; Mark scrambled back before it touched his
boots. The mere sighed, a dank breath of rotting blossoms.

"Oh shite."

Quickly he started to his right, threading between the
cherry trees. *One chance,* he thought. *Just give me one piece
of luck now and I swear to do the rest.*

Luck was with him. On the bank he found a rowboat,
with two oars stored neatly inside.

He sighed with relief. . . .

. . . *Wait. Husk said lots of heroes had come this far. So
they must have wondered how to get across the moat.
Maybe some poor bastards tried to swim—uggh!—but
surely others would have found this little tub and rowed
across. Yet no hero ever returned from the Red Keep. So
how came the boat to be back on this side?*

Mark swallowed, thinking of the apple he had tossed in,
the moat's dank sigh. Maybe nothing waited beneath the

sick black water of the mere: but he was taking the damn boat.

He studied it as best he could for leaks or snakes or spiders, then finally stepped into the bow, careful not to wet his boots in the dreadful mere, and sat down quickly as the little rowboat wobbled under him. Hunkered in the stern he planted both oars against the shore and shoved mightily, driving forward.

It was almost daybreak; a crimson light seemed to smoulder in the Red Keep, as if its stones were embers waiting to kindle at the sun's touch.

Mark's little boat glided bravely across the mere, cutting a dark wedge through the cherry blossoms. *Hello,* he thought, drifting into nightmare. *I'm back.* The red stone ahead, the weirdly glowing cherry blossoms, his own thick forearms that rested on the thwarts: he recognized them all, drifting into memory, visiting a place he'd lived in as a boy, but forgotten every morning when he woke. Once, when he was seven, he'd been lost here for many weeks, running a terrible fever, blind to daylight. I'm here again in dream-world, he thought, surprised. *This is where I went.* Behind his back his childhood shuddered like a shadow thrown from a growing flame.

He always thought he'd had a happy childhood, living with his Ma, but he had forgotten what the nights were like, forgotten the bitter world of dreams. Here everything was weightless and uncertain: a breeze could make his heart flutter like a leaf, could sculpt the granite Keep like a heavy crimson cloud.

His boat began to slow. The ripples spreading out from her bow were heavy and smooth. Reluctantly Mark unshipped his oars, held them high above the water, then suddenly brought them down and pulled with one powerful stroke.

Something caught on the right oar, skewing his course.

Cursing Mark jerked it free; from the corner of his eye he glimpsed something sliding off the blade, a pale blur like a clutching human hand.

He let himself drift. He had enough speed to make the far shore, and he didn't dare touch the thick black water again.

Apple falling as if in mud; slow heavy swell. A sigh of rotten flowers.

With a gentle bump he fetched up on the far bank. Stepping out he turned and looked back at the moat. His stomach felt cramped to the size of a walnut. He grinned tightly. He had solved Husk's riddle and crossed the dreadful water. "Ower two stiles and not even breathing hard," he murmured.

Well, actually your heart's hammering like a mad smith and your ears are pricked like a scared cat's: but then that's why the King is going to owe you a barony, ain't it?

Before him the greensward sloped twenty paces up to the Keep's outer wall, a great barrier of thick red granite blocks, close-mortared: a difficult climb, but not impossible. He had come a fair ways east of the white path. On his right, the Scarlet Tower rose into the night, jutting from the eastern wall like a bloody spearpoint. A thin quarter moon drifted overhead, a pink petal on dark blue water.

How did the boat get back to t'other shore?

Mark paused. Even if he broke the enchantment on the Keep, he'd have to return over the moat. He looked around, but saw no pontoons for a floating bridge. *Drawn up behind the walls no doubt; probably too heavy for you to muck wi' anyhow.*

His nerves screamed for speed, but instead he settled down to watch the rowboat, ready to grab it should it start to drift of its own accord.

A sudden tramp of footsteps came from behind the door at the top of the white path. Mark loped quickly into the shadows at the foot of the outer wall. A set of keys jingled, turned. The door opened and a flicker of rushlight leapt out.

Two men in livery walked through, carrying torches. Behind them came a great lady, swathed in black satin. She walked proudly, but her strong face was drawn with fear. Behind her, another liveried man swung the door shut. His sword was drawn.

Ghosts! Ghosts or devils or some damn thing you better hope doesn't notice you, Shielder's Mark.

Although . . . they look pretty solid, he thought, trying to ignore his racing pulse.

"Cursed scow's drifted again," one of the torch-bearers complained.

"Fetch it up, Donkle," said the man with the drawn sword.

"Safe passage." Even in fear the great lady's voice retained a tone of cold command. "The Prince my son hath bade tha make my passage safe, boy."

"Harler am I clept, milady, and a man. I am no woman's 'boy' any more," Drawn-sword answered softly.

The lady's hands twisted around a silk purse at her belt. "Gold have I, and silver too, and colour-glass to grace thy lady's throat. Thy heart's desire in gleam and gew-gaws have I, if you only set me free: I swear it. I'll make no trouble, cause no stir: marry, walk will I with spider's feet, and talk with fish's tongue."

Harler laughed unpleasantly. "Mice is ever kind to cat, milady. Thy son must also fear thy influence, should his father . . . pass away."

The Queen's eyes darted frantically around her, but there was no place to run. She drew in her breath as if to scream, but quick as thought Harler had his sword-point at her throat. "Tisn't dawn," he whispered. "No birds yet sing,

Majesty. Roost a while longer, or I'll put a last stop in thy flute."

The Queen turned, whispering fiercely at the other two men. "And ye? A second brace of cuckoos bent alike on killing the Queen who holds in bond thy honours and thy lives?" Donkle shrugged uneasily, dragging the boat over to where the others stood. The third guard smiled, drew his knife, and cut the silk purse from the Queen's belt.

"Art tha answered, i' faith?" Harler asked.

The Queen nodded, and her proud head faltered. "Answered, yea: but not in faith."

So the servants mean to slay their Queen, half for gain and half to protect her son. Does he mean to slay his father, the King? She's been a raspish mistress, you can bet: they took like rats turning on the crippled cat.

Still, can't hold wi' traitors, especially when they're about to filch your damn boat. Besides, a proper hero's always on the lady's side: let's see if we can't add a Queen to our list of rescued damsels, Mark thought, stealthily drawing another apple from his bag. *"One squirrel" hasn't much of a shine to it.*

He tossed the apple in a high arc toward the moat and waited for the thick splash. He rose as all three guards whirled to look into the water.

"What was that?" Donkle hissed.

"Nought!" Harler said. "Trout gawping at fly, belike."

"Well someone's caught a bug," Mark said pleasantly, nuzzling Harler's back with the point of his sword.

"Who i' the Devil art tha!" Donkle cried.

"My name is no job of yours; nor is the murder of your Queen."

"Slay me these traitors!" Her majesty commanded.

Softly Harler said, "I do not know your motives, pilgrim, but I wis tha'rt slow at reckoning. Three against one is long odds by any counting." The other two guards drew their swords.

"Two to one," Mark said tersely. "I'll stick you the moment one of your pigs puts out a trotter."

Harler nodded. "Marry, thy words have some merit," he said. "Mayhap might we—"

He dropped suddenly to the ground and whirled, but Mark had been waiting for such a trick. He met Harler's sword with a numbing parry, and stepping inside his guard, he kicked him in the stomach, hard. Already off balance, Harler tumbled backwards down the slope and fell heavily into the moat. He spluttered and shook his head, struggling to gain his feet.

Then he screamed as something jerked him under the water. Cherry blossoms heaved and roiled. Once, Harler's face rolled above the surface, whooping for air. Some time later they saw one hand claw the moat, fingers splayed, straining for an endless moment at the sky.

The water closed over Harler, smoothed, became still.

It's not real it's just a nightmare shite it's just a nightmare nowt more than that. Mark looked at the other two guards. "Care to try another throw?"

Donkle shuddered and shook his head.

"I don't mean to gut you," Mark said. "I've no quarrel wi' you, but I need your boat and your silence. Now: drop your weapons."

Donkle did so at once. Abandoned, his friend glanced at the moat, then laid his sword upon the ground.

By God you're getting the knack of this, Shielder's Mark. "Good. Now: up there." Mark pointed with his sword to the base of the outer wall. Slowly the two liveried men walked up the greensward, Mark behind them. When they reached the wall, Mark drew his knife and used the butt to club the unnamed guard. He crumpled to the ground.

Donkle winced.

"These villains must be brought before my son!" the Queen cried. "This treason must be doused with blood, ere like fire it spreads, to turn our state into Inferno."

"O shite," Mark grunted. *Should have gagged her first.* "I don't kill for any pleasure: especially not yours."

Kill? Had he really killed a man? *No! A dream, no more. A spell, some damn witchery.* Mark's hands were trembling as he laid out the sapped guard. *An I'd hit him any harder, I'd maybe have two bodies to my score.*

There's more honour in Squirrels Saved than Men Killed, Shielder's Mark.

Shite.

He looked uneasily at Donkle. "You see how it is—"

"Of course, of course! I wis tha can'st do no other," Donkle said quickly. "Sorry to be such a bother!"

"I *can't* be dragging you both around after me."

"Tha speaks sooth, i' faith. Tha knows best thy business," Donkle said. He looked down at his unconscious friend and grimaced. "We'll wake in the morning, yes? That is, a wee throb in the noggin, sure, but mayhap no worse than if we'd drunk a bottle too many?" He looked anxiously at Mark

"How should I know?" Mark snapped. "It's not like I've practised, mate. Maybe I'll crack your skull like an egg."

"An it please God," the Queen sniffed, retrieving her purse from the unconscious guard.

Mark gave her a dirty look. "Bloodthirsty awd bitch. Hey—Donkle: come here." From his pack he fished out the line he meant to use for scaling the Tower. *If it's short, it's short. An extra yard or two won't make much difference.* "Hands behind your back," Mark said.

Donkle eagerly complied, face alight with gratitude as Mark trussed him up. "Great thanks, sir. This skull o' mine thanks tha, my wife thanks tha, and three wee kiddies—"

"Open up," Mark said, reaching for another apple.

"Me awd Mum thanks—Aaaaah: ulpgh!"

Mark examined his handiwork. "A nice pork you make, with an apple in your snout," he chuckled. "But this way I don't have to bash you."

Well pleased, Mark arranged Donkle against the wall as carefully as he could, checked to make sure he was breathing well through his nose, and gave him a friendly pat on the head. Gamely, Donkle hummed a little tune.

Now: the Queen. For a moment, something tingled in Mark's brain. Something about her was familiar. . . .

. . . But if he had seen her face before, it was across the moat, on the other side of dream, where he could not find it. Here the past went back no farther than the water's edge, and dawn might as well be the end of the world, so distant was the future.

He had to do something with Her Majesty *now*. "Two pigs safe in poke," he said, holding up another span of rope.

She gasped in outrage. "You cannot mean to—Hast tha no respect for the sacred person of a Queen? For duty, or for thine own honour?"

"'Honour buys no bread,' we say at home."

The Queen looked at him with infinite contempt. "Aye, an' it were clear tha never gentle wast, when tha kicked thy foe. Churlish were it; only baseborn duel thus."

"We weren't duelling, we were fighting," Mark snapped. "I saved your life, damn your eyes. Doesn't that count a brass button to a Queen?"

Slowly she nodded. "Aye . . . Aye: for thy timely rescue, much thanks."

"Why did they want to kill you?"

The Queen sighed. "Of late my son has roosted oft in yonder Tower; but never hath he suffered me to enter there. My heart's-dread evil whispers. Arts there are, as black as yonder moat, as fell as graves, to which a colt might turn, a-chafing at his master's bit. He has for many moons been smithing on a darkling thing, a dagger all acreep with dread, of iron cold as the Devil's heart."

Mark nodded, feeling a quick burst of triumph. *Now we're getting somewhere. A dagger, then, lies at bottom of this enchanted Keep, a dagger the son means to use upon his father.*

He felt quick, shrewd, planful. "We both need this boat, if we want to flee this place. But—afore I go, there's summat I must do within," Mark said, trying to speak as the Queen did. "Marry, an I choose not to bind or beat tha, will you give your word not to call out the guards or take the boat yourself and leave me behind?"

Slowly the Queen nodded. "Aye."

"How can I trust you?"

The Queen stared at Mark with contempt. "A Lady am I, and a Queen, boy. My word must truer be than gold or blood or colour-glass."

"Oh. Right." *'Art tha not cloddish, i' sooth?'* "Look, is there someplace we can hide the boat, in case someone else wanders by here?"

"Beneath yon Tower a tangle is, of rushes and of sallows. There might I with the coracle crouch," the Queen said, with a strange, rueful smile, "—and tarry for my prideful champion." She bent to grasp the boat's prow, then stopped, drew herself up to her full height, and held out a fair hand encrusted with rings. "Arina's Regina's Testibon's Royal Lerelil."

Awkwardly Mark bowed. The hand he kissed was smooth as milk and smelled of rosewater. "Shielder's Mark," he said. "Honoured."

"Tha'rt meant to say, 'Thy thrall,' but tha dost not know, I wis." And with that Queen Lerelil began walking along the edge of the greensward, pulling the little rowboat beside her.

Mark stood a moment and watched her go. *Will she wait? A noble's promise to a common man is about as good as an oath sworn to a cow,* he thought sourly. *Still, surely she won't betray the jack who just saved her skin!*

Anyway, he wasn't going to club anyone else on the head. And looking at the Tower, he didn't think he had much rope to spare for tying up stray royalty.

He started off toward the Tower, stooping to pat Donkle as he passed. He walked in the shadow of the walls, even though he'd seen no sentries.

Now that was odd. No one on the walls. No lights lit in the Tower either. No voices eddying from the great hall, no lovers strolling through the cherry orchards, no horses whinnying from the stables. The Queen and her guards were the only people he had seen.

No soul had lived in the Ghostwood for fifty generations. But here, tonight, a Queen ruled, a son plotted, guards schemed in this nightmare country he remembered from his childhood, where trees hissed secrets to the dark wind and witches lay in wait for little boys.

Somehow the Keep was snared in grandfather days, before the Time of Troubles when the magic stopped. Each step into the Forest was a step through the years from the present into the past.

The Tower loomed above him as he reached its base.

But if tonight was a night long ago—the "one black night at the heart of hell," Husk had called it—why was the Red Keep dead? Why weren't rushlights burning in the windows, voices calling the watch, booted feet hurrying across the courtyards inside? Why only silence and a stink of dead flowers?

If other heroes had been here before, how came the boat to be on the other side of the moat?

The moon had fallen farther eastward now, singed to a flake of ash by the approaching sun. The sky was finally beginning to pale.

Something had gouged his foot. Squatting down, he found the grass littered with chips of granite. *Must have fallen from the wall.* He picked up a flat piece and slung it sidearm out into the water, listening for skips. It hit only once, and then was swallowed in blossoms.

Chink!

A ringing sound, steel on stone. Mark yelped as a piece of rock smacked into the ground beside him. He stared at it in the dim grey light, and felt his heart freeze.

A flat chip of granite, identical to the one he had just thrown into the mere, had fallen exactly where the first one had lain. Exactly. Not a single new blade of grass was bent.

A spasm of pure fear rippled through Mark's body, made the skin crawl on his back like water ruffled by the wind.

Chink!

Mark leaned against the red stones, sick with fear. *Steady lad. Work it through.*

What if they *had* gone across, Harler and his henchmen with Queen Lerelil between them? *Of course. They went across, and stabbed her, and left her body for the crows.*

But summat threw all that off. What? You, of course! Just like when you chucked that stone into the moat and it got replaced. So when you took the boat, it cut against the grain of what happened that night long ago. The boat had to be on the other side, because that's where Harler left it that night.

Here it's always today, the day Queen Lerelil dies. That's why Husk said not to linger: after a day passes inside this moat, it will be today again. Stay an hour too long, and you'll be trapped in that last day of the Red Keep's life, a living ghost.

Mark swore softly to himself, shuddering. *O God, there's probably heroes here who never died at all, but stayed too long and were limed by the Red Keep's spell, doomed to relive one day for all eternity.*

Shite. But the whole day was not happening again: not at all. Only when something was disturbed was it put right.

Chink!

Looking up Mark saw the shadow of a man on the Tower wall.

The shadow bent a leg, straightened it, climbed another few inches, swung back a careful arm:

Chink!

Spikes!

Some bastard stole your idea! He's scaling the Tower wall. Goat's-piss and sheep-shite! All his work gone for nothing. Mark watched helplessly as the climber moved surely up the stone face. He had been beaten. "No bloody luck," he swore. *Tonight of all nights, some pig's-pizzle hero beat you to. . . .*

Hawd on. Think. Tonight of all nights. . . . "There isn't any other night! Anyone who dares the Ghostwood always gets to the Keep 'tonight.'"

Well, whoever was scaling the Tower clearly had the jump on him. Mark pulled a piece of cheese from his pack and settled himself on the grass, watching the climber.

So this might be a hero from a hundred years ago. Brought back by . . . by me chucking that stone, I guess.

If the climber had come here at some time in the past, clearly he had failed to break the enchantment and been caught in the Red Keep's spell. If so, Mark stood to learn something by watching him.

The climber was almost at the top now. If he got the

dagger and broke the spell, Mark would have to do without a barony. But he *had* rescued Queen Lerelil. That had been a neat piece of work: his first really story-worthy deed.

He decided again that he needed a name for his sword. *Violent? Blood-drinker?* Too . . . brutal. *Thief?*

Thief. That was a fit name for a sword of his. Nothing pretentious, nothing overblown: but a steel thief who robbed wrong-doers of their weapons, or their lives.

The climber had reached the topmost window. For a long moment he hung there, as if angling to reach inside. Then he stopped, jerked and hung suspended, feet scrabbling against the stone for a dreadful moment before tumbling back and out, screaming as he dropped through the night. He landed with a sickening crash only yards away.

Mark's heart hammered in his chest. He stared, horrified, at the crumpled figure on the grass before him. He thought of the spikes now lying in his pack, and cold sweat crawled along his limbs.

A low, mournful melody whispered from the shadows by the dead man's body, a song like the wind passing over a bed of reeds, lonely as November.

It called to Mark, that song: called to places left empty when his father went away, hollows never filled. It sang to Mark of a thousand days alone before the dawn, driving to make himself faster, stronger, better, so that one day he could show them all, he could say Look! And they would know they had been wrong, everyone who had mocked him, scorned him.

Left him.

Dream-slow he stepped toward the fallen body. At its side, a flash of fallen moonlight and a whisper-song, thin steel sliding from a leather sheath.

"Sweetness!" Mark breathed. The most storied of the

great weapons, its steelsong lost forever when Stargad the Shrewd challenged the Ghostwood and did not return.

But tonight Mark was back in grandfather days, and Sweetness sang for him.

Desire kindled in Mark. Here was a treasure to wrest from the perilous wood! He stooped to unbuckle the half-sheathed sword from its dead master's side, averting his eyes from Stargad's face.

A pale hand crawled from beneath Stargad's cloak and settled on the pommel of his sword.

Mark leapt back with a yell of fright. Slowly the shadow before him gathered itself to all fours, then knelt, then finally stood.

"You! You're alive!" Mark breathed.

Stiffly Stargad threw back his hood, showing a face horribly crushed by his fall. "No," he sighed. "I am the dead."

"Shite, shite, shite!" Fear jumped and crackled through Mark. He whipped out his sword: it trembled like a dowsing rod in his shaking hand.

"I am the dead," Stargad repeated. He was a tall man and spare; his face, before his fall, had been long and gaunt. One eye jutted from its socket; the other gazed at Mark with cool sorrow. "And though it gives my heart no joy to say it, you too must die."

"I mean to die well," Mark said. "I was thinking of taking another two score years to get ready." *Fine words, fine words. Tell your shaking swordhand to be so brave.* "What happened up there? What was waiting for you?"

A spasm of pain passed over Stargad's shattered face. "The brooding Tower have I climbed too many times. Inside one waits who has a soul as cold and hard as iron. Each time he slays me with his touch, and I see my Death within his eyes. Now like all the others I have returned to guard the Keep."

Sweetness whispered its terrible song. "As I climb, I always on my fifteenth step glance down upon the Great Hall's shingled roof. Thrice now have I seen Four-fingered Fhilip creep across the slates, and once the larcenous Silverhand, paused before a lamplit window. To his cheek he raised his hand; I knew him by the silver bracer proud round his wrist. I think he wept."

Stargad gazed at Mark with his one good eye. "Can you guess why we return, Warm One?"

Mark shook his head.

"Because it is our duty. Stay the dagger must, or else the heart will bleed! The heart will bleed. . . . We were wrong, thrice-curst fools to try to break the spell that chains the black wind within these walls. The tines of sharp ambition spurred us forth on this mad quest to wake the dark. As you are spurred."

Stargad, prince of a line already old in grandfather days, bowed sombrely to Shielder's Mark. "My greetings to your honoured father; sorrow to your dam. Prepare to die."

And then Sweetness leapt out with a cry like larksong at first light and cut Mark's sword cleanly in two, so the top half flew clattering against the wall of the Keep.

Mark flung the haft at Stargad and bolted. Fast as fear his legs carried him, racing back to the door Queen Lerelil had come through. He ran within and slammed it behind him, then stood, chest heaving, listening for Stargad's footsteps.

Shite. Shite! His muscles were screaming to run, fight, anything, but he forced himself to stillness.

No sound of pursuit. *Wine and ribbons and all pretty girls defend me! Sweet, sweet air of life.*

He felt a warmth spill down his chest. He'd been cut. It

was only a scratch, but he stood halfway to fainting, trembling like a first-day foal.

Hell.

Still no sound. *Maybe Stargad can only prowl the ground he walked when first he came; never got inside, so he can't come in now.*

A duchy at least, Mark swore to himself. O God, that bulging eye, that flat, dead voice. *The King owes me at least a duchy.*

Faintness shivered through him, as if he hadn't eaten in two days. So much for Thief. "Better stick to saving squirrels," he murmured.

Another chance at honour gone.

Men had dueled, stories said, for the privilege of falling before Stargad's blade. *But you're not here for honour lad, nor glory either; just to fetch the dagger and break the spell. Fighting dead heroes is none of your business,* he told himself, gasping against the door, ears straining for any sound of Stargad's approach. *Running away was just good sense.*

Still no sound of pursuit. He was safe—for the moment.

For the first time he looked around. He was in the Red Keep's large courtyard. A line of stables had been built against the Keep's west wall. Mark stood facing the Great Hall. At night the servants would have rolled out their mats and slept there. Two buildings flanked the Hall: on one side, an elegant wing the size of a great manor house. Where the royalty lived, no doubt. A squat wooden building jutted from the other side of the Hall: kitchens, probably.

And where the manor house touched the Keep's eastern wall, the Scarlet Tower stood, its flanks flushing with the dawn.

Frustration clenched in him. *If Stargad failed scaling the*

Tower, you've got no bloody hope, lad. That was your best idea, your ace to play to break the spell.

Now he didn't even have a sword. After a lifetime of training he had run out of plans. *Why didn't Duke Aron get around to this place when he was thrashing the Ghost-King in the Time of Troubles, eh? Wi' no spells, how can a man hope to. . . .*

Unless. . . .

He blinked. *Must be something wrong wi'. . . .*

Shift the ground, shift the ground. If you don't have the answer, change the question!

By God you're a genius, Shielder's Mark! He let out his breath in a long soft sigh. "You're a genius."

He scanned the courtyard: emptiness, silence. He slipped quietly across it until he stood under the eaves of the Great Hall. He stopped, listened, waited. Nothing. He crept toward the Tower. As he passed one of the open kitchen windows, a gleam of ruddy light caught his eye and he froze. Light? No torches burned in the Red Keep's brackets, no lamps hung above the stable doors. Unless he disturbed things, the Keep should be as silent as the grave, as dark.

Mark peered through the window.

An old man sat cross-legged on the kitchen floor, stirring in the ashes of a tiny fire, all dull coals and cinders. His head was pale as a mushroom, bald and wrinkled with age. He sat in profile to Mark; the white line of an ancient scar ran raggedly down behind his right ear.

If the Old Man saw Mark, or heard him, he gave no sign, but only sat and stirred his ashes, as if looking for a secret hidden in the cinders.

But I didn't do nowt to summon this Awd Man, Mark thought. *Uncanny awd bastard.*

Like a rock rising from a river the Old Man jutted from the Red Keep's enchanted sleep. He seemed real, where even Stargad had been half a dream. Fear flowed from him, and age, and terrible patience. The darkness of death was in the Old Man's black robes; in the shadows that mantled him; in the coals from which he did not raise his eyes.

So why, cased within his fear like a seed within a nut, did Mark feel a great desire to go to him?

He shivered. *You've a job to do, Shielder's Mark. If you aren't here to battle heroes, then you aren't here to hark to an awd man's tales neither; your business is wi' the dagger, nowt else.*

He forced himself to go on, passing the kitchen, until the red glow of the little fire was lost.

Why had Stargad said he should not take the dagger? Enchanted, of course. Obviously each failing hero was enspelled to defend the treasure he came to steal.

And yet. . . .

On t'other hand, t'Awd Man wants you to take it.

Angrily Mark shook his head. Why should he think such a thing? The Keep was whispering strange thoughts into his heart.

When he reached the east wall it took him only a few moments to find what he was looking for, a stair leading up to the battlements. Reaching the parapet, he walked swiftly to where the outer wall abutted the east wing of the manor. As he had expected, there was a door there: this was the way someone coming from the royal apartments to the East Tower must pass.

He knew Queen Lerelil's son meant to kill his father with the dagger of which the Queen and Stargad had both spoken. Either he had come to the Tower from the Great Hall, crossing the courtyard, or he had come from his own chambers. On balance, Mark thought his chambers more likely.

The door was a solid one of iron-banded oak, and opened

outward. Mark drew his knife and reversed his grip, holding it like a club. Then he pulled the door open, stepped into the shadows behind it, and waited for the Prince to come out. Because of course the Prince must have come this way, and closed the door: and must do so again when Mark left it open, sure as any summoning. This way Mark could get to Prince and dagger before they ever came to the Tower. This way he would never have to face whatever had killed Stargad.

It only took a moment for a tall, proud man in his early forties to emerge, clenching a black dagger in his fist as if it were an adder. As he closed the door, Mark clubbed him. He fell with a groan and lay twitching on the parapet.

Got to practise that.

The fallen man moaned. He was badly dazed, but when Mark tried to take the dagger from him he clutched it fiercely. "Thief!" he cried.

Mark looked around in panic, waiting for the rush of torches, servants' running feet. He clubbed the Prince again, much harder, and grabbed the dagger from his nerveless fingers.

Magic lay in the iron dagger, heavy as time; sorcery clotted its dull blade like blood. It burned ice-cold; Mark yelped with the touch of it. Swiftly he flung his old knife over the battlements into the moat, and jammed the iron dagger into its sheath. He sprinted down the stairs and burst into the courtyard.

No servants had come at the Prince's call, just as no one had come at the ring of steel when Mark and Harler fought. Mark slowed to a walk, grinning like a madman. He had done it!

Then the earth began to heave. The air filled with a weird, sighing sound. A dark wind gusted in the courtyard.

Mark quickened his pace. In the breaking daylight a

shadow shuddered across the courtyard. Looking up, Mark saw the Scarlet Tower begin to sway. Running grooves appeared in its tall granite walls, as if its stone were melting into crimson cloud, cut by the wind rising throughout the Keep.

Mark yelped and ran.

The dagger was a spike of ice along his leg; suddenly he had the feeling that it was not the stone walls and towers that were weightless, but the dagger that was heavy. Like a real knife stuck through a painting, it was the one true thing in this night of dreams. It was the dagger's weight alone that kept the rising wind from whirling him up like a leaf, or blowing him apart like a man of mist.

Mark leapt through a small door in the outer walls; a blast of wind roared out with him, wild and damp as a spring storm.

Fierce exultation gripped him, a delight almost like rage. He yelled—

—until a horrible thought cut his triumph short.

What if the Queen's buggered off?

He almost cried with relief when he saw her crouched among the rushes. "You haven't left!"

"There's some words weightier than thine," she said haughtily. "I told tha: I am Queen."

Mark gripped her by her astonished shoulders and bussed her on both cheeks. "And pretty as a milkmaid," he cried. "Now, into the boat! We're almost free!"

The Queen stood her ground. She squinted in the grey morning light. "Caught a gash you have, boy." She moved his shirt gently to one side just below his right collarbone.

"It's nowt but a scratch. Look, this whole Keep is coming down around our ears, so get—"

"Where camest tha by thy talisman?" Queen Lerelil whispered, staring fascinated at Husk's charm. She ran her fingers over the crude carving as if not trusting her eyes in the dawnlight.

Mark shrugged impatiently. "Its nowt but a trinket some awd madwoman gave me."

"Some old madwoman. . . ." Lerelil murmured, still as a statue. "Tha saved my life, boy. I have not forgotten it. There is a gawd I would joy to give you." And so speaking she reached under the collar of her elaborate gown and pulled out a golden chain from which hung a silver medallion. On it, a golden serpent with ruby eyes was biting its own tail.

Mark touched the wooden charm hanging around his neck, staring at the Queen's gift. *By God it's a bastard child of Lerelil's amulet!* His eyes met hers, standing by the rushes of the eastern marge of the Red Keep, and for a moment they shared a mystery.

A great ghostly murmuring rose from behind the walls, a babble of faint voices, barking dogs, clattering horse-hooves, shouts and orders, screams and whispers. Overhead, the Scarlet Tower began to melt and run like a great red candle consumed by a terrible heat.

"You waste our time!" Lerelil cried. Dropping her medallion over Mark's head she turned to clamber into the boat. He jumped in behind her, and pushed off with one tremendous shove. Rushes swayed and creaked around them, and then they were gliding across the moat. Dawnlight turned the water grey as dead men's flesh; cherry blossoms clotted their prow. When they were almost becalmed he risked one hard, chopping oarstroke, forcing himself not to look down even when he felt his oar snag and then tear free of something like seaweed, or tangled hair.

Mark shipped his oars when they reached the far shore. Lerelil stepped from the prow, and began to fade. "No!" Mark shouted, but understanding came too late, and he could only watch as with one stride she stepped from the one eternal night of the Red Keep and into the future.

And then she was gone, a year from him, or twenty, or a hundred, and he had so much left to ask her.

Shaken, Mark held the dagger well before him when he stepped from the boat. The very air tightened against him. For one sickening moment it was like walking against a hurricane; he feared he would slip back and fall into the moat.

Then the dreamy world split like meat around the iron dagger and Mark pitched sprawling onto the bank.

A great wind sprang up. For the space of three heartbeats the air was a storm of blossoms, a thousand years of cherry petals bursting from the bud, flowering, dropping in an instant.

When they settled to the ground, the moat was only a grassy ditch. Here and there the sun's first rays glinted on what might have been metal, or bone. The walls of the Red Keep were stone, sagging and moss-eaten. The Tower roof had fallen in. A shadow passed off the Forest like a ghost at cock-crow, blown to tatters by the wind.

Quickly Mark jammed the black dagger back in his sheath.

You did it.

You did it! Did what all the high born bloody heroes failed to do, the princes, the kingdom's greatest sons for a thousand years. Four-fingered Fhilip and Devid that Dared, lightfingered Silverhand and Stargad the Shrewd: you kicked their arses all! Delight filled Mark again, hot as rage, sharp as steel. *You showed the bastards!*

He would be a great man and ride a great horse and live in a manor with five hundred men. He would be a Duke and live behind stone walls high enough to keep out an army, thick enough to baffle any wind. He and his would be *protected*, where no war could come. No more would loneliness creep in to take his family away.

He started down a thin path where once white stones had lain. Far underfoot now. He imagined a wave of time sweeping across the Ghostwood, washing away old dust and old dreams, leaving the Forest glistening and ready for life, eager for the sunrise.

Oops.

Shite. No pack. He'd left it behind when he fled from Stargad.

He faltered. So much for his food, his tent, his spare pair of socks. They were all gone now, lost a thousand years ago.

Husk's little hut was long empty, its branches blown apart. A few cherry stones still remained beneath an ancient oak, and a pile of tiny bones at the bottom of a black metal pot that might once have been a helmet.

Husk. . . . Thoughtfully Mark took out his two medallions, one cedar and one silver. Two serpents hung about his throat, swallowing their own tails. Who was that old moon-mad woman? A woman, maybe, who had died a thousand times one night: and lived once, wreathed in squirrels.

Like a fierce blaze that falls to embers, Mark's exultation dimmed; he was filled instead with wonder. He was happy, yes, happier than he had ever been, but it was the happiness of a child. He looked back at the shattered Keep with new eyes.

He, and the boy he had been, had fled together from the Red Keep's ruin. That boy sat inside him, waking from a long sleep, remembering what it was to see marvels in a spider web, to hoard up secrets and run from witches.

Steady on. Mark settled himself on the grass and waited

for sunrise. He was too full of feeling to go. Not now, not yet.

Besides, the incomparable Sweetness lay just across a grassy ditch. He'd never have a better chance to get a sword worthy of a Hero; and he wouldn't even have to make up its name!

Mark remembered the way the sword had sung to a hollow place in his heart. He shuddered, recalling Stargad's crushed face.

"Well, he won't miss it," he growled.

2

Before the King

What a bloody joke, Mark thought a fortnight later as a pair of beefy men in livery started forward to throw him out of Swangard Palace. *What ever happened to happily-ever-after?*

It had taken him two weeks to trudge back from the Ghostwood: two long, cold, hungry weeks without his pack and blankets. Each night he had eaten just a morsel of daydream to fill his belly, and warmed his hands over the thought of his triumphant reception before the Crown.

But after getting to Swangard it had taken him all day just to get inside the Palace and up to the Spring Room where the King was holding court. By now it was beginning to occur to Mark, as the guards drew their broadswords, that things weren't going to get any easier for a dirty country boy in this rich man's world.

'Art tha not cloddish, i' sooth?' . . . *I guess this means no parade.*

Bastards.

Mark was hungry. Weary. Filthy. Enraged. And really tired of beefy men in livery. "Stand back, damn your eyes!" he swore. Then he drew Sweetness.

For one eternal instant, time stood stiller in Swangard Palace than it ever had at the Red Keep. Across the room the King froze, halfway out of his chair. Beside him the Queen's fleshy face sagged in shock. Her eldest daughter recoiled, her second gasped.

The youngest princess grinned.

On the King's other side his two councillors, gaunt Anujel and stout Vultemar, glowered in outrage. Behind the throne Sir William, the King's champion, looked on, greying eyebrows raised with interest.

Sweetness murmured its grim enchantments, freezing the ladies and gentlemen of the Court who stood between Mark and his King. *Whole village wouldn't pawn one lady's dress or one Jack's cloak and boots,* Mark thought, stuck between awe and anger. The men were dressed soldier-style, all epaulets and medals and braid. The monstrously thin women wore hoop-skirts with rigid hems just below their knees: *They look like butter churns wi' legs,* Mark thought sourly. *But you must admit that all the girls are handsome, and all the fellows pretty.*

"Thanks for your attention," he growled.

Shielder's Mark was not a pretty young man. His brown hair was shaggy and unwashed. His long narrow jaw was covered with black stubble that looked like a boy's bad first beard. His hands were too hard; his fingernails were blunt and dirty. His cloak was travel-stained; the leathers on his boots were parting from their soles. And frankly, he stank.

He bowed with a flourish and raised his magic blade above his head, so that every corner of the room was filled with its keening, crying song. "This is Sweetness, greatest sword of grandfather days. I picked it from between Stargad's bones in the Red Keep, where he lies. I've broke the Ghostwood's spell, and come to claim my reward. I've had two weeks walk, little food, less sleep, and no thanks. I've spent half the day trying to get past your bloody doormen and stewards and under-ministers of this and bloody that, and I'm sick of being polite.

"I will be heard, and I will get what's owed me! If any

man doubts my word, he's welcome to come wi' me to the Ghostwood, and look for himself."

He dropped his sword-point, and the spell was broken; everyone started jabbering at once.

At a glance from the King, Vultemar bellowed for silence.

Sinking slowly into his throne, His Munificence Astin IV, his spare frame draped in the royal black, studied Mark with a profound lack of enthusiasm. "And do you know those harsh and rigid medicines the Law prescribes in case your claim be proven false?" He nodded at Sir William, who alone among the men in the room was plainly dressed, in brown silks without lace or military honours. "In such a case would we our champion ask to chastise your impertinence."

"If I were lying, he could try," Mark growled. "But can you doubt your ears? There's only one sword as sings: Sweetness, that was lost in the Ghostwood as everyone knows."

Eyes glanced across the chamber; whispers twittered from every corner. Mark looked slowly around the room, feeling dirty and wild and fierce. Like songbirds under a hawk's shadow, courtiers cringed beneath his gaze.

Sir William, the King's champion, dropped his hand from his sword-hilt. "The boy speaks sooth."

Astin IV turned in astonishment. "William! Are you mad? One thousand years has darkness lain upon that Wood, and spilled its gloom upon our hearts, a tristeful tributary, fouling with its melancholy spring the shining Sea that is our kingdom. Stargad tried to break this spell, and thumb-less Fhilip; Silverhand and countless others. Can that blot not even Aron could erase have now been lifted, by,"—the King waved an angry hand at Mark—"By a ragged cloak and pair of mildewed boots?"

Sir William shrugged. "One sword only ever sang, Your Majesty. I must believe my ears."

Mark's fierce elation drained away before the older man's level gaze; he felt like a boy, and a bragging boy at that. Sir William gave him the ghost of a smile. "Beside this, I am a fair judge of young men; my heart tells me that he speaks the truth."

Mark looked at him gratefully. *Now that's more like a knight should be. When you're a Duke, make that man welcome in your castle any time.*

"We . . ." The King faltered. "We confess ourselves amazed. Anujel, Vultemar: advise us." Two head bowed down to whisper in his ears, one gaunt and grey, the other pink and fat.

The Queen waved her ample arms. "Well if he must remain, at least he should be clean. Lord Peridot, your honour and your courtesy would like arise in our esteem were you to be a gentleman and give this boy your cloak."

A courtier in fawn- and peach-coloured silks bowed, a smile quirking his thin face, and unbuckled a flowing apricot cloak, trimmed with ermine.

The Queen turned to a lady-in-waiting. "Cousin Lissa, an you will, take the mantle from this gentleman,"—her nose wrinkled—"and have it burned. Ready a chamber, and in it salvers of steaming rosewater, and a ball of soap." She frowned at Mark. "Perhaps two balls."

In her place beside the youngest princess, Lissa nodded.

A smile lit Her Majesty's plump face. "You swear that this is not some prank, set to tease the humour of the Court? 'Tis very like your sense of wit, Lord Peridot, to send a cloddish knave to us, enwreathed in borrowed glories."

Can't you hear the sword, you daft awd sow? "No joke, Your Majesty, though I look like a scarecrow and stink like a sty."

The Queen clapped her hands. "Ooh! And witty to boot!"
O Lord.

Should I have bowed when she yapped at me?

Mark had felt strong and free when he despised them all,
all the preening courtiers. But now his moment was slipping
away, sinking between the King's scowl and the Queen's
silly smile. He glanced at Her Highness, trying to guess if
she was waiting for him to kneel or something.

. . . And found his eyes caught by the youngest princess, the one who had grinned when he burst into the room.

Mark had always imagined princesses as tall and willowy, with straw-coloured hair and a distant expression;
rather like Lissa, the lady-in-waiting. But Princess Gail was
short and stocky; she had a vixen's face, shrewd and small,
with short brown hair and gold-brown eyes. She wore tights
and tunic of the royal black, belted with a gold sash at the
waist: *Too short for the butter-churn style,* he guessed. She
even had a knife jammed through her sash; no toy neither,
but a good dagger like the one he'd left in the Wood, with
a broad blade and a worn bone handle.

Gail looked at him like an archer staring down a target.

Mark's heart stopped; jumped; and died, a stag shot
leaping.

"What fun!" the Queen exclaimed. "Lissa, also Master
Civet find, and Master Bolt," she said, as the lady-in-
waiting approached to take Mark's grimy cloak. "By their
craft those tasteful gentlemen must turn this Shielder's Mark
from duckling into swan, if he will paddle in our pond."

Lord Peridot was bowing to Mark. Mark's jaw snapped
shut and with a supreme act of will he dragged his eyes off
the Princess.

Peridot was a small man, and slender. As he bowed he
held his right hand across his chest; Mark saw that he was

missing the index finger. "My greetings, cousin. May I offer you my cloak while yours is . . . on its way?"

"Th-thank you," Mark stammered.

"Is something wrong?" Peridot's thin lips quirked into a sharp smile. "Perhaps, my country cousin, you find in my disfigurement the footprint of the Devil. Do you long to hold your fingers horned to ward against my Eye, or step so that my shadow does not fall across your own? You would not be the first to blanch at my affliction."

"No, no, not at all," Mark said, flushing. His eyes fled Lord Peridot's hand.

Sir William was staring at him.

So was the Princess.

He wished himself under the earth.

. . . No, goddammit!

He had braved the Ghostwood, and broken the spell not even Aron could undo. *Is the man who holds Sweetness to piss himself before a roomful of perfume and ruffles?*

Stocky Vultemar and slender Anujel stepped back and stood quietly behind the King. The King stroked his pointed beard with fretful fingers. "Attend us, Shielder's Mark. Perhaps you *have* done what you claim. We shall this day a troop dispatch to investigate your tale." A smile flickered briefly across Astin's face. "But Sir William have we trusted in farming many boys, and never found a better husband-man to harvest from them rich crops of men. If he believes you, then so will we—for now. And if you speak true, then ancient law is clear: what you ask, the Crown must give." He laughed without great warmth. "Great will be your name, boy: it will all the honoured titles in this room outlast, including ours. The fourth to bear the name of Astin later years will know but by his gift to you. So tell him: what will you have?"

O, fine fields and orchards heavy with fruit; tall stone

walls walked by men in blue and silver livery. Mark drew his breath. "Your Majesty, I thank you. An you will, I'll take . . ."

He faltered, feeling a pair of narrow eyes trained on him. "I'll take . . ."

Half against his will, he turned to face the Princess.

Like a spear her gaze passed through him, heart and soul, and he was lost.

"You'll take what?" she asked, her eyes aflash with triumph.

"Hush, Gail!" the Queen fussed. "No time is this for boldness!"

"The King is waiting," Anujel said.

Mark's life, his whole life and all his plans, went spinning out from under his feet. He was a wild man in this Court, shaggy-haired and stinking of the road. A keen wind blew through him, lifting him up like the spring breeze under a hawk's wing. Daring, he felt; fresh and brave as rainbows. "Your Majesty," he said, bowing with a flourish of his borrowed apricot cloak, "I guess I'll take your daughter."

The crowd gasped. Lord Peridot stiffened. Slender Anujel bent to whisper outrage in his sovereign's ear. The Queen stared at Mark's travel-beaten gear, then looked anxiously to her youngest daughter.

The Princess smirked. "Which daughter, bold stranger? The King has three."

"Shall I say the fairest?"

Gail laughed. "Oh no! That would be my oldest sister Teris, and she's already married to Duke Gerald."

When Gail laughed, her narrow brown eyes got even narrower, shrewder, and more mischievous. Mark felt as if he and she were two children sharing a joke no grown-up could understand.

The King's councillors conferred in anxious whispers. A

thunderhead was building on the brow of his August Majesty, Astin IV.

Mark didn't care; he had eyes only for Gail. "Then I'll marry the cleverest," he said.

Gail shook her head. "That would be Willan. She reads three books a week, if you'll believe it, and talks to the Bishop about, ooh, deep things. But alas! She is married to Count Laszlo." Gail pointed to a portly man of middle years, who bowed coldly in return.

Mark threw up his hands. "Well, then, I guess I must ask for the *boldest* daughter of Astin IV."

"Ah!" Clad in matching black hoop-skirts, the two older princesses nodded drily. "Now that," said Teris, who was pregnant, "would be Ered's Gallant's Reynold's Ferdinand's Royal's Gail."

Gail curtsied as well as a short woman in a tunic can.

There was a long, tense silence.

Lord Peridot, resplendent in peach, his slight chest gleaming with his grandfather's medals, caught the King's eye and coughed, twice.

The King shook his head. "Now listen, Shielder's Mark. While we are charged to offer you the choice and pick of this our kingdom, what you ask exceeds the bounds of all impertinence. You cannot require the last unpluck'd fruit from the royal tree, our daughter, she to whom the kingdom's greatest men years of anxious courtship have addressed, to wed—forgive us—so far beneath her station." He glanced at Lord Peridot. "Though you could not know when first you made this startling request, there have for years been . . . expectations in this matter. Gail is to another purpos'd; stealing her beneath the sable cloak of hoary statute were no honour nor no credit to you, and could not help but foul that pure baptismal water that your deeds have earned to cleanse away your commonness."

Slowly, carefully, thoughtfully, Mark spat on the floor of Astin the Munificent. "Is the lass engaged or isn't she?"

"Well—"

"No, I certainly am not," Gail snapped, glaring at her father.

Behind the throne, Vultemar and Anujel were shifting like nervous hens. Astin stilled them with a wave of his hand. "Consider, boy: imagine us reversed, you King, and I petitioning the hand of your last daughter. Ask and we will grant you what you will, but girlish hearts are not ours to give."

"But your daughter's girlish hand is," Gail said. Smiling. Lethal.

Mark bowed as coldly as he could. How dare, how dare they treat him like dirt, the man who broke the Ghostwood's spell! "The Princess is not engaged. I've asked for her hand and now you get to grant it. Or has some witchery turned the King's gold word to lead? If your daughter can't marry an honest man without a title, then make me Prince o' Pigsties."

The Court held its breath, shocked.

Hunched in his great plush-covered chair, Astin the Magnanimous chewed moodily on his moustache. At last he sighed. "We will not be forsworn, boy; king's words *are* gold, and must be honoured more than any coin. Our statutes clearly state that we must give you what you ask. But they do not force respect, nor amity, nor friendliness between us. Nor do they ask us to rejoice in wedding our great line to yours."

"No doubt we'll get on better once I've won your daughter's heart," Mark said, shrugging.

Gail looked a flight of arrows through him. "My heart cannot be won," she snapped. "It's mine to give."

Mark gulped.

Beside him, Lord Peridot allowed himself the pleasure of a thin smile. "Young man," he murmured, "time I think will prove to you that woman's heart is harder won than castles: and far more difficult to keep."

Turning to the King, Peridot bowed with flourish. "My liege, were Duke Richard here, my noble patron and my lord, sure I am that he would want to make the first congratulations on this startling felicity! How glad, how happy must a father be, to graft a noble daughter to such a legend-making tree!" His eyes lingered on Gail. "From so fair a bud, what ripe fruit must swell!"

Willan and Teris glanced away, shivering with distaste; Gail looked to be throttling Peridot in her imagination, slowly and with great thoroughness.

The courtier continued unperturbed. "And too I must confess a certain satisfaction for my master. Sweetness, so long lost from Stargad's line, has now returned against all hope, fetched hither from the Ghostwood by your future son-in-law." Turning, he made another deep bow to Mark. "Duke Richard will be pleased indeed to meet the man who found his long-lost property!"

Mark started, his hand straying to the precious sword belted at his side. "What do you mean? Sweetness is—"

"You need not be concerned," Lord Peridot said, dismissing him as if he were a stable boy. "The Duke is known for his munificence: your pockets will be heavier by a flock of Swans, no doubt. Or payment can be made in any form which better suits your needs: raiment, beer, or what you like."

Mark felt himself go white with rage. "I am not a village beggar, lord. I won this sword fairly, and if your precious Duke Richard wants it, he'll have to take it from me."

"We will no longer stand these threats!" the King roared. "Shall you now add banditry and boasting to the tally of indignities you thrust upon this Court? We have no assurance how you came upon this blade, by theft or duel or dicing. We *do* know Sweetness was for Stargad made, and Stargad's line. Your one request you made and we will grant it should your tale prove true. Now unless you wish to face the peril of our direst wrath, yield up the sword, that it may straight unto its lawful owner go!"

"Straight into would be more like it," Gail muttered.

Carefully Mark drew Sweetness from his sheath. The room fell deathly quiet but for its lonely steelsong. Tension danced like lightning round the ancient blade. "Make me. Sire."

The King looked to his champion.

Sir William sighed. "Well, sorry am I, Shielder's Mark, but I am sworn to act for Astin and his Court. A fine blade, Sweetness is, and finer too I guess the man who won her: but give her up you must." He stepped down from the royal dais, making no move to draw his sword.

"*You* know this is crooked as a witch's back," Mark cried. "I won it fair!" He and Sir William were suddenly alone: Lord Peridot and all the other be-medalled men had melted back, to watch from the edges of the room. Mark gestured at Sir William to keep his distance. "I know how to use this," he warned.

"I'm sure you do, my lad. And I know how to use mine." Sir William shrugged. "And if we fight, perhaps I win: then you give up the sword. Or perhaps you win, and wed, and hang for killing me. Either way, this rashness leads to death, for your pride may stand no stiffer than the honour I have pledged my King. That honour owns the last drop of my blood: does your pride cost you so much?" A small smile showed in Sir William's beard. "Too old am I, and you too young, to die for a yard of hammered steel. Humour me, lad, and give it up. What honour comes from killing old men with grey beards and creaking joints?"

Mark flushed with shame, "I . . . . That isn't what I wanted." He looked at Sweetness, and its song filled him with longing. He ached to grasp it, and the high, noble, magical world it meant, so different from his village past. It seemed to him now, even surrounded by princesses and palaces, that in this one blade, clean honest steel that sang of battles gloriously fought, and nobly lost, was all that he had striven for those cold mornings in the Commons. Was everything his heart had longed to be.

He held the sword out, hilt first. Sir William took it from him, but beneath greying brows his eyes were grave. He smiled and shook his head, gripping Sweetness with the ease of a man well-used to weapons. "Good work, lad."

A queer, shaky gratitude filled Mark's breast. That smile and those three words from a man like Sir William almost made up for losing Sweetness.

Almost.

The Queen clapped her hands. "Oh good! I *do* like weddings more than funerals!"

The King nodded coolly at Mark. "Our third and youngest daughter is engaged, and stands to wed the man who—perhaps—has lifted up a curse that has upon our kingdom lain from grandfather days. Whatever were our differences, tonight we should rejoice! Prepare the Halls for banqueting, that we the pledge our ancestor swore may redeem in coin of meat and wine."

Buzzing and glittering like a nest of wasps, gentlefolks swarmed from the Spring Room, scrambling to prepare for the unexpected ball.

"Princess Gail is famous for her . . . spirit," Lord Peridot murmured, suddenly at Mark's elbow. A delicate honeysuckle scent clung to his neatly trimmed beard. "I am sure that were my patron, Richard Duke of High Holt here, he would be the first to wish you well." Peridot's thin, elegant face crimped into a smile as he watched the Princess stride off behind Willan her sister. "Indeed, coz, I admire your boldness. I shall savour your prógress like a work of art: it promises to enlighten while it entertains."

Mark's heart sank. He had always imagined they would hold a banquet in his honour. But now that he was here, he was getting the feeling that nothing that happened in the Palace was going to be much fun. Watching the courtiers mince and flounce and slither away, he knew they must think him a village fool, not the Hero he had always longed to be.

Well, at least the damn food should be good.

3

Palace Entertainments

"I'm a hero, not a whore," Shielder's Mark snapped at his unhappy valet, striding from his room without so much as choosing his epaulets or pinning up his hair. "I'll wear my worth on my heart and hands, not my back!" *And damned if I'll pull a village around my shoulders, or belt a town about my waist,* he thought, stalking off to dinner.

And yet . . . . And yet, when he reached the Dining Hall where supper was to be, and saw the glistening throng within, he found himself lingering at the threshold. He was dressed in a cinnamon-coloured cloak and tights, and a fawn-coloured tunic. All his clothes smelled of hibiscus flowers, and they'd put rosewater in his shaving bowl. *Rose ower dung-heap still smells like sweet shite,* he thought sourly.

He'd never given a tinker's damn about his clothes— until now. But watching the courtiers bow and chat, he realized there was an art to dressing that he didn't grasp, a way of standing to advantage, of moving well. There were no pockets in his tunic and he didn't know what to do with his hands.

Without military medals, he pulled out the talisman Queen Lerelil had given him and let it dangle on his breast. In this room of twittering birds, the ruby-eyed serpent seemed old, cold, and brutal.

You're in ower your head, lad. You know less than nowt

*about this world, and you haven't made many friends since
you got here.*

It went against all his instincts to fight on his enemy's
terms. And so he hesitated under an archway, studying the
gentlemen of fashion for some clue as to what to do with his
hands, his movements, his words.

To Mark's left, Anujel and Count Laszlo met and bowed.
The Count had changed into a tunic of red-brown velvet
with gleaming gold buttons. Ribbons and medals adorned
his chest. His round, high-browed head sat atop a platter of
lace. "My dearest Anujel: how fares your honoured father?"

"Well, well. I only hope to be as fit as he is now, when I
at last permitted am to drop the load of Policy, and retire to
that good garden that the ancients of my line maintain upon
our small estate."

"A happy man is he who turns his back upon the fray,"
the Count said mechanically, as if he didn't believe his
words and didn't particularly care whether anyone else did
either. He was married to the middle Princess, Mark
remembered. The clever one: Willan.

"Of your honoured father I must ask in turn: how fares
he?" Anujel inquired.

"Splendid, I believe. Angling is his passion of the
moment." Count Laszlo's fingers toyed with the jewelled
hilt of a dagger that hung at his hip. He glanced at Mark,
then away. The tiniest hint of a smile crept to his lips. "So:
the last and boldest Princess is to wed. The King must be a
happy man."

Anujel's eyebrows rose. "I doubt his happiness outstrips
your own in any way, or that of Gerald, Duke and consort
to his eldest heir," the councillor remarked.

Count Laszlo's cold eyes twinkled. "Of course, the Duke
and I must joy to see our sovereign glad."

"Of course," Anujel said drily. He bowed before an imposing dowager. "Duchess."

Quickly Count Laszlo bowed. "Here I take my leave of you, dear coz. Your health, and health unto your father." And then, "Duchess! Your servant. Could you condescend to take a turn about the room with me?"

The Duchess, a grim, horse-faced woman in her late fifties, nodded imperceptibly and continued her stately cruise with Count Laszlo behind her like a round-bellied merchantman in tow to a battleship.

Mark stepped back from the threshold as Anujel walked by; they pretended not to notice one another.

What the hell? The Count's smug as a pig in mud ower you wedding Gail, but why? And why should Duke Gerald be whistling too, as Anujel seemed to say?

Gerald and Laszlo are about to be your brothers-in-law. Don't seem the types to be happy about having a workman in the woodpile, and yet . . . .

Mark shook his head, puzzled.

His fingers fretted for a bit of string or a loop of wire to fiddle with. *Wish they had pockets in these damn tunics.* He settled for resting his right hand on the butt of the black dagger belted at his side. It was cool to the touch, real as stones, sure as winter. It made the scene before him seem to fade, as if he were standing outside in a cold street, with a wind blowing and rain starting to spatter on the cobbles, peering into the Dining Hall through the slats in a shuttered window. . . . All those cloaks and candles meant less to the real world than a breath of wind.

Mark shook his head again. He held on to the dagger, as if it could shield him from the plots he felt weaving round him. *They're waiting for you, Mark my lad. There'll be a bow bent behind every bush for you, you can bet on it.*

*You're not a sportsman, you're not Somebody's son, but
you've poached on their hunt.*

Ah!—And there's the fox you beat them to!

Followed by Lissa, her lady-in-waiting, the Princess Gail
entered through another archway. Mark guessed her mother
must have been working on her, for now she wore a
fashionable knee-length hoop-skirt and high-necked black
doublet on which gleamed a golden necklace. A circlet of
golden wire held back her short brown hair. Two more drops
of gold, like dragon's tears, hung from her ears; they
shivered as she strode into the room.

Brass-bold and sharp as steel, Mark thought admiringly.
What lambs a ram could make, on such a ewe!

At last, his one ally in the Court had made it to the Dining
Hall. Mark squared his shoulders, tossed his cinnamon-
coloured cloak gallantly over his left shoulder, and strode
into the room.

"Princess!" he said when he caught her, bowing low.

His cloak piled in cinnamon folds on the tile floor; he
stepped on one corner of it and almost fell.

There must be a trick to this bloody bowing business.

*Steady on, steady on. Probably she never noticed; try a
little charm. Show her you've got the hang of the gentle
speaking.* "May I have the honour of your company for a
turn around the room?"

Gail's lips pressed together in annoyance. They were thin
lips, he noticed: more used to commands than kisses.
"Lissa," Gail said. "Inform the honoured gentleman that his
conduct is improper."

The lady-in-waiting curtsied respectfully to Mark. "Sir,
with all respect unto the customs of your birthing-place, in
Swangard, prior to an introduction by a friend or member of
the family, one may not importune an unknown lady."

"But she's to be my bride!"

(Soothingly.) "Of course she is! Which makes it all the more important you conduct yourselves impeccably until the jointure of your single states into a wedded sanctity. Any impropriety that touches on a Princess is sweet to Scandal's tongue. Would you subject your bride-to-be to calumny, or allow the Gossip's dirty fingers to leave stains upon her honour?"

"Oh great," Mark growled. "Fine. Whatever. Please, madam, would you do me the honour of introducing me to your mistress?" Tall, awkward, and swathed in his horrible cloak Mark felt like a cinnamon-coloured lighthouse. He flung the bloody thing savagely back over his shoulder.

Lissa's voice was soft, her manner pleasing. "Only a gentleman, one known to both the Princess and her kin, could make this introduction with propriety."

"Bull-pizzles!" Mark snapped, looking directly at Gail. "We're to wed! You can't tell me we can't chat about the bloody likelihood of rain."

Eyes were fastening on them like leeches.

Lissa turned to the Princess. "Claiming an acquaintance on the strength of pending marriage, Shielder's Mark believes no harm could come from brief and clearly innocent remarks when made in full view of the Court."

"Tell the gentleman he does neither of us credit by making a public jackass of himself," Gail hissed.

Lissa turned politely back to Mark. "The Princess has observed that while you—"

"Shite and swan's-piss! I'm going, all right? I'm going!" Holding his cloak out with one arm to keep it from piling on the floor Mark bowed and fled to the appetizer table at the back of the room. Here, standing before trestles laden with food and drink, he stared fixedly at bits of fruit bobbing in tureens of bright pink punch.

This was it: he had hit bottom. All his life he had looked

forward to this day, his triumphant return, his hero's welcome. Instead, he was alone among strangers and enemies.

So much for happily ever after.

Wasn't it every boy's dream, to marry a princess with flashing eyes?

He'd been so sure Gail wanted him to ask for her hand. *Damn it, she made me do it!* But now she was acting like any other high-born lady, despising his manners, his birth, his breeding. The feast he had come to so hungry, after so many years of lonely toil, had turned to ashes in his mouth.

"Delicious, isn't it?"

The speaker was perhaps five years older than Mark: a young man still. His clothes were soft, comfortable, and expensive-looking. His small mouth was all but hidden by a magnificent beard, carefully trimmed, of warm brown hair soft and silky as ermine. He frowned at a pair of silver epaulets on his forest green tunic, as if they were a brace of toads he'd found squatting unexpectedly on his round shoulders. His hands were soft and pale; on his little finger he wore a silver ring set with an emerald. Instead of a dagger he carried at his hip an odd copper cylinder, narrower at the top than at the bottom.

Most remarkably, he wore a strange contraption on his nose: a bridge and two circles of wire, holding discs of glass through which peered his pale grey eyes. His arched eyebrows gave him an eternal look of faint surprise.

He seemed friendly. "I prefer the trout, myself. Some like the almond-spears: too sweet before a meal, I think." As he spoke he turned a flake of trout deftly onto a small cracker. A round pink-rimmed hole appeared in his silky beard; he popped the cracker in.

Mark wondered how long it would take him on handyman's wages to buy just one of those crackers, topped with flaked trout. He felt his hackles rising.

The courtier finished his cracker, looking like a small brown owl snapping down a mouse. "Magnificent! Atrexides' Avayar's Valerian's Archibald's Valerian," he said with a bow. "*Your* name of course is known to all. May I have the honour to inquire on how your honoured father fares?"

"Dead," Mark snapped.

Valerian blinked. "Er. Um. Allow me to express my—"

"I don't know he's dead: I only hope so. Like as not he just abandoned us."

Valerian took the contraption from his face, and polished the glass discs with his satin tunic-hem. "The only trial of spectacles: they get so easily smirched." He frowned, held them to the light, settled them back on his nose. He peered at Mark as if trying to work out a difficult sum. "At Court the Truth, like vinegar, is a better garnish than a beverage," he remarked, biting into a second cracker. Bits of flaked trout clung to his beard. "For instance, when I inquire about your honoured father, you say 'As well as we could hope.' You shake your head in sorrow, to give me time to sympathize, without encouraging a further question. Then in turn you question me about my honoured father; listen; nod; and echo my trivialities."

Mark smiled in spite of himself. "Tell me, sir: how is your honoured father?"

Valerian swallowed. "Cross as a crab and sick of the sight of me," he said frankly. "Would you stalk one angry leftward stride? I'd like to try the punch."

Deftly Valerian ladled pinkness into a crystal cup. He nodded to Mark, blinked, and smiled. "Advice unsought I know is rarely welcome. Yet allow me one cautionary word. Every person in this room is drawn to you like filings to a magnet. Greatness is the breeding-ground of flattery, and intrigue, and all the other plagues that power can bestow. Well it were for you to know these courtiers are not your friends: they mean to use you, if they can."

"Except you of course! You want to help me from the goodness of your heart, right?"

Valerian laughed. "Of course not. Actually, I do mean well, but I also have a use for you. A drink?" he asked, holding up a ladleful of punch. Mark nodded; Valerian poured. His hand trembled, and behind his spectacles his pale eyes blinked more rapidly. "But unlike these others, I don't want your power. I will aid you any way I can; if my service seems of use, then all I ask is leave to attend you when at last you settle on your new estate, wherever that may be."

"Estate?"

"Of course. Was that not your master-stroke? A princess cannot wed a commoner; in asking for his daughter's hand, you force the King to make you son and noble too. A lesser man would not have played his card so well." Valerian goggled anxiously at Mark. "That *was* your thinking, was it not?"

"Um,—of course."

Valerian seemed relieved. *Nervous ower summat else, though: he's blinking like a bat in sunshine.* "You were telling me how you meant to use me," Mark prompted.

"Er, right. Who's near to you is near to Gail, and who's near to Gail is near to—Lissa!" Valerian said her name as if it were a butterfly he meant to pick up with his breath.

Mark chuckled. "And you're the ram who's out to straddle her." He glanced over at Gail's lady-in-waiting. Blond, willowy, discreet: come to think of it, Lissa would make a better princess than the Princess did.

"St-st-st-straddle!" Valerian squeaked. Above brown beard his cheeks flushed punch-pink with agonies of embarrassment.

"Allow me to assure you, sir, that my intentions to that fairest of all women—that shaft of sunshine! She upon whose brow discretion vies with wisdom! She who—"

Mark waved his hands, smirking. "No straddling, then. But you want to come wi' me, to, er, warm yourself in that shapely shaft o' sunshine, right?"

Valerian puffed his feathers; blinked; shifted from claw to claw. "Er . . . more or less."

Mark guffawed. "At last. Someone in this bloody place I understand."

Valerian shrugged. "I am small, and have no power, so I am the first to greet you. Some have more to lose, and thusly more to fear. When they have drunk a tumbleful of courage, they will find you."

"Fear? Why should any man fear me?"

Valerian frowned. "You underestimate yourself. Why, every cheek you look upon turns white beneath its powder. Ladies blanch beneath your gaze, and fair hearts speed: but not for love."

"But why?"

"Why!" Val drained his glass and filled it up again. "You broke the spell that lay upon the Ghostwood! Where you succeeded, Stargad and Fhilip and Aron Duke of Swans had failed. You came before the King in boots begrimed with Red Keep dust. From your sheath you drew a weapon out of legend, claimed the greatest prize in Astin's realm, and dared him break his direst oath!" Valerian waved a hand out at the room of nobles. "You think this happens every day? Can you not see that you are terrible?"

"Oh." Sheepishly, Mark shrugged. "It slipped my mind."

"Hmmmph! . . . Then too, there is the matter of the Crown." Thoughtfully Val stroked his soft brown beard. "One of Astin's daughters will be Queen. That daughter's husband will be consort, second greatest power in the land.

Duke Gerald and Laszlo, Count of Maltis, worked for years to win their places. We know them, and they know us. But you! We know nothing of you."

"That reminds me—" and Mark told Valerian of the conversation between Anujel and Count Laszlo, which seemed to imply that Laszlo and Gerald were strangely delighted at the prospect of having him for a brother-in-law.

Valerian bobbed owlwise, like a schoolmaster. "The Count and Duke believe the King will never make you Consort, nor let your blood besmirch the royal line. Gail seemed once a likely choice for Queen: there is steel in her. Gerald and Laszlo and the other dukes fought like dogs for years to keep great Richard, Duke of High Holt, from forcing Gail's engagement to himself. It seemed that they had lost when Anujel came in on Richard's side. But lo! in Shielder's Mark a hope unlooked-for! They think the King will not allow a workman's child to sit astride the throne. The Duke and Count must now believe they have the contest to themselves."

"So the buggers have no reason to fear me," Mark said, anger edging his voice. He caught a glimpse of Laszlo across the room, his round head riding on its plate of lace, talking to a Bishop.

"To underestimate a man like you is not the kind of error those men make," Valerian said, frowning. "Nor will Duke Richard. The powerful will think: a man so great as he must be, who broke the Ghostwood from its ancient spell, once having married Astin's daughter may find it no great matter to reach out and pluck the Crown as well. Greatness will not sleep tonight, my friend, but pace its floor with furrowed brow, and gaze upon the moon, and curse at fate for bringing peril to the palace, shaped as Shielder's Mark. Can you imagine Astin has thought of aught since you arrived, but how to keep his kingdom from your clutches, and your knife out of his back?"

"But I didn't mean . . . I didn't *know*—"

Valerian grinned. "Poor Mark," he drawled. "My eyes drop millstones for you, thrust abruptly into greatness, power, wealth and wife."

Eh?

Mark grappled with the idea of himself as one of the great, wrestling for power and influence.

Power.

All he'd ever wanted was to break the curse and earn a safe place for himself and his family. But how safe were grey stones and soldiers in livery if he still had enemies?

But if he used his position well, took advantage of the power it offered him, he and his could be safer still.

He looked thoughtfully at Valerian. "Is that why the King filched Sweetness? He didn't want its name added to my own?"

Valerian sipped his punch. "A voice would carry farther, that sang to Sweetness' song. And his Majesty knew something must be salvaged for his vassal, Richard."

"Who is this Duke Richard? Everyone seems to be watching ower shoulders for him."

Valerian nibbled a piece of crumbly Rhenant cheese. "Duke of High Holt, Richard is, and greatest noble in the land. He has many friends at Court. His strings are fine as cobweb: hard to see, but sticky, running everywhere. He's like to be your closest, kindest, deadliest enemy." Mark blanched. "No great act is without its consequences, good and evil," Valerian said quietly. "If you will set free a shadow chained a thousand years, there will be changes in the land, and in your life, and nothing says those changes will be good. Or had you never thought of that?"

"You . . . you make it sound very complicated," Mark said.

"Power is rarely simple," Valerian replied. "At least, not here."

As Mark digested this unpleasant thought a bell rang to announce dinner, and they were seated.

How do the lasses sit while wearing those hoop-skirts? Mark wondered, mystified. But manage it they did, and flawlessly.

The King and Queen sat at the head table, along with their daughters, Duke Gerald, Count Laszlo, and the horse-faced woman Mark had seen earlier, whom Val identified as the Duchess of Fenwold. "Heavier than lead and tougher than mutton," he whispered.

The rest of the company was arranged six to a table. Mark and Valerian were to dine with the Countess Malahat; Talyard Cirdon, the Bishop; a sharp-featured young woman named Janseni ("Brilliant musician!"); and Lord Peridot, dressed in a peach doublet with blueberry lace and hose. "He looks like dessert," Mark muttered as they sat down.

Val stifled a smirk.

If nothing else about Mark's reception had been what he had hoped, the dinner at least lived up to expectation. Seven magnificent courses, punctuated with excellent wines and ices; truly a feast worthy of a hero.

And the hero needed it. Still, after the turtle soup and the wildflower salad, the stuffed quail and the braised peacock in mustard sauce, Mark began to slow down, trying to savour the glorious food.

You might eat like this the rest of your life, you lucky bastard!

Never go hungry again. Never wake up wi' belly snarling at darkness, knowing there isn't a mite for breakfast. Never hammer your face into a smile and shake your head at

*someone's charity while your legs feel like willow-wands
from hunger. Never forage for sloes and fiddleheads to
throw in the pot because you have neither bread nor grain.*
At the thought, a looseness spread from his belly to his
back, as if his stomach had been clenched around hunger all
his life and only now relaxed its grip.

He spied on his tablemates. They had smooth skin and
soft hands that had never known a plow or scythe or
hammer. They did not know how special, how holy a
wonder this dinner was that their servants set before them,
platter after plate.

Lord Peridot controlled the conversation at their table,
Mark soon saw, always ready with a well-placed question to
start someone talking, or a well-placed thrust to finish them
off. As the butlers served the fifth course, pheasant braised
in garlic butter on a bed of watercress, Peridot was asking
Janseni her opinion of Sir Avedut, composer to the Court
and songmaster in the employ of Councillor Anujel.

"His work is . . . well-proportioned," she said cautiously. "It always gives the ear what it expects, which
satisfies an audience."

"But can, perhaps, not move them?"

"Precisely my thought too, mi'lord," Janseni said with
some relief. The musician leaned forward with increasing
passion. "Is it the place of art to merely give the people what
they want? Or should we teach them to want more, expect
more, hear more! Art, real art, something more than balance
and proportion must possess. It must have fire, and passion.
Art must have a vision, a challenge and a lesson to bring
before its audience."

"I like a challenge too: but not at dinner!" Lord Peridot
remarked. The Countess Malahat smiled, half *for* him, half
at her.

"Not a challenge then; I mis-spoke myself. Say rather, I

would hope my music held a hand out to its listeners, and led them to a place where they had never been before."

Valerian nodded. "Or seen once long ago; or dreamed; but thought they had forgotten."

"Exactly," Janseni said. "Just so." She coloured, and abased her eyes beneath Peridot's amused smile. "Of course I cannot promise that the piece your Lordship asked from me will reach these lofty goals; perhaps at least it will amuse."

"Oh, it will at least amuse, dear girl. Have no fear of *that*." And though Peridot's smile seemed kindly, Janseni blanched. After that she spoke seldom, and reluctantly.

All dinner long, Mark noticed, Janseni was constantly watched by a young man two tables away, whose wan face and ardent gaze told everyone in the hall how desperately he loved her.

The Countess Malahat was what Mark's friends called a Rain-in-April Woman: one who could stir even the deadest root. *Must use wire in the bosom of her gown to push 'em up,* Mark thought. *You want to knock 'em with your knuckles to see if they're ripe.*

He chatted a little with her, and then a little more, kindled by the sparkle in her eyes. There was a moment, as their glances met and tangled over the remains of the cold snipe, when he found himself thinking wistfully that if only he had known about the amiable Countess, he might not have been in such a hurry to dicker for Astin's strong-willed daughter.

The Bishop was going on at length about angling, a passion of his, and Mark tried to pay attention. Much better to think about fish, than to let his mind wander in the dangerous direction of the Countess Malahat's bewitching green eyes. Mark caught the Bishop looking at him, old eyes cold and bright with lazy amusement. Mark blushed and looked at his hands, twisted together on the tabletop, his muscled fingers monstrous by the delicate dessert spoons.

"I lust for trout," the Bishop remarked. "The cunning lures, the careful seduction of a teasing fly or wriggling spoon; the strike's fierce consummation!"

Like soft fingers Mark felt the Countess' eyes running over his back, his neck, his arms.

"—And the desperate, hungry battle between the angler and his prey. . . . Ah," the Bishop sighed, eyes glittering like frost. "Nothing like it."

"Ha! The Queen is tristeful," Val said suddenly.

All eyes darted to the head table. The Queen was frowning at a butler, but just as Mark looked up, Gail happened to be looking at *him*. Her brown eyes were fierce and alarmed.

Her look ran through him like a crossbow bolt; his nerveless fingers went numb upon the table.

Valerian blinked blandly at him. "Remember something?"

Sharply Mark drew in a breath, tried to smile, shook his head.

Steady on, steady on. You and Princess Gail were meant for one another, lad. He remembered that afternoon, the feeling just before he asked for her, taking his life into his hands like a jug of ale he meant to drain at a gulp. He sat, stricken to the heart that he could have thought of turning from her.

She won't be easy, I guess: but to shy from her would be base treason, breaking faith wi' all that's fierce and proud and free in both of you.

A silence dragged out for quite some time before he realized everyone was waiting for him to speak. "Beg pardon?" he gasped.

"I asked you your opinion on the Ghostwood's game," the

Bishop asked, "and if there would be hunting there, now the spell is ended."

"Uh, well. Squirrels, of course. Good hunting if you like squirrel pie." The Bishop's nose wrinkled. *You're babbling, lad.* "Some nice trout in the Boundary though."

"A fine little river," the Bishop reflected. "Fine trout I had there, three years ago, and carp, too, if you can believe it. But as for game, now, I should like to try the Wood itself. Picture it! To hunt a glade no man has swept with hounds before!"

Countess Malahat shuddered provocatively; Mark watched the shiver travel from her closed eyes down past her ripe mouth, her soft throat, her silky shoulders, and some long time later, down into the folds of her plum-coloured gown. When he looked up he found her watching him, and smiling. "Would you not think it dangerous," she suggested, "to seek your sport in a—forbidden place?"

The Bishop chuckled. "Not after what our friend has done. We sportsmen all owe him a debt, for making good another great preserve. The spell is broken, the Wood is safe."

"Think you so?" Janseni said softly. "I think so long a song of mourning must an echo leave."

Mark nodded. He did not believe that sunlight soon would gladden the Ghostwood's eaves. Too much lay buried under dry needles there. Too many years lost. Too many lives.

He shuddered. *By God you let some loneliness out when you broke that spell, Shielder's Mark, and it's followed you home. No great deed without its consequences, good and bad,* he thought, looking at Valerian. For the first time doubt blew into his heart like a puff of wet spring wind, damp and cold and cloudy. *Could he have been wrong to break the spell? 'A mad quest to wake the dark'—that's what Stargad said.* Under the table Mark touched the cold black handle of the iron dagger. *'Stay the dagger must, or the heart will bleed.'*

The Bishop chuckled. "It is a woman's place to shiver at a name, a past, or anything which local legend has invested with an awe and sense of dread." He smiled at the Countess, reaching for his wine glass. "This curse was laid in grandfather days. The Time of Troubles, of ghosts and magic chained by Aron, Duke of Swans, has long since passed. From out of superstition's dusk to daylight have we come since then. How runs the ancient adage? 'Faith is a candle, where Reason is the sun.'"

"I have heard it," the Countess said, smiling and widening her eyes. "But I never thought a Bishop said it, Father."

The Bishop smiled again and swallowed his wine. "That I do not know."

"Ask Valerian," Lord Peridot suggested. "He knows everything."

Valerian frowned warily. "Why tease me, cousin? Never have I made that claim, nor never will. My moiety of wisdom exceeds not by one drop the portion held by any at this table."

Peridot grinned. "Of course! You surpass us all in all, including modesty. . . . And you *do* know whom the Bishop quotes, I wager."

"Well, yes," Valerian admitted. "It was Aredwyth the Sage, a theologian of Duke Aron's court."

Lord Peridot raised his hands to the rest of the table. "You see? I told you he knows everything."

"Not a fraction of a fraction of it," Valerian protested. "Theology by chance is one of my amusements, and Aredwyth a writer not easily ignored."

"He can't be *that* important if the Bishop didn't know him," Mark pointed out.

There was a long moment of silence around the table as everyone but Mark looked away from Bishop Cirdon, who was studying something at the bottom of his wine glass with great care.

Oops.

Shite.

As Mark began to blush, Valerian dove into the silence. "The passage, though obscure, is interesting because nobody remembers the second half. In full, the famous lines of Aredwyth should read,

'Faith is a candle where Reason is the sun;
No one needs a candle: until darkness falls.'

You see, the meaning of the adage changes considerably in the context of the whole."

"Yes," said the Bishop at last, turning to signal a steward for more wine. "I see that."

As the remains of the seventh course were being cleared away and a last round of lemon ices served, the King stood to make a speech. It was about the dawning of a new age, and seemed to take one. The lemon ice was consumed, the bowls removed and replaced with salvers of rosewater. Heads were nodding by the time the King announced that before the wedding Mark was to be knighted and given charge of Borders, the Keep that stood across the river from the Ghostwood. He would be made a Duke, and the Wood itself would be his preserve, including the Red Keep, should he choose to restore it. Of course the King's men would first sweep through the Wood and the Keep, to make sure all things lost there were restored to their rightful owners.

Mark leaned over to Valerian. "That means they're going to loot it before they turn it over, right?"

Val nodded.

The King then congratulated Mark upon his title, his land, his heroism, and his choice, if he did say so himself, in brides-to-be. Everyone sipped from their glasses, and there was a scattered round of polite applause.

Lord Peridot clapped the loudest. Pushing back his chair he stood and bowed. "Your Majesty! Allow me to present a present to the Crown." The King nodded; Janseni tensed. "In honour of your daughter and your new-found son-in-law-to-be, may I present the first recital of a song commissioned from Janseni, the wonderful young woman whose tunes propose to teach us all a lesson!" Turning, he signalled to a far archway.

The sound of flutes wound into the room, two of them, laughing and quarrelling. Finally, a kind of harmony emerged from their strife; the same notes that had struggled the moment before were now part of a beautiful melody, merry and haunting at once, like children seen playing from a distance.

It was strange music. At first Mark thought it odd for oddness' sake, and ugly at that: typical of the Court. But when the melody popped out, he realized it was a tune he'd known all his life, sung by the children in his village. Only here it was richer and more complex.

He glanced over at Valerian, who smiled and shook his head in wonder.

Two flutists entered and stood on either side of the archway leading into the hall. Marching in behind them, dressed in sombre robes and grave expressions, came three midgets. They waddled, trying their best to keep in step. As the flutes began their melody for a second time, the dwarfs began to sing. Or rather, to croak.

Midgets Two and Three looked frankly scared to be parading before so glittering a company; their voices faltered.

Their leader kept grimly at his task, but he was hopelessly tone-deaf, and each note was agonizingly off.

A nervous titter started from the back of the Hall. The lead singer frowned, but his juniors, clearly trained as clowns, clutched for that laughter like drowning men. They began to caper, bellowing their parts and making droll faces.

The laughter grew, and their antics with it, until soon the flutes were lost, and all that was left of the song was the first midget's part, yelled above the crowd.

The clowns clambered up onto a table, dancing together. The aristocrats of Austin's Court laughed until tears streamed down their cheeks. *Twice as funny because the bastards were embarrassed first,* Mark thought, revolted.

Janseni was deathly pale. "Why?" she whispered, unable to meet Lord Peridot's lazy eyes.

"Come, come, girl. Your music is a hit! See the merriment it brings before the Court."

Countess Malahat laughed, bright as sun on ice. "I must admit that something in this music took my hand, and led me where I'd never been before."

Two tables over, a young knight flung back his chair with a crash. The flutes faltered and the crowd fell silent as he strode over to their table. "Lord Peridot?"

Peridot glanced up at him. "Deron, is it not? Count Berkeley's son. The passing of your father was a wound this kingdom will not easily survive."

Deron's handsome young face was white with rage. He was the fellow who'd been mooning at Janseni all night, Mark remembered. How horrible, to see the woman you loved so humiliated. "Sir, you are no gentleman. This music is a work of great passion, by a lady of unparalleled artistry. To demean, to sabotage it with these antics I would have thought too low a thing for even you to do."

Peridot shrugged. "A matter of opinion, sir. You are free to yours."

"He's giving you an out," Janseni said in a low voice. "Take it, Deron."

Deron stood a moment longer, jaw working. "I do not think I can," he said at last. And then he slapped Lord Peridot so hard it snapped his head around.

Peridot rubbed his cheek thoughtfully with his right hand, displaying his missing finger. His voice was light, but he gazed at Deron with serpent's eyes. "Is it now in fashion, striking cripples? Or is it only old Count Berkeley's son who is so brave? Well well, 'tis clear I am no man of arms. A sword I will be forced to borrow. Your Majesty," he called, turning to the throne. "I hate to bother you, but this young man has challenged me, cripple though I am. I must petition for Sir William's loan."

Deron swallowed, glancing up at William, the King's champion, but said nothing.

"Sir William!" Gail cried. "Father! Letting Lord Peach-blossom mock my wedding is one thing, but giving him the satisfaction of murdering Deron in the bargain is too much!"

"Be quiet!" Astin roared. "This squire before us all did willfully challenge Lord Peridot while knowing him to be unfit for combat. It was a churlish act, and if Duke Richard's trusted man begs of us the service of our champion, he shall have it!"

Janseni's head sank into her hands. "There Deron, what did I tell you?" she said listlessly. "With one night's work he's killed us both."

4

Gail

The following evening Mark and Valerian were talking in Mark's chambers. Valerian was hunched before the fire, peering at an embroidered cushion through a large disc of glass that made small things look bigger. He clucked in admiration. "To think of sewing all those stitches! Women's work would drive me mad. What clever fingers, what knowing hands!" He frowned at his own hands: soft, pale, plump.

Mark paced the flagged floor. "Why would Peridot stick his knife in Janseni? Had she jilted him or summat?"

Valerian pocketed his seeing glass. "If you can't cut down the tree, you may at least collect its fruit," he observed.

"What?"

Valerian stroked his beard and ventured a smile. "Shielder's Mark grasping Court intrigues is like a man clutching at a cloud. Well, you'll learn. . . . The ancient theologians wrote that bodies were mere husks for souls. Within the orbit of the Crown a like phenomenon may be observed, for people here are pails to carry power in, each face and heart but boots, cloak and breeches for the true political reality. I cannot see Lord Peridot's heart, assuming that he has one, but it isn't hard to make a guess or two. Janseni is a brilliant newcomer, a challenge to the status quo. Thus she threatens Avedut, music-master of the Court for many years."

"Now I follow you," Mark breathed. "Peridot was drawing swords for his friend Avedut!"

"I do not think the men acquainted," Valerian said briefly. "In truth, I never prior to last night had heard Lord Peridot reflect upon a single note of song, nor take pleasure in the art. The point is that the patron of Sir Avedut is the honourable Councillor Anujel." Valerian blinked meaningfully at Mark, as if this made the whole matter quite plain.

Mark's shoulders slumped. "And so . . . ?"

"Anujel gave Richard his support for Gail's hand, and the Consortship, of course. For Peridot to attack Janseni is for his master, Duke Richard, to support Avedut and thus Anujel, his ally at the shoulder of the King. This much is clear as glass."

"But Anujel's support doesn't matter now that I'm going to marry Gail, does it?"

"Well, no, but it mattered when Peridot originally commissioned the song. Going ahead with the parody at a feast in honour of the engagement was a mistake, though: pure viciousness on Peridot's part. Richard will be displeased with him for that, I think. After all, were you to suffer an . . . accident, then Gail's hand would once more be free, and Richard wouldn't want to have burned any bridges."

Mark gulped as Val had begun to muse. "For Peridot it was a lucky chance that Deron loved the lady. He is Duchess Fenwold's nephew; eccentric as the horse-faced Duchess is, the taint of his hot-headedness will surely mark her. Fenwold is hers, not her husband's; she is too great for even Richard's arm to shove aside, but she can be pushed out of the lists and into the stands, if he is shrewd about it. Had she interceded with the King for Deron's life, she would have put herself in debt to him, and so reduced her influence. Thus would there be one fewer Power with whom Duke Richard must contend. . . ."

Val trailed off and shook his head. "Too complex for me!

Divine Lissa, that angel who attends upon your bride-to-be, could give you deeper reading. In matters such as these her mind is like my scrying-glass, that makes the tiny clear. If a duke were plotting for the Crown, she would sniff it in his wife's perfume, or read it in the trimming of his beard."

Mark paced from the fireplace to the window. It was dark out, and cloudy: all he could see in the glass was his own faint reflection, pale and powerless and angry as a ghost.

"At least Deron was not badly maimed," Valerian observed.

Mark grunted. "Sir William let him off easy."

Oh yes, that bloody duel was an education, wasn't it? Intrigue's not the only thing you don't understand. You thought yourself a warrior. But watching Deron and Sir William was the end of that little fancy. Soldiers, real knights, fought sheathed in steel from boots to helm. "Bastards wear a bloody smithy on their backs, and feel it no more than a fish his scales," he murmured, awed and angry.

"Any knight can dance a galliard in his plate, my friend. The years that you spent stooking corn or plowing fields or shearing sheep these men spent at tilts and butts and buffets, with masters for the sword and lance and bow. Every noble's son can make a warrior, if he wills it." Valerian winced, glancing wryly at his own soft belly and white uncalloused hands. "I never took to it, myself."

"They're so bloody good," Mark said, shaking his head. "I thought I was neat, but even Deron could take me to pieces."

Valerian grinned at him. "You're lucky then you had such mercy on Sir William's creaking bones, to forswear beating up old men and let him have your precious Sweetness."

Mark shuddered. "Aye. I would have had my coxcomb trimmed, and deserved it. He probably would have killed

me by accident, thinking I was half his match." He paced
back to the window and stood, head bowed before the night.

"Don't decide to carry millstones, Mark: the world is
heavy as it is," Val said kindly. "These men had tutors, time
and money; but it was Shielder's Mark who did what no
knight had done in a thousand years of trying: broke the
spell that lay upon the Ghostwood." Valerian took a
brass-handled poker from its hook on the mantle and stirred
up the fire, which hissed at him, spitting sparks. "Why do
you say Sir William let young Deron off? I thought he
fought well."

Mark shook his head. "Deron's blows came fast and hard,
like darts. Sir William cut one moving line: he even picked
up speed from Deron's blocks." Mark stopped, trying to
phrase what it was that made Sir William special. "For three
springs I worked as a shepherd, with an awd man who'd
done it all his life. It was a big flock, and every time we
moved the sheep, I'd have to count them out by rhyme. But
t'awd man never counted a lick: he could tote up that weight
of sheep wi' one glance, and know if it were light or heavy.
It was the same today. Deron sees blow, parry, step, strike:
but William sees all one thing. When he parries, he doesn't
just block a blow, he changes the shape of the whole
fight. . . . God, Val, I'd give my right hand to be his
squire."

Valerian glanced sideways at Mark with the ghost of a
smile. "You are eloquent."

"I'm an idiot," Mark said gloomily. "I can see it, but I
can't do it."

"I feel that way about Janseni's music." Valerian sighed.
"Sad it seems to me, that Deron risked his life for one who
does not love him."

"She doesn't!"

"Of course not. Did you not observe? He wore no favour.

I do not blame Janseni; no more can she command her heart than can the rest of us. But it seems hard, that such a love as Deron bears could leave her heart untouched." Valerian peered down, frowning at his toes, speaking as much to himself as to Mark. "But women seldom love the men that love them best."

"Not if the men are sappy about it," Mark said absently. "Look, Val, remember what you said yesterday, about the Ghostwood changing my life?" Valerian nodded, peering solemnly at Mark through his spectacles. "Well if you had asked me about my life a month ago, I would have said it had been pretty good. My dad left when I was young, but I was too little to really remember him."

Mark walked to the window, looking out through his own reflection at the night. "But something did happen in the Ghostwood. At least, ever since I left the Red Keep I've been thinking about my childhood. Things I'd forgotten for years, like how it felt to dive into a pile of autumn leaves and how they smelled when . . . when my Dad burned them one time and it started to rain. Once I even remembered my Grandma the day before she died, the exact way she looked and the sound of the fire and the way the embers glowed when I blew on them to keep her warm. . . ." Mark trailed off, then turned to his friend. "And the funny thing is, now I don't know if I was happy or not. Isn't that queer? If you asked me now if I was happy as a boy, I wouldn't know what to say."

Reluctantly, Val said, "All spring I too have been thinking of my father."

Mark tapped his finger on the butt of the black iron dagger at his hip. "Was I happy?—It seems like the sort of thing I ought to know."

●   ●   ●

Later, after Val had gone, Mark put another faggot on the fire and sat hunched before the grate, hooking his boot heels on the rungs of his stool, thinking again of the duel between Deron and Sir William.

So you aren't a warrior after all.

That hurt. All that sweat, all those lonely mornings practising with sticks in the Commons, dreaming of fame and honour, kindling every muscle with slow fire, hammering himself into what he thought was a hero's shape. But if you weren't Somebody's Son, it didn't matter.

Mark looked at the backs of his hands. He had strong wrists, very strong; he could take a calf over with a quick jerk, he could crack walnuts with his fingers. He remembered how he used to love the swing of the scythe, twisting at wrists and belly, knowing that what was a chore for every other boy was training for him. His mother walked behind, bundling the cut, and each bundle was another enemy slain, another harvest of future glory.

A web of veins and tendons ran over the backs of his hands. *Don't see those in Val's hand, in Peridot's. Theirs are smooth. Smooth petal flesh that smells of rosewater, sheathed in kidskin gloves.*

A faint white welt ached in his right palm, a seam of frost lying under the flesh. *Must have got it when you grabbed the iron dagger from the Prince. Best be ware about showing that around, or bloody Astin will find some reason to steal it too.*

"Aye well: sword for daughter's not a bad bargain."

Mark laughed at his own audacity. He had reached out with his dirty hands and grabbed the chief treasure of the kingdom from its King. *Stared t'awd bastard down.*

Well, all right: that wasn't all of it. The girl chose him as much as he chose her. What a strange, proud, fierce, fox-faced woman! Quickness in her small hands, her narrow gold-brown eyes.

His hands were stained by wind and sun: *but she'll be used to hands as pale as fresh-cut pine.*

Mark's heart sank.

He'd heard people say that before, but only now did he feel it, feel something sag in his chest, just beneath his breastbone; turn sick and hollow inside. She would want white hands, soft fingers—

Mark spat on the floor. *No. No! She picked you out where you stood wi' the stink of the road still on you. She's seen what you are. She'll not turn her back on you for that.*

But what about Deron, risking his life for a lass who didn't love him? And a cold little voice said, *How can you know her reasons? P'raps the Princess thought you were Somebody's Son, aweary from your labours. After what you'd done, how could she guess you were nowt?*

An even if she knows you're dirt, how can she know what that means? All her life she's seen only gentlemen: she'll want things, expect things . . . and you'll never guess what they are until she's gone, and someone like Val tells you, and says it was clear as glass she'd leave you from the start.

Angrily Mark jumped up from his stool.

How exactly d'you . . . do you swive a Princess? You don't have to court her, thank God. But afterwards, on the wedding night. . . .

Mark had swived a girl or two before. He went at the thing with as good a will as anyone, and liked to see his partners laugh: they seemed to like it.

But you're no expert. He'd kept his pizzle tethered, for the most part. If you didn't get out fast enough, the girl might have a baby, and if she had a baby you ought to marry her, and if you were married to someone you should never leave them, and if he was going to the Ghostwood he might very well not come back. So he had tried not to think about girls, and made love to his fist when he had to.

Most of what he knew of swiving was from watching rams on ewes. A Princess now: a Princess would have expectations.

They must know things, these thin-fingered gentlemen. Probably that's summat else you get taught if you're Somebody's Son.

Gail wore tights and a tunic the first time he laid eyes on her. Tights! What did you do about tights? The girls he had lain with were wearing dresses and nothing else: you didn't need to be too handy, and they were helpful anyways. But tights! And corsets! These women wore corsets. Mark groaned. *Nails to nuts the wedding dress will be a lace-and-button nightmare.*

How long d'you think she'll wait while you paw and fumble? How long d'you think she'll stay with a jack who doesn't know how to please a lady?

She'd take a lover. He knew it. And everything he had worked for would be in ruins. His house would be a cuckoo's nest, some smirking courtier would be slipping his powdered pizzle into his wife, his servants would sneer at him, his soldiers would make horns behind his back.

"Shite!" He grabbed the brass-handled poker and jabbed at the fire, breaking its red heart.

And another thing: you swear too much.

Well.

No point in getting sick ower things that might never happen. Hell, the only times you've seen her, she hasn't had much use for well-dressed pricks like Peridot.

The looks she's given you, good and bad both, have been proud and sharp and straight as arrows. She'll not take a

*lover behind your back, Shielder's Mark. If she wants quit
of you she'll stick a dagger in your belly from the front!*

*And you could learn. You've clever hands for most things:
no reason swiving should be different. It won't be your body
that lets you down.*

She liked him well enough to look at, or she wouldn't
have challenged him with her eyes, daring him to ask for her
hand. She'd seen him dirty then, and it hadn't been his silver
tongue that caught her fancy.

He had come back from the Ghostwood.

He could be a husband now, and a father too.

And to be a father. . . .

They would be man and wife, after all.

A sudden memory rushed over him from some tipsy
holiday night, the press of skin on skin, the smell of a
woman's hair in his mouth, her laughter smothered against
his shoulder. Her stomach pressing up hot against his and
his hand in the small of her back.

Mark drifted slowly to his bed, sat on the edge and pulled
off his boots. Unbuckled his belt.

That could be Gail, nipping on his shoulder, her slender
arms vined around his back.

A spark jumped through him. The salt taste on his lips
could be her royal sweat; it could be her brown eyes kindled
with candlelight, her thighs that made a valley for him to—

There was a knock at the door.

Goat's-piss and puppy-guts! "Coming, coming!" Blinking to rid his mind of his fantasy of Gail Mark leapt up,
swore, ran to the door in his stocking feet and wrenched it
open with what he prayed was an easy smile.

Lissa, Gail's serving woman, stood on his threshold. Her
eyes flicked from his stockinged feet to his strained smile:
adding him up like a manor steward toting rents. *She's got
you pegged to the last penny-piece, lad. O god.*

"I beg your pardon, worthy sir, for my untimely interruption."

Demure, attentive, and unthreatening, Lissa was just what Mark expected a princess to be: tall and willowy, with wavy gold hair that framed her face. Earlier it had been plaited into an elaborate coiffure, but now, long after bed-time, it fell free, and rustled against her satin shoulders as she walked.

She was leading him down one of the darker, narrower, draughtier corridors in the Palace. Clearly the way was not much used; instead of glass lamps, empty torchbrackets hung upon the walls.

Lissa walked ahead with a taper in her hand. "We thought it best to be discreet; some gossips out of malice love to speculate, and could to their advantage turn the seeming impropriety of your visit to my Mistress' chambers."

"So why give them the chance?"

"The Princess willed it."

Ah. "I bet this wasn't your idea."

Pause. Carefully, Lissa said, "The Princess is so well-equipped with judgements of her own, she seldom feels the need to borrow mine."

Mark grinned. "I'll bet."

Thrown by the light of Lissa's taper, their shadows snuck after them like cut-throats. "What if someone sees us going into Gail's chambers?"

Lissa turned and cast Mark an amused glance. "Anyone who wishes to outface the Princess is very welcome to try."

Gail's quarters were not what Mark had expected.

On a peg near the door hung a heavy, ravelling felt cloak that had once been brown. Below, a pair of battered leather walking boots leaned like drunks against the wall.

Still smelling of smoke, bits of newly cured leather were scattered across a worktable under the far window. Also on the table was a woman's corset; a strip had been cut from it, as if to make a belt. A stuffed goose stood just left of the fireplace, peppered with spark-holes.

Somehow Mark had imagined more lace. More pinkness. More finery. He looked at his bride to be.

"I shot him," Gail said.

She was sitting on the edge of her bed, hunched over the worktable, sharpening a skinning knife as long as her forearm. The whetstone circled expertly up and down the blade: sliz sliz sliz sliz.

Mark looked at Lissa, but her smile was blank as winter. "Uh—shot him?"

"The goose. On my fourteenth birthday. I'm a good shot. Very good, for a woman of the Court. I practise most days. I ate him too," she added. Sliz sliz sliz. "I hope you're not one of those stupid people who kills for sport."

Mark looked at Lissa again, beseechingly. She replied with a tiny, definite shake of her head.

Gail put away her whetstone and wiped the blade of her skinning knife with a rough oiled cloth. "I was hoping you would break the rules and try to see me, but frankly you don't seem the wooing type, and I hate waiting."

"You said I wasn't supposed to—"

"Of course you aren't." Gail frowned up at him; it made her triangular face even sharper. "I just hoped you would try. But you are here now, so let me tell you how we will proceed."

"Princess." Mark bowed as correctly as he knew how. Turning, he bowed also to Lissa, a little less deeply. "My lady." He stepped politely back into the corridor. "I look forward to seeing you both at the wedding."

"Where are you going?" Gail demanded. "You just got here."

"I am going to bed," Mark said. "I'm not a servant, Princess, nor a dog neither. I come when I'm asked, not when I'm called. I'm a free man born. I didn't grovel for your father, and I won't do it for you."

Gail was looking at him in genuine surprise. "But—"

A spark smouldered in Mark's voice, of anger and desire. "Your eyes, your hands, and even your bloody proud highhanded manners are in my heart like fishing hooks, Princess, but by the Devil you'll get a fight before you land me."

Gail blinked. "Lissa? Was that a curse or a compliment?"

"I would ask the gentleman," said Lissa diplomatically, biting her lower lip and trying very hard not to meet Gail's eye.

Gail turned to Mark and cocked her head on one side with the strangest expression, commanding and vulnerable at once. A real person peeped around the Princess then, like a child peering shyly from behind a mask. "Well?"

Like iron leaping to a magnet, Mark's spirit jumped to meet her, the woman who would be his wife. "I meant to curse, but my tongue tripped ower my heart."

To his amazement Gail flushed. "You're a better wooer than I deemed," she whispered.

Mark felt Gail touch him with her eyes, with herself. As some women bared their flesh she bared her soul, and from across the room he was stung by the shock of her nearness.

He could know her, if he dared.

That was the challenge in her eyes.

Mark's fantasy returned to him, of holding her naked beneath him. He blushed, shamed to have such a picture in his mind while the real woman sat before him, head bowed and strangely vulnerable. For a panic-stricken moment he was sure she could see his vision of them making love. Resentment and tenderness and desire swirled in his heart.

He stood awkwardly in the doorway until by chance his hand brushed the iron dagger at his side. At its cool touch a weight settled through him, anchoring his heart firmly in his chest.

Gail said, "Please don't go."

Mark stepped back into the room. A moment hung between them then, clear and fragile as a bubble thrown up by a waterfall, drifting, delicately dancing between them.

Lissa closed the door behind him, and the moment was gone.

Better say summat, lad. You can't stand around stiff as a plank forever. "What is all that?" Mark asked, pointing at the worktable with its scraps of leather and gutted corset.

Gail smiled mysteriously. "You'll find out on your wedding day. —Which is what I wanted to talk about." She sheathed her skinning knife and put it on the table. She was wearing her gold earrings, Mark noticed, the long teardrops that swung in tiny circles as she looked at him. "I'd like Janseni to do the music."

"Good. Yes."

"Do not answer quickly," Lissa said. Her voice startled Mark; he had almost forgotten he and Gail were not alone. "Such a choice is not without its consequences. It will seem an insult to Lord Peridot, and through him to Duke Richard."

"That's the point," Gail said. "'If you can't strike the master, kick his dog.'"

Lissa frowned. "No hope of any marriage to the Duke can now remain, Princess. You need not fear his band upon your finger: why antagonize him? The Lord of High Holt may decide to yield before inscrutable Fate, but never will he pass a challenge by, if you choose to offer one. He is not a gracious loser."

"He better learn to be," Gail snapped.

"Good by me," Mark said. "Janseni will do the music. Was there owt else?"

Gail uncrossed her legs and swung her heels so they thumped against the edge of her bed. "Well, there was one other thing," she said reluctantly.

There are certain things a young man does not like to hear about his wedding night.

"What!"

"I'm sorry," Gail said firmly, "but it's out of the question."

Mark stifled a curse. "Can't we at least fight about it in private?"

"You mean Lissa?" Gail's head drew back, and her earrings whirled in angry circles. "You think I am the sort of woman who tarries alone with a man before her wedding day?"

Mark stared at her amazed. Her gall left him speechless. "As if it would matter!" he spluttered at last.

"Lissa is my oldest friend and closest companion. I suggest you get used to her. Wherever I go, she comes with me."

"Even when you come, she doesn't go," Mark muttered.

"That kind of comment is ill-suited to a gentleman," Lissa snapped.

Great. Now he had angered even the statue. "Did her remarks become a bloody lady?"

"Princesses don't have to be ladies," Gail said. "It's the best thing about being one. Look, it isn't as if I'm saying *forever*. Just, not now, that's all."

Guess I should be bloody honoured. I bet not many folks hear the vixen plead.

Gail looked at him with a shy smile, as if to say, I know I'm being very difficult, but we have a special relationship, you and I: I know you will understand. "I can't stand all these cages! City walls, castle battlements. . . ." She held up the drooping corset and laughed. "They tie the cages to our bodies! I can't breathe here for all the perfume! . . . I need to get away from that. When you came before my father like a hawk among the songbirds, you brought a taste of free air on your wings, Mark. Don't ask me to give it up now."

A shiver ran down into Mark at the sound of his name on her tongue.

"I want to go with you, be with you, travel the wide world. And I can't do that if I have children," she finished simply. "I'm an heir of the royal line. They'll say it's too dangerous for me to go out while I'm pregnant. Then will come the confinement. I might die, Mark. Some women do. And if I don't, I'll be a mother . . . and that's a cage that never opens."

"You've never been out in the wide world," Mark protested. "It's cawd, Gail! It rains and it's muddy and it's full of bandits and pox. You say you want to go out there, but how do you know? You've been a Princess all your life; you don't know what you're talking about."

"I shot him," Gail said coldly, pointing to the stuffed goose. "I shot him and I gutted him. I handle a bow a damn sight better than you, I'll bet. I had a tanner teach me to cure leather and a dyer showed me how to draw colours from madder and woad and blackberry root. Don't you ever patronize me, Shielder's Mark.

"You will not come into my bed until I wish it. Nobody else can see how I can bear to wed myself to such as you.

If I implore this marriage be annulled, the Bishop will comply before you can count ten—if you can count to ten. My father will have paid you what was owed, and you will then be left with *nothing*." She glared fiercely at him. "Nothing! Is that clear?"

Bull's-eye.

Slowly, Mark said, "When boys fight, they have rules. Because if you don't, people get hurt. We have only known one another two days, Princess, and already you've drawn steel on me. Was it fun for you to tell me that everyone here despises me, Princess? Was it nice? Was it *smart?* In fifty years of life together we will have plenty of chances to bare our steel at one another.

"Tell me, Lissa. Is it well-done to throw my birth at me like this? Is this how nobles talk to nobles? Or is this how they talk to their servants?" Pale-faced, Lissa stared at the flagstones and did not answer.

"Who do you think you're dealing with?" Mark yelled at Gail. "Your butler, your stable-boy? Or does everyone let you get away wi' shite like this because of who your father is? Is that what being noble means? Hiding your bad manners behind your father's cloak?

"I may not be some Duke's son, but I'm the only man to make it back from the Red Keep. I walked through time and crossed the moat where the dead things live. If I was good enough to break the Ghostwood's spell, then I'm good enough for you."

"Is that a threat?"

"It's a promise." Mark tried to master his rage. "Gail, I will be the best husband I can be. I'll love you and respect you. Once I take my oath I'll never swive a serving-girl or leave you for another, but I must have my own respect, even if I can't have yours."

"You have mine, you have mine, you idiot," Gail snapped. "Weren't you listening?"

Lissa choked with laughter.

"Oh, bloody right then," Mark sighed. "That's settled. I'll get your respect; just not your bed."

"If you don't ask, you won't be refused," Gail wheedled. "It's only for a little while, Mark. A few years, no more."

"Years!"

"You're attractive, Mark, you really are—in a shaggy, awkward kind of way. And I'm . . . I'm curious," Gail stammered. "But the step from bed to cradle is so short, you see?"

Bull's-eye again. She was right, but Mark couldn't bring himself to say it.

"A village woman most oft is married when she is how old?" Lissa gently asked. "Twenty-seven? Twenty-eight? The titch of land each freeman has cannot support too many babes, and common folk are smart enough to know it. So they bide their time, chafing and impatient I am sure, until they feel the moment right to wed and have a family. Only at the Court, where daughters are another good for sale, like cows or beans or eggs, are women wed so young as Gail now is. You demanded of the King her hand, and it was given unto you; you purchased her as if she were a she-goat or a strip of land, because by ancient statute her father had no option but to sell her for the coin you held: the greatness of your deed.

"And Gail is willing to abide by such an arbitrary sale, closed between two men without the need for her consent, because it is her duty; and she likes you. All she asks is that you give her but a little time to grow into a woman: less than she would have if she had played along beside you in the fields of your youth, and sparked her eyes on yours in the village where you were raised."

Eyes downcast and unchallenging, Lissa gently stripped back Mark's indignation to reveal the narrow-minded, selfish churl he was.

Oh she's got you there, lad. You're just a boy who cries for pudding before dinner. What an ass you are, Shielder's Mark. What a . . . what a common man.

You're a pig, he told himself. *You are a pig.*

Pig. "It's such a strange thing to be . . . told you cannot share the marriage bed," he mumbled. "And in front of someone else!"

Blandly, Lissa said, "You will find the Princess loses little sleep in fretting over other people's pride."

Gail winced. "Ouch," she said. But she didn't disagree.

5

'Til Death Do Us Part

Two weeks went by in a whirl of balls and receptions. A rider returned from the Forest, breathless and panting, to announce that Mark had told the truth: the Ghostwood was no longer wrapped in shadow, and the Red Keep lay in ruins within, open to the sun, though no other man yet dared to enter it.

Mark was officially given the Keep at Borders, just across the river from the Ghostwood. He didn't care a damn about being titled Duke of Borders, but being knighted by Sir William was an honour that cut him open to the core. It was the greatest moment of his life.

Valerian, working hard to earn a place near the Divine Lissa, guided Mark through a maze of manners, customs, clothing, perfumes, delicacies, and wines which otherwise would have quite unmanned him.

Finally the wedding came. The ceremony was lengthy and complex, full of chants and rings and rituals to lay the Troubles that could beset a marriage bed. None of this mumbling made much sense to Mark, but he performed his part with deadly gravity. The wedding guests had buzzed, hearing that Janseni was to provide the entertainment, but when she started playing all gossip stopped, and for a brief time her soaring, joyful music made them all better than they were.

At last Mark stood with Gail while the Bishop intoned a sheaf of solemn verses, and proclaimed them man and wife.

Joy cracked Mark open then, spilling from his eyes and his absurdly grinning face. He felt Gail free and alive as spring beneath her mail of lace and silk. Her lips were like warm rain when they kissed, and kissed, until the crowd began to snicker; and Gail's mouth was as thirsty as his own.

"What was that?" Mark muttered, when at last the Bishop cleared his throat and prodded them apart.

Gail grinned back at him, eyes dancing. "A promise," she said.

"What a haul!" Mark surveyed the cartloads of presents strewn around their new quarters. Most of them had been presented in an extremely long and tedious ceremony earlier, so each giver could show off his gift before the assembled Court. Only a few more private presents remained to be unwrapped. "We should get married more often."

Gail cried in triumph as she defeated a silk bow and stripped away the plush cloth wrapping of another present. "Oh. Scent." She frowned, disappointed, and pulled the stopper from a crystal decanter. A wisp of spring snuck out, a tingle of breeze and blossoms.

Lissa forgot the wedding ledger in her lap. "Master Civet's best!"

Gail shrugged, wedding dress rucked up to her knees. "You want it?"

Lissa's blue eyes widened. "You mean I—!" Catching herself, she settled back into her armchair, folding her long, slender legs with the easy elegance that marked her every movement. "I really think the gift was meant for you."

"Take it," Gail grunted through a mouthful of cloth. She was trying to chew through a knotted silk ribbon that stood between her and her next present. "You love it and I never wear the stuff. Besides, it's from Richard."

Lissa cradled the decanter of scent in her slim fingers, shook her head and laughed. "Thank you, Gail." She started to put the bottle by her chair, stopped, opened it once more, touched her finger to the rim and put a tiny drop behind each ear. Spring stole out from her, fresh with new life. Seated there, slim and elegant in her long bridesmaid's dress, her blond hair winding around her white shoulders, Mark thought again how Lissa looked so every inch the princess.

"Damn!" Gail swore, pulling at the silk bow with her teeth. "Wish I had my knife."

"Alas! By a tragic oversight I forgot to tell the seamstress that your wedding gown must have a place for cutlery," Lissa remarked.

Gail stopped, peered down at the lace waterfalling around her shoulders, and laughed. "Don't let it happen again!"

"If you really crave your implements of doom, a serving-maid would not be hard to find, to send back to your maiden quarters in search of steel."

"Here," Mark said. "You could borrow—"

"Ah, don't bother," Gail mumbled, gnawing through the ribbon.

Mark reached for a long, flat gift wrapped in red velvet. "Here's something from your father. I wonder why he didn't want me to open it in public?"

Lissa turned back to her ledger. "Richard Duke of High Holt: one bottle scent."

"O Lissa! Shooting gloves!" Gail cried. She held up two gloves, one small and black, the other, much larger, a handsome scarlet. Gail leapt to her feet and hugged Lissa until she gasped. "Real friends give you things you want!"

"You like them?" Lissa said eagerly, eyes sparkling.

"Like them! Come here," Gail said, dragging Mark away

from the King's present. "Put this on. No, the right hand, dummy! There: a perfect fit! But of course it would be. Lissa always does everything perfectly. It's her worst fault."

Mark flexed his fingers and looked doubtfully at his wife. "I never took three shots wi' bow; I doubt I could hit a cow at ten paces."

"What!" Shocked. "A still cow or a walking one?"

Lissa grinned. "Gail loves to torture other folk with archery lessons."

"First thing tomorrow morning," Gail declared. "We'll be at the butts at dawn."

"Well, first you have your wedding breakfast to prepare, and then you are to entertain a delegation from the town: Swangard's mayor will be there, with seven cygnet aldermen," Lissa said gently. "After that, the two of you are due to stand for Master Brush, the portraitist. Then lunch, of course, and after that—"

"All right, all right!"

"—You will be making preparations for your trip," Lissa finished.

"When we get to Borders, I'll be an eager 'prentice," Mark promised. He untied a second ribbon on Astin's gift. "Why do we have to visit this Richard anyway? There's work enow to do on my own Keep; I'm not keen to dawdle in another man's house."

"We have to cross Duke Richard's land to come to Borders anyway," Lissa said. "'Tis only courteous to call. And then, his Majesty believes it would be . . . gracious if his daughter were to bring with her a gift or two, to token the esteem in which the Crown still holds the master of High Holt."

Gail picked a bit of ribbon from between her teeth. "We have to buy him off so he won't be too mad that he didn't get to marry into the royal line." She shivered. "I'd rather sleep with a snake."

"But not wi' me," Mark said.

Gail glanced at him uncomfortably. "Don't make this unpleasant, Mark."

"I guess I need not note my own gifts in the ledger," Lissa said. "What have you there, milord?"

"Mark. 'Milord' makes me uncomfortable."

"You don't do the title much grace yourself," Lissa remarked. Her smile was bright as winter sun, her voice as smooth as cold satin.

Mark blinked. *Did she just insult you, lad?*

Impossible.

He saw Gail give her friend a quick sharp glance. Well, maybe Lissa had meant to insult him. And yet, he didn't think the cut in the comment was really meant for him. Rather, it was as if he were hearing an echo of an old conversation between the two women. *Must be a lot of water has flowed between these two. Deep water. Strong currents.*

Still smiling as in jest, Lissa nodded sympathetically. "You and 'your lordship' soon must learn to co-exist in comfort: you are Duke of Borders now. Your name is seated in a high place, and the rest of us must even so approach it, with 'milord' and bended knee."

"If you can call her Gail, you can call me Mark."

"I know the Princess. To her, I am a friend as well as servant," Lissa said.

"You're no servant," Gail said impatiently. "Just my friend. My best friend."

Blandly. "Friends are not required to walk two steps behind."

"I don't require that!"

"No," Lissa said politely. "You do not."

"Well I'm sick of all these rules," Mark said. "I'd rather have a friend than a servant, and that goes down to my last man in livery too."

Lissa's eyes narrowed. "He and I are honoured, sir, by such familiarity."

Uh oh. Mistake. Mark felt his belly clenching. *Talking to these people is like walking in a bog: one mis-step and you're up to your bloody crotch in it, and every struggle only makes things worse.* He fled the conversation and finished unravelling the long flat package from His Majesty, Astin IV.

The King's gift was a longsword in a beautiful scarlet sheath. Mark looked ruefully at it. "I guess this is to make up for t'one he stole."

The scabbard was of tooled leather, wound about with vines. The hilt was wrapped in silver wire, and a red gem glittered in the pommel. Worshipfully he drew out the blade, which like the scabbard was etched with a tracery of vines.

"Its name is Harvest," Gail said gravely. "It is among the finest weapons in the Treasury, forged by Redwine's Smithson's Dal in grandfather days."

Mark laid the sword across one finger. The balance was superb: his finger sat less than an inch above the hilts.

He hefted it. Though longer and heavier than Thief, Harvest felt lighter and more responsive. "Beautiful," he whispered. "It isn't Sweetness, but it will go a way to settling that score." He sniffed in puzzlement. "What's the smell?"

"Clove oil," Gail said, surprised. "Didn't you keep your old sword oiled?"

Mark laughed. "My sheath was lined with sheep's wool, like this one, and sometimes I might dabble in a drop of neat's-foot oil, but I never cared if the blade smelled pretty."

"A lining well-soaked in oil of cloves is best for steel this fine," Lissa said, turning to Gail. "But remember, clove oil dearer is than silver."

"Really? All my knives just . . . came with it."

Lissa looked at her Princess as if to say, *Quite.*

"She's a beauty," Mark marvelled. "A man needn't feel ashamed wi' such a lady at his side. Strange, though . . . she's taller by far than the girls that danced wi' Deron and Sir William."

Gail beamed. "Your friend Valerian, the fluffy one: he told Sir William you'd never used a shield, so William thought a longsword would be best for you."

The thought that Sir William had picked the weapon made it even more precious. Mark wondered that the great knight should waste his time thinking of presents for a braggart who couldn't make him break a sweat, were they to fight. *God: maybe there's a chance he'll talk wi' me! Maybe even show a stroke or two. . . .* Mark held the hope cupped close to his heart like a candle flame, warming himself with the image of Sir William setting his stance right, teaching him strategy. Moving him through a cut, his wise hands firmly guiding Mark's arm.

"It took Sir William and I hours to convince Father that he should give you this. He is so stingy sometimes."

Mark grinned, elated. "He'd already given me his best treasure of peace," he said gallantly. "It'd be hard for t'awd sod to give away so great a prize of war."

There. Val 'ud be pleased with a line like that.

"When added to a Dukedom and a Keep," Lissa remarked wryly. "Princess, could you really think your father would take kindly to the thought of giving such a weapon to his terrible son-in-law?"

Gail paused, fingers half-buried in a pile of fine linen. "I hadn't thought of it that way."

"You can be sure your father did. Why else do you think

he did not give this gift in public? Even so, others will be certain to remark upon it. To you, a sword a goodly gift must seem, to give a warrior husband. But to others, it will seem a mark of preference; and a hint of where the Crown may go."

"Well don't blame me," Gail said. "I never bother with that sort of thing. Sir William should have thought of it."

Lissa said, "Perhaps he did."

Mark stared at Lissa, startled, but her calm, elegant face revealed nothing.

"Besides which, everyone in the family knows I won't be Queen. I told them years ago. I won't scheme against my sisters or creep around the Palace for that." Snorting with contempt at the thought of scheming for something as base as the Crown, Gail flung aside a pile of wrappings until she found another package to heft. "More towels," she grunted. "I can just tell."

At last all the gifts had been opened and duly noted in Lissa's ledger; their velvet wrappings lay scattered across the floor like bodies on a battlefield. Still robed in her wedding gown, Gail retired to the next room. Like a surgeon bringing out her scalpel, Lissa produced a button-hook and followed.

The women were gone a long time. Mark wandered through the room, gathering the velvet in one pile and the silk bows in another. There was a fireplace with wood already laid. Mark lit it from a rushlight on the wall.

The room was dominated by a vast enclosed bed, with oak doors carved in a hunting scene, and overhead a canopy of lace. A real bed, with real walls, so no one walking through the room could see a sleeper sprawling there. Or doing summat else, for that matter.

All this time, Mark knew, Lissa was in the next room,

undoing button after button, slowly revealing Gail's neck, shoulders, back. . . .

No use thinking on it, Mark told himself. But that didn't get rid of the hollow feeling in his chest. *It should be you in there with her, your fingers on her bare back. It should be your eyes she smiles for.*

Shite.

He jumped off the bed and buckled Harvest to his belt to see how it hung. He practised drawing it as fast as he could, left hand pulling back on the scabbard while the right whipped out the glittering blade.

Still the women did not return.

Finally he took off his sword belt, threw the bed-doors wide and lay on his back under the white lace. *Think of summat besides your wife, Shielder's Mark. . . .*

Flesh of your flesh, now. Yours for the taking.

But not for the asking.

When Gail returned she wore a simple black nightdress. The hem fluttered just above her ankles as she pattered to the doorway. She hugged Lissa and wished her good night.

Lissa bowed to Mark, pressed Gail's hand, lingered. *Worried? Tired? Jealous?*

. . . And closed the door behind her as she left.

Turning, Gail blew out a long sigh. "What a day."

"A day!" Mark said, rolling onto his side, head propped on one hand. "A week at least."

"Hah! Just be glad you weren't wedged into what I was wearing!" Gail seemed subdued and anxious; in the shapeless nightgown she looked rather plain.

"You were very beautiful," Mark said.

"That's . . . that's very nice of you to say." Gail looked around the room, taking in the piles of velvet, the flickering rushlights, the fire. The bed. "I wish there were a window on the south wall. I like to see the moon at night. When we were little, Lissa and Willan and I would sometimes sleep together in my room. The moon would shine this magic silver light on us; we'd put out all the candles and tell ghost stories until we screamed into the pillows."

Something in her words, her voice, made Mark think of Husk, and the firelight flickering in her little hut of cedar-boughs, and the years lying in drifts behind her house. "I can't imagine owt scaring you!" he said with a smile.

Gail shivered. "Oh, you're wrong. They could both scare me. Especially Lissa. Twenty times I ran to Mother's room, and then felt like a fool when she asked me what was wrong."

Mark tried to imagine the demure Lissa telling blood-curdling tales of terror. So much time, so many passions lay between these people, so many unexpected sides.

He felt again how much he was a stranger.

Lissa knows some parts of Gail that you will never, ever see, Shielder's Mark.

The thought made him jealous, and a little sad. "I'll stick to the bargain, you know. I'll not force myself on you."

"O no! O no, I know you wouldn't. You would never do that," Gail exclaimed. "It's just. . . . It sounds silly, but I miss my old room. I know that must seem stupid to a great traveller like you."

"It doesn't seem stupid at all," Mark said softly. How strange it was, to see this side of Gail. *Not everybody sees her like this,* he thought, honoured. *Tired and quiet and thinking of the past.*

He took it like a gift, something of herself she dared to show him. He wanted to protect it, to hold her mood like a butterfly in his hands.

"Childish," Gail decided. She came and sat beside Mark on the bed, scowling sideways, as if he had done something wrong. "That's all it is. It's been easy for me to stay a child:

you get your way when you're a Princess. And Lissa was always so capable, so mature; I never had to bother. But I'm a married woman now." Her small feet dangled over the edge of the high bed; she swung them in little circles. "I guess it's time to grow up."

"You sound like we're halfway dead! I'm too young to be a ghost just yet!" Then, greatly daring, Mark held a goosefeather pillow cocked overhead. "One more moan and I'll have to thump you."

Gail giggled. "You must feel like a nanny, not a husband."

Like everyone else, Mark had always said he hated silly, giggling girls. He discovered he was wrong. Giggling made Gail infinitely prettier, like sunlight falling into water. "Well, an older brother maybe."

She looked archly at him. "I didn't mean to kiss you like a sister this afternoon."

"No," Mark admitted, looking again at her thin warm mouth, her gold-brown eyes. "I didn't feel like your brother then."

Gail grinned and put a hand over her mouth. "We'd better change the subject."

"I liked it just—"

"Really. I mean it."

Mark thumped her lightly on the head with his pillow and then slumped back, defeated. "So ... ." *Ah!* "Say: when I came to your room that first time, there was something on your worktable, a deerskin and a dead corset. You said that on our wedding night you'd tell me what it was."

Gail blushed.

Blushed?

"Oh, that was nothing," she muttered.

"Come on!"

Gail mumbled something.

"What? You sound like my friend that got his teeth kicked out while gelding the dyer's mule."

"A present," she snapped, glowering. "It was going to be a present for you. It didn't work out."

"Oh. Can I see it?"

"No!"

"Why not?"

"It's stupid," Gail said fiercely. "It's stupid and I'm embarrassed to show it to you, all right? Are you satisfied?"

Mark paused to consider. "Nope," he said at last. "I'd like to have a peek."

"Well you won't, so get used to it."

"Princess," Mark said gravely. "Do I have to remind you that you're talking to a man who braved the Ghostwood? Who dared the Red Keep? Who crossed the moat where—"

"O Mark, it really isn't very good," Gail cried. For a long moment she stared at the floor. "Will you promise not to laugh?"

"Cross my heart
And swear to God
On pain of death
and Aron's rod," Mark chanted.

Blushing furiously, Gail shuffled into the far room. She returned a moment later and put something in Mark's hand.

"It's made of leather," he said, frowning and shaking the thing out. "There's a kind of a bulge here: sort of *hedgehog-shaped*—"

"It's a hat, stupid." Gail snatched it away and held it right ways up. "Here's the brim and here's the crown. You wear it on your head to keep the rain out. I made it for you. There: are you satisfied?"

Gently Mark retrieved the hat. It was without a doubt the most misshapen, lopsided abortion of a hat he'd ever seen.

It looked like a tiny leather quilt with an upset stomach. "It's so, so *pink,*" he said, trying to keep a straight face.

And indeed pink was the word for it, though the dye was badly blotched and mottled; some parts of the brim were burgundy, while much of the crown was as pale as cherry blossom.

"I wanted to make it myself," Gail said, red with mortification. "I shot the deer and skinned it, I hung the leather to be cured, I gathered madder to do the dyeing and then I tried to sew it all together but it's a horrible mess and you promised you wouldn't laugh and I'm stupid and that's all there is to it."

"You did all that?" Mark said wonderingly. "You skinned a deer? Princesses don't skin deer."

"This one does. Very badly," Gail added. Her eyes were bright; Mark couldn't tell if she was going to cry or kill him. "It seems like it ought to be easy, but I was never very good at sewing and anyway it takes forever to get a needle through leather. I couldn't figure out how to make the, you know, the crown *stiff,* so I thought I could use part of a corset to firm it up. And the dyer gave me the same mordant that he used to make your cinnamon tunic, but I guess it works differently on leather than it does on wool and anyway it's all ruined."

"You did all that, to make me a present?"

Gail nodded.

Mark looked wonderingly at the ungainly heap of leather in his hand. *A Princess skinned a deer for you. And that's a bigger miracle than anything that happened in the Ghostwood, Shielder's Mark. And what did you get her?*

Nowt. Just because they all seemed so rich, you never even thought to give something that was worthy of her.

But she did not use her riches to make your gift. She made it with her own fine hands. While your hands, which you thought so hard and tough and clever, you left idle. You that are so smart wi' knife or file or hammer didn't make her so much as a wooden box to put her jewellery in.

Mark felt like dirt. "Well I think it's the best hat I've ever had," he said, clapping Gail's gift on his head. He could feel a ring of little ridges where the whalebones in the corset bulged through the inner lining. "I'll wear it every weather."

Gail couldn't stop a giggle. "Even in bed?"

"In my bed, in my bath, in my grave!" Mark proclaimed. His heart leaped as he saw her grin despite herself. He marched over to the window and studied his reflection. As a courtier's hat, it was a joke. But Mark was from the country, and as a plain, country hat, it could just barely pass.

Mind you, it was pretty damn pink. "Why were all my gifts supposed to be red?" Mark asked.

"Lissa says it's your best colour. She's clever with that sort of thing. . . . I hope she likes the perfume. It's so unfair that I should get all these clothes and things. They're quite wasted on me. But Lissa is so beautiful. If she weren't so tall I'd give her my whole wardrobe."

"Just because Lissa's a swan doesn't make you a duck, you know."

Gail shrugged. "You're married to me: you have to say that. Besides, anyone walking around in a hat that pink can't be trusted on matters of taste, Shielder's Mark."

Mark held up an imperious finger. *"Never* insult this hat," he warned. "Men have died for it."

"At least it will keep off the rain." Gail studied the mound of presents that took up one corner of the room. "Can we have that all taken by wagon?" she said suddenly. "I don't want to dawdle along with valets and grooms and cooks and the rest of it. Can't we just go on our own? That would be wonderful!"

"Just you and me?"

"And Lissa."

Mark sighed. "And Lissa." Which reminded him; he owed someone else a debt. "Would you mind if Valerian were to come wi' me? I'd like another fellow about, to help me dress and all."

"Well, I *suppose* he can come. But I mean to set a hard pace!" Gail said gleefully. "Oh, for the open road! No more corsets and no more stupid skirts!"

"No more feather beds and satin sheets," Mark pointed out.

"No more tiresome receptions, no more tedious 'entertainments.'"

"No more seven course dinners wi' five kinds of wine."

"No more snake-hearted gossips and cruel scandal-mongers!"

"No more baths, with all the hot water you want," Mark sighed.

Gail bounced with excitement on the edge of the bed. "No more servants waiting on you hand and foot!"

Mark groaned and fell back upon his feather bed, feeling the bruises of a hundred nights of sleeping outside gather in his back. "Oh shite," he groaned, pulling the brim of his hat down over his eyes.

When he looked up Gail was dragging something in from the next room. With a grunt she threw it to the floor. It was a sleeping pallet. "There," she said, shoving it over near the fire. "That should be plenty warm."

All the disappointments of this wedding night flooded back into Mark at once. "Ah: I see my bed is ready," he said nastily.

Gail's thin lips pursed with anger. "What do you take me for? This is my bed, not yours."

Anger and shame, anger and shame. *How many times can a prince turn into a frog?* Mark wondered. *Ribbit.* "Don't be stupid," he snapped. "I sleep on the ground all the time; I'm used to it. Princesses don't sleep on the floor."

"This one does." Banging open a linen pantry Gail dragged out a pillow and a blanket.

It's not fair she should be most beautiful when she's bitchy. "Look, I—"

"Mark, shut up." Gail lay down on the pallet. Softly she said, "Don't let's fight about this. I'm the one who's denying you your . . . husband's rights. It isn't fair for you to suffer any more than that. I have to feel I'm doing something to make up for it, however small. All right?"

Slowly Mark nodded. "All right."

Lissa's slim fingers, unlacing one button at a time. Gail's narrow vixen face, her tiny feet pattering on the cold flagstones. Her wedding dress rucked up to her knees, sitting amidst a wreckage of presents. Her fire-brown eyes, sparking with anger.

Her childhood, awake with ghosts, cupped in his hands like a butterfly.

'Til death do us part, Mark thought. For the first time he felt the years before him, piled in drifts as deep as those behind.

'Til death do us part.

6

Lullaby

The next day they prepared to set off from Swangard. Gail stalked around her old rooms, badgering the servants to be careful with her brushes and bottles. Her knives and hunting gear she packed herself.

Mark's duty was to stand by and look as if he were really in charge, even though everyone knew that it was neither the Duke nor the Duchess, but Lissa who ran the show.

Mark's only slip came early on, when four servants moved to take out Gail's huge panelled bed, and he started forward to help them heft it.

The lightest brush against his arm held him in place. "I never cease to wonder at the canniness of craftsmen," Lissa remarked. As she spoke, a pair of cabinet-makers' 'prentices began to take the massive bed apart.

Mark, who'd slept on straw pallets and never seen a wooden bed, laughed out loud. "That's bloody clever!" he marvelled. And ignoring Lissa's wince he crouched down beside the 'prentices to see how the cunning bed had been made, that it could so easily be moved. By the time the whole canopied-monster had come down, Mark's carpenter curiosity was well-satisfied, and two patches of wear showed on the knees of his new silk breeches.

Someone snickered as he brushed them off. "I hope you find yourself improved by study," Lissa remarked coolly.

Uh oh. Let me guess: the Duke is not supposed to muck about on the floor and rub shoulders wi' the servants. He risked a quick glance at his wife. The embarrassment Lissa managed to conceal was clear on Gail's face.

Shite.

"I like, uh, a neat bit of woodwork," Mark mumbled. A blush was crawling up from his lacy collar. *You're a Duke now, not a handyjack. Now you've shamed us all again, even the servants. What are they to make of their master sweating onside of them? .*

For the rest of the day he nodded gravely, said as little as possible, and kept well out of Lissa's way. He was relieved when the endless parting ceremonies drew to a close and they left Swangard at last.

On their first night out of the capital they stabled their entourage in a pair of inns along the road. After dinner Gail summoned the steward in charge of the movables and informed him that on the morrow she, Mark, Lissa and Valerian would walk ahead. "I do not want a wagon closer than two hours behind," she warned. "I mean to walk unheralded and unattended, without horses to fuss about or servants underfoot at every step."

"But Princess! You won't be safe on the road alone!"

Gail snorted. "Pshaw, Davin! You sound like an old woman. Will I not be travelling with the man who broke the Ghostwood's spell, the greatest hero of our time?"

"Oh." The steward nodded. "I had forgotten," he said, bowing deeply to Mark. "Of course you will be well. Forgive my impertinence." Gail sent him off with a flick of her fingers.

"Gail!" Lissa hissed. She didn't sound convinced that the Hero of the Ghostwood could shield them all from harm.

She's bloody right too, Mark thought unhappily. *O Lord.*

But Gail could not be swayed. The next morning she got

them up before dawn and marched them from the inn before their retinue was stirring.

A first pink seam ran along the eastern horizon; overhead stars still glittered in a night-blue sky. "I never knew how cold this hour could be in spring," Valerian remarked through chattering teeth. His breath steamed from him. Fog gathered in the ditches on either side of the road.

Mark smirked. "Bracing, isn't it?" It was nothing new to him to be up before the sun, but Valerian kept Court time. *I'll bet every swan I own he's been up for hours, primping an' preening, knowing he would pass the day wi' the Divine Lissa.*

Indeed Val was a picture of elegance, with a charcoal-coloured cloak draped easily over a dove-grey doublet and breeches. His copper tube was sheathed at his side, and on his head he wore an excellent felt hat with an emerald-green plume that just matched the stone on his ring. His beard was neatly trimmed and his fingernails gleamed. *Pity he can't keep from yawning,* Mark thought gleefully. *And every time he looks at owt too long his little glinty eyes go wide and bleary. Makes him look like a well-dressed owl after three beers too many.*

Wouldn't be so bad, if it weren't for the one bit o' landscape he can't keep from staring at.

"Your pardon, sir," Lissa snapped. "Is there a stain upon my dress, or mud upon my cheek?"

"Er, n—!" Val squawked.

"If so I beg you, tell me like a gentleman so I may fix myself, and leave off this, this staring."

"Oh!" Val squeaked. "O, O no! Your habit is perfection, your countenance divine! My eyes are but a trifle weary from too little sleep, and as a tired man would rather rest on heather than on rocks, so these orbs of mine without my thinking sought the gentlest bed on which to take their rest."

Gail snickered. "Now now: let's not have anything bedding on my Lissa."

Lissa glared at Gail and Val in turn. "Indeed," she said frostily.

Valerian gulped; fluffed; pushed his spectacles higher up his nose.

"Nice nip in t'air," Mark said quickly.

"O Lord it's barely *light*," Lissa groaned.

But despite the hour she was her perfect self in a rich blue swallow-tailed jacket and knee-length walking skirt, gold tights, and calf-high boots, also golden. Her long blond hair was triple braided; a gold hairpin held it gathered just above her neck. She wore a pair of fine silk gloves: gold, of course.

Gail had whipped Mark out of bed with barely time to tuck in his shirt-tails. He looked at Lissa in awe, wondering when she managed to achieve such stylishness.

The Duke and Duchess don't measure up at all, he decided. Gail was dressed all in royal black, thinking to be dramatic, but in the pre-dawn light the effect was rather drab, and spoiled by the dirty brown cloak and boots she insisted on wearing.

And as for you, Shielder's Mark, you look like a slaugh-tered sheep. Gail had laid out a white shirt and pants, with blood-red boots, cloak, belt, and scabbard. Any style he had was completely shot by the monstrous pink leather hat he had clapped upon his head.

Ah well; you're a Duke now. You can do what you bloody like. Besides, you don't want to look like the breed that whelped a cur like Peridot.

"Come on!" Gail cried impatiently, stumping ahead of them all. "Do you want our baggage to catch us on the road?"

"Captured by a feather bed," Lissa muttered morosely. "God send me so cruel a fate!" But when the sun began to climb into a vast blue sky dappled with white clouds, even she had to admit it was a fine day for walking.

It was hard for Mark to believe that just one month ago he had left the Ghostwood and come trudging up this very road. Then he'd been a filthy, common man, breaking ice in the ditches to drink each dawn. Now he was a Power in the land: monied, landed, wived.

The barren land was under plough now; the slanting early sunlight glistened on black clods slick with dew. Every third field was unploughed, a tussocky meadow of long grass and frogcalls. "What are they doing out here?" Gail asked, pointing at a farmwife wandering the fallows with her two young daughters.

"Herbing," Valerian said. "Shepherd's purse, this time of year, and sweet violets, from which the herbwife brews a remedy for coughs. They also say it helps to clear a clogging in the chest."

Mark gaped. "How the hell would you know village simples?"

Val blinked. "Um, well. It's, er, a hobby of mine."

Prompted by Lissa's questions he went on to talk about other spring medicines: broom tops to strengthen sluggish hearts, Black Willow bark for fevers and pain, and elder flowers, which made the best brew when you had a cold.

Unfortunately Val was not so good at chatting as he was at lecturing. When the talk turned away from herbs, he remembered all at once it was Lissa he was speaking to, and his eloquence failed. Mark sighed. *What a pudding.*

Gail stumped beside Mark, her short legs eating up the road, straight bangs going swish, swish, swish.

Running from Swangard to the High Holt, the West Road was banded with hoary poplars. Their pale leaves were still damp from the bud, delicate as butterfly wings. Larksong rustled from between their boughs, or soared up out of the farmlands beyond. The road was one of the principal highways of the kingdom, and they passed many people as they walked. Carters who would have kicked Mark out of their way a month before bowed as he passed, and touched their forelocks.

A brace of young women went by, curtsied to Mark, then burst into giggles once they were past. *Damn hat*, he thought, regretting that he'd ever sworn to wear the pink monstrosity.

Instantly he was shamed to have thought badly of Gail's gift. *And what care you what a canty lass thinks, eh? You're a married man now.* The thought surprised him. *And your eyes aren't to dawdle below a girl's neck no more neither.*

Gail stumped on beside him, tireless.

They passed inns like mile signs: the Prodigal Son, the Jolly Carter, the Green Ghost, the Cob and Cup. As the sun sank slowly in the west, each one seemed more bewitching to Mark: his nose tingled to the scent of bacon frying, and his mouth was parched for a pot of cool brown ale.

In the early evening Lissa groaned as the Dancing Duck receded slowly behind them. "It's turning cold and cloudy, Gail. You know what rain will do to my boots."

"That's *Adventure*," Gail grinned. "The wind, the sky. Look at the sunset! And the way our shadows stretch out behind us, like giants."

"I never knew a shadow was so heavy," Val complained. "The bigger mine grows the wearier I am." A great yawn came over him, and his spectacles slid down his nose. He pushed them up, blinking, and smiled. "With luck when darkness falls I'll feel much lighter."

Lissa laughed. "That's a pretty paradox."

Beneath his soft brown beard, Val smiled a small pink smile.

Sic 'em, Mark thought. *Atta boy!*

"There, Lissa," Gail cried. "Let the wind of adventure fill your sails!"

"Wait a minute," Mark complained. "I'm with her. I'm a Duke now. I don't have to sleep outside any more."

"What sort of hero are you?" Gail demanded.

A cool wind came up as darkness fell, muttering among the poplar leaves. Empty fields stretched around them, and a line of low cloud came in from the west, bringing nighttime and the smell of rain. They were a clopping of pony's hooves then, a creak and sway of saddlebags in a tunnel of hissing poplar leaves. The road had emptied with the coming of nightfall; of other travellers they saw only a single lantern swaying in the distance. Then it too swung off to the left, headed for a lonely farmhouse.

Val fumbled with their lantern and got it lit at last. The bull's-eye threw a swaying yellow shadow down the road before them. "The miles squat heavy on my feet and shoulders," he grumbled. "I pray we reach a tavern soon!"

"If we don't find one we can always sleep outside," Gail said cheerfully. "That's why I set aside bedrolls for us."

"Ah," said Lissa. "Bedrolls. Yes." She sighed. "It happened that I saw them, Gail, and thought they were misplaced. I sent them back to Steward's Davin last night. It had not occurred to me—and for this I take all blame—that you would wish for us to bed down in the ditches overnight. Really, it was thoughtless of me."

Gail drew a deep breath. "No bedrolls?"

"None."

A long silence followed. The wind seemed suddenly colder, and the night more dark. Warm yellow light spilled from the windows of a farmhouse far away across fields of mud; it might as well have been on the other side of the moon.

The wind turned damp. Mark felt a tiny cold kiss on his brow. Then another on his hand, his neck, his cheek; and the sky began to stream in earnest.

"It's raining," Val observed.

"The tent? The tent didn't make it onto our pony either?"

"My apologies, Princess."

"Ah."

They walked on through the rain.

"It's strange," Gail said at last. "What the darkness does. It's as if the whole world has dwindled down to just us four, and the pony of course. As if nothing else exists: only us, walking down this road. . . ."

"Which has no start or ending," Valerian said softly. "And we always have been walking, and the world's a cage of leaves around the wind, and footsteps mark the only time, each washed away as swiftly as knife-cuts in a river."

Gail shivered and smiled. "How different it is from balls and dinners and a palace full of lanterns! Only Lissa's cloak rustling and the pony's hooves, and our voices. . . ."

A strange mood had come upon Mark, melancholy and yet distant, as if he stood in a high place and looked back along his life, a path stretched far behind him, and far below. How many times had he walked alone, in rain and darkness? Feinting and lunging and dodging in fields soaked with rain until he was a man of mud, too tired to move, his whole body shaking with cold and wet. Each day another patient hammer-blow, forging himself into Shielder's Mark, Hero. Legend.

At the palace he had been a 'prentice again; Gail and Lissa and Valerian had been his masters. But here, out with the wind and the rainy night, what seemed so strange to them was like a child's secret hiding place to him; as achingly familiar. As full of memories. "The world seems small because you listen to nowt but yourselves," he murmured. "Pull down your hood, Gail. Hear how big the darkness really is."

Slowly she raised her hands and drew back the hood of her battered old cloak, so her pale face emerged from its shadow like the moon sliding from behind a cloud.

For the space of many heartbeats all four walked bareheaded. Rain slicked Mark's hair and trickled down his cheeks, and the sound of it rolled in from every side, gusting through the trees and streaming into the ploughed fields around them. Their footsteps rang suddenly on a plank bridge; a streamlet hurried by beneath them and was gone. The air was heavy with a smell of wet earth.

"You're right," Gail whispered. "We aren't everything. We're so small we're barely here at all."

"No less than fox or marten," Mark said. "And not much more."

"A sobering thought for a Princess," Gail laughed. "I'm not so sure I want to listen often to the world."

Mark laughed with her, love and sadness strangely in his breast at once. "But that's what Adventure is, Gail. That's what it means, if it means owt at all."

"And that means rescue!" Lissa cried, pointing down the road. There, at the top of a long, gentle rise, they could just make out a faint glimmer of light at the edge of the road. "Better than a palace!"

It would be a damn poor palace, Mark thought, that had less to offer than the Ram. There was one rushlight over the bar, one embering fire in the big hearth. Long black cats of smoke, unwilling to get wet outside, skulked around the roofbeams. Mark hung his dripping cloak and hat on a peg by the door. The tables were knife-scarred and stained with spilt beer.

It was a small, sad, decent little inn, the sort of place a

carter might stay on his way to Swangard. Not where Mark had imagined bringing the Duchess of Borders, his lady wife.

"Paradise!" Valerian said, slumping into the first chair he could find.

"I always pictured Paradise with windows," Lissa remarked, brushing out her skirt and sitting down. "So you could watch God stroll by." Her blue swallow-tail coat was splotched with rain and mud clung to the sides of her golden boots. Her blond hair was plastered to her skull. Mark guessed she was wearier than she had been in years. It was impossible she should look as elegant and stylish as ever, but of course she did.

Gail looked like a waterlogged gnome. "Told you we'd be fine," she crowed. "I'm hungry enough to eat the Devil."

"We only serve him Tuesdays," said the innwife, coming out from behind the bar. She wore a kerchief around her head and her apron was stained with grease. "Is there owt else I can get to please your honours?"

"Anything hot would be a marvel," Gail said. "Beef stew or baked potatoes, chicken pie or sausages; perhaps a roast of pork. Pan-fried fenceposts would do, or boiled rocks. Just so long as it's hot!"

The woman laughed. "I hate to tell it, but you're a mite too late! Kitchen's closed, milady. We can heat you up some wine, if—"

"Closed! The kitchen's never closed to Quality, you stupid woman!"

The innkeeper, a tall, thin man with a silver hoop dangling from his left ear, smiled apologetically at the table of gentry. "We've a pork roast we can do, or bacon if you'd like it quicker. Plenty to follow, and hot as you can stand it, I promise. Janey, fetch these fine folks two loaves and a dish of butter."

His wife stood still a moment, fighting to hold her smile, and then did as she was bid.

The innkeeper rolled his eyes. "You must forgive the missus. A good soul, but she doesn't deal much wi' Quality."

"You're sure it isn't any trouble?" Gail asked.

The innkeeper answered with a vigorous shake of his head. "No, madam, none at all. We hadn't really shut down all the way; Janey just don't like to do more work than she must, if the truth be known."

"I wonder why," Lissa said, so softly Mark could barely hear her.

Valerian peered wistfully through foggy spectacles. "Did someone offer us mulled wine?"

Soon Jane had returned with four cups of hot wine and two fat loaves of oatbread. "This is wonderful!" Gail said. "I didn't know you could make bread from oats."

"It's good bread," the innkeeper's wife said defensively. "I make it myself and I've never had complaints."

"No offense meant, goodwife. The Duchess is just too rich to know any better." Laughing, Mark cut himself a slice. "I never ate white bread in my life before I came to the Palace, Gail. Real people eat oatbread mostly, and rye."

Gail blushed. "I'm so sorry!"

Jane shook her head. "I didn't have any call to get edgy. Just something in the air these days. I haven't been myself."

"Well, there's worse could happen!" the innkeeper said, popping into view with a grin and a platter heaped with rashers of bacon. "Is she whistling about the wind? You've heard too many stories, our Jane." He rolled his eyes again. "We're no examples, to shiver at ghost stories at our time of life."

Valerian looked curiously at the innkeeper's wife. "What sort of stories?"

"I—"

"Nothing worth mentioning. You know how it is," the innkeeper said. "The awd wives have nowt to do all day but chatter, and an innkeeper's wife gets more chances than most to listen to any lie that comes along." He looked around anxiously to make sure their cups were full. "Carter's Kev, I am. If there's anything you need, anything at all, just ask it. I'm having the girl make up our best rooms."

"Pray," Lissa murmured, "If it please you, we would like to hear your goodwife's tale." There was the slightest edge to her voice, so faint Mark barely caught it.

Their host was better used to dealing with Quality. He snapped to attention. "Of course! Well, Jane? Don't just stand there! Tell their worships!"

Jane reddened and stared at the floor.

Lissa glanced at the innkeeper. "I do not have to tell you, Carter's Kev, the Princess does not care for lumpy mattresses. Make sure a ewer of hot water waits in both our rooms. You will find my purse as open as your feet are swift, and your fingers diligent."

"Prin- prin- . . . the Prinsssss!" the innkeeper gasped. He started forward, peering in the gloom at the black tunic just visible beneath Gail's weather-beaten cloak. "Oh, yes ma'am. Thank you, ma'am!"

Discovered, Gail winced and shrugged off the dripping cloak, letting it hang over the back of her chair.

Lissa turned back to the innwife, doffing her grand manner like a pair of gloves. She smiled a warm, conspiratorial smile. "To tell the truth, Gail here adores a lumpy bed."

Jane chuckled in spite of herself and then bit her lip. "He means well, miss. We . . . we don't often see such fine people as yourselves at the Ram."

Lissa looked down at her mud-spattered boots and

laughed. "Well, we're not so fine as we were this morning, but the Duke in truth is generous, and his lady wife. Weary as we are, I'm sure we would not notice were our beds but blankets over boulders. I pray you, do not be offended. I dearly wish to hear your stories, but it seemed they were not like to come, with our good host a-hovering by." Lissa glanced at Mark and Valerian. "If it please you, I can make these fellows disappear: there are some things only silly women can really understand."

Jane laughed out loud. "Oh, 'tisn't much, miss. Last moon I started having funny dreams. I soon found out I weren't t'only one. We started hearing stories in here. Someone said there'd been a spook in High Holt three nights running. 'Like a sojur on the battlements,' they said, 'Only awder, and dressed up for a funeral.' Then too, folks have been . . . remembering. Remembering things as we've worked hard to forget," she added quietly.

Sadness settled on them, soundless as snow falling into water.

Then Jane blinked, and sucked in a big breath, and smiled, all business. "Kev's right; there's nowt to it. Just spring turning. Make a start on your bread and bacon, and I'll have you some fried taters in a minute."

Gail shivered with satisfaction as the innwife left. "Ghosts! It must drive Richard mad, to have something at High Holt he can't boss around."

"Now we know the real reason the Duke chose not to join the celebration of your nuptials at Swangard," Val mused. "A spirit! Think what it must be like to breathe, and know before you stands one whose chest rises with air ten centuries old."

"I think Richard had his own reasons for not coming to the wedding," Lissa said.

Valerian took another sip of his mulled wine. "Last moon,

the innwife started having her strange dreams. . . . About the time that you, friend Mark, your mighty deed all done, strode forth from out the Ghostwood eaves to claim the prize you had by heroism won."

Mark nodded. "You said it would change things, didn't you? . . . You know, of all of it, t'Awd Man is the thing that bothers me," Mark said softly. "All the rest was like a dream. But I'll bet he lives there still, sitting in the kitchen, stirring in his ashes, looking for some horrible secret."

"Don't!" Gail cried. "You're just trying to scare us now." She shivered. "You told me you took that old dagger you wear from the Red Keep—I asked because I wondered why he kept a knife so dull—" she explained to Lissa. "But why didn't you tell anyone what it was?"

"The man who's robbed at the door, leaves by the window," Mark said drily.

"Oh. I guess you're still mad about Sweetness, hunh?"

Mark grunted.

"Dearly would I love to look upon Queen Lerelil's gift," Valerian said. "I have a passion for all ancient things."

Mark took the medallion from around his neck and passed it to Valerian.

"It's a magic charm," Gail said decisively.

Mark scowled. "Don't play the peasant, Gail. We don't believe in charms nor magic spells nor t'evil eye neither, even in the country."

"You don't believe in magic! How do you explain everything that happened to you!"

"I think there was magic once," Mark said slowly. "But I've never felt it, outside the Ghostwood. And I think . . . I think you'd know, somehow, if there were any in the world. I guess I wrecked the last magic left in the kingdom," he said with a little laugh. But inside Mark's heart was pierced with longing, and great grief. *What if that were*

*true? What if you broke the last spell there was? Now no
sunset will ever be so beautiful, no song so sweet, no story
so grand as it had been once.*

He felt again the great, dry, empty drift of years behind
him. *What if you've broken the last bridge there was
between the present and the past?*

Lissa said, "I don't believe in magic either."

"Lissa!" Gail cried, hurt. "You used to believe."

Lissa raised her cup and sipped her wine. "Yes I did.
Once."

"Do you believe in magic?" Mark asked Val.

Val looked up from the medallion. Carefully, he said, "I
believe in poetry, and I believe in God. Is magic something
different from these two?"

"You're the only man I've met that truly believed in
God," Mark said, wondering and strangely envious. For the
first time in his life he wanted to believe, but that well
within himself was dry, empty as the Red Keep's ruins.

"Nobody believes in God," Lissa said. "Not even Bishop
Cirdon."

Valerian shrugged and handed back Queen Lerelil's
charm. "I know it's not in fashion, lady. But years of peering
through these spectacles have made me marvel at the
confluence of things, and left me with a wonder that will not
go away. There is little bit of everything in all. At certain
moments, staring through my scrying glass, or looking at a
sunset, or listening to the brook that runs behind my father's
house, for an instant I forget myself, and lose the thing I'm
thinking on, and catch a tiny glimpse of everything instead.
There is a place the soul goes, between one thought, one
time, one heartbeat and the next. . . ." He faltered, as if
embarrassed to have said too much.

Lissa said, "You are eloquent."

Mark cut himself a thick slice of bread and covered it in

butter. When they had first stepped into the Ram, with its embering fire, its low chat and beery, smoky smell. he thought he'd left the wind and rain behind.

But now the night came creeping back into his heart; a darkness of rain falling on abandoned fields, forgotten houses. Things lost, or buried, or left behind. He could feel it pressing against the tavern's thin walls.

After washing down a piece of bread with a gulp of wine he said, "I've felt it. The memories. Like she said. All my life I've pointed straight as a signpost: Ghostwood, 3 miles. And after I went, it would just be, you know,"—he smiled at Gail—"happily ever after."

"Hah! I am no man's happily ever after!"

Lissa coughed.

Gail scowled at her. "What I mean is, this is just the beginning! I expected I should be married to some dull Duke and keep house and practise needlepoint and be generally dead from the moment I married. But you! You rescued me from that." She shrugged and laid three strips of bacon across a slice of buttered bread. "But I know what you mean. You never thought of life after your trip. For a woman, it's marriage you can't see to the other side of."

Valerian fluffed himself, and a quick smile flashed within his beard. "I fear no woman's vision extends even to this side of the nuptial river: not with me standing on the bank, that is."

"You were a great disappointment to us," Lissa suddenly remarked.

"Eh?" Val looked up, a square of bacon impaled on the end of his fork. Mark, caught sucking his fingers, glanced around at the others. A sick feeling roiled in his belly. *They eat bacon wi' knife and fork?*

Shite.

A strange expression was on Lissa's face, mixed from memory and mischief. "It is not permitted for young ladies of the Court to mingle with young gentlemen, of course. But no father's word, nor wizard's hand, ever yet has stopped determined maids. We used to watch you very closely. You and all the other gamecocks strutting through the Palace."

"I confess I don't remember you," Val said, colouring slightly.

"We were children," Lissa said. "Little girls are by young men infallibly ignored, if there are bigger girls around. But my tale was saying you surprised us when you fell in love."

Gail grinned, licking her greasy fingers. "I'd forgotten that. He had a crush on Teris, didn't he?"

Lissa ignored Val's strangled squeak. "We were disappointed, sir. Every coxcomb's heart was tangled in the lime she placed so artfully on her cheeks, or caught in that crevasse of bosom Master Bolt's dresses kept showing off. We guessed that you would fall for Willan, who had a finer mind, though smaller breasts. But you were dull and loved her not; we thought you very stupid, and swore to think of menfolk nevermore."

Gail giggled. "Oh, that was awful. Even then I knew I wouldn't have big, uh, that I. . . ." She trailed off into silence.

Valerian bobbed and peered and huffed. "I trust . . . I trust my taste improved with time, and with it my discretion."

Mercifully, Carter's Kev chose this moment to come downstairs and approach their table, hands clasped respectfully before him. "Is everything to your satisfaction?"

Gail and Lissa burst out laughing. *Steady on, lad: no smirking. Stand by Val as he's stood by you,* Mark thought, desperately crushing down a snigger.

"Everything is wonderful," Valerian sulked. "Marvellous. Couldn't be better."

Mark nodded gravely. "I think we'll tipple a little more of t'awd grape-juice, Kev."

"Oh yes." Valerian stuck out his glass like a beggar's cup. "Yes please. A great *deal* more wine."

"Jane!" the innkeeper yelled. "Wine! You've left their glasses empty."

"I've been cooking, dear, and we do have other trade, in case you hadn't noticed," Jane said, appearing from the kitchen with a copper kettle in hand.

"Half your 'trade' is drinking on credit," Kev snapped. "They can wait." He turned and shrugged, looking at Mark. "She's a good cook, as I think you'll agree, but she hasn't much head for business. There's women for you: no sense for money."

"Oh?" Lissa's fine eyebrows arched.

The innkeeper blanched. *Of course Lissa's wearing the price of the Ram on her back, poor bastard.* "Women, uh, women like our Jane, that is. . . ."

"I'm not greedy," Jane said imperturbably, pouring mulled wine from the kettle into Val's glass. "Is that what you meant, dear? It's your worst fault, Kev: being greedy. You needn't be proud of it."

The innkeeper managed a sick smile. "Just trying to keep a roof ower your head, and dresses on our daughters," he said. "Nowt wrong wi' that."

Jane smiled and pecked him on the cheek. "No. There's nowt wrong wi' that at all."

"There is a school," Valerian remarked as their hosts retreated, "to which all women go, where they learn to outwit men."

"Oh sir, let me assure you," Lissa said, smiling sweetly, "the feat is not so difficult that it requires lessons!"

The fried potatoes, when they came, were garnished with mushrooms and altogether excellent. They ate and drank as only people out walking all day can.

But however much they drank, they did not grow merry with it. They had spent much of the day thinking ahead to Mark's new Keep at Borders and chatting about what they would find there. But now they were no longer on the road, and their thoughts, like their feet, went no farther forward, but back, back, always back. Valerian told a funny story of a grasshopper collection and his father's armour. Looking back with shining eyes, Lissa told of scrapes and scamps that she and Gail had shared.

"By the Devil's big black hat, you two were a pair of vixens in the henhouse," Mark said at last. "Is there no end to these stories? I'm surprised t'awd King didn't sew you up in bags and toss you i' the moat like kittens."

Lissa gave Mark a curious look. "Many were the lives you changed, when you took Gail to be your wife. She used . . . she used to tell me she would marry one like you. Some day. A dashing prince would ride up to the palace and carry her off. And I always knew she would be right."

"But I can't even ride! What a disappointment I must have been."

"Not for Gail," Lissa said. She looked into her cup of wine, as if she saw a day long past, drowned there in the dregs. "We were mad for horses. We used to run about the garden screaming, pretending to be stallions. Perhaps we did not sound like horses, but that is what we said we were. Once Gail fell, and twisted her ankle, and I ran to fetch her nurse. When we got back Gail wouldn't tell us what was wrong, but only neighed instead."

"Until nurse cuffed you."

"She was so scared she had to hit someone, and she didn't dare touch you."

Gail nodded slowly, shaking her head in wonder. "I'd forgotten that."

Lissa took a long slow sip of wine. "You forget things," she said.

Aye: a lot of water gone by between those two. . . .

Mark signalled the innwife for more wine. "All girls are mad for horses. In my village the grandmothers sang the boys to sleep this way:

> *Hush little soldier,*
> *Time to go to sleep*
> *In your dreams gran will give you*
> *A silver sword to keep."*

"My nurse sang that too!" Val laughed, holding up his cup so Jane could fill it with more wine.

Mark held out his goblet. "But if it was a *girl*, they sang:

> *Hush little Princess*
> *Time to go to sleep.*
> *In your dreams gran will give you*
> *A silver mare to keep."*

A second voice had joined him. Looking up Mark saw the innwife standing by their table. She was still as a statue, except for her hands, which pulled and twisted on her apron hem. She sang so softly they could barely hear. Her eyes were full of rain and darkness.

> *"You shall have a bridle*
> *And saddle of gold,*
> *And your little mare will take you*
> *Wherever it's told.*

Hush little Princess,
And always be good
Or Aron will take you
Down into the Wood.

Hush little Princess,
Ghosts are all gone,
Your Troubles are over
Until the next dawn . . ."

She fell silent; one tear tracked down her cheek like a bead of rain.

The whole inn had fallen whisper-still. Carter's Kev came slowly out from behind the bar. "All right, our Jane, all right," he murmured. "It's ower now, long long ago." He reached, awkward as a scarecrow, to put his arm around her shoulders.

She whirled and slapped his hand away. "Don't touch me," she hissed.

"There weren't nowt to be done for her, J—"

"All these years I've let you touch me." She untied her apron and put it on the bar. "You'll have to finish up, Kev."

Stick thin and brittle, he watched her walk back through the kitchen, and away.

Gail and Lissa slept in one room, Mark and Val in the other. The long day and the mulled wine had Val snoring softly the instant his head touched the pillow.

Mark was not so lucky.

Hush little soldier . . .

Like a mill-wheel the lullaby turned and turned within his heart, each turn bringing up a new wash of grief.

Part of it was Janey the innwife, of course: singing for

some daughter lost or sick or fallen. Many a mother had such a ghost to haunt her.

But the grief ran deeper still.

It was his mother's voice that sang the song, Mark realized. His mother singing that song to him . . . while in the background his father made to go.

A silver sword to keep . . .

He couldn't find his father's face.

This memory was like all the rest: angry footsteps, a clattering shield, part of a leg walking by, a man with his back to Mark's bed, bending over to stow something in his pack.

Tension like a wire round his heart.

And in the air his mother's song, trying to soothe him, trying to make him go to sleep.

Make him go to sleep *so they could fight. And it was rage that stiffened your dad's back, rage that made your mother's voice tremble as she sang.*

And you always knew it. You never told yourself before. But you've always known, haven't you?

Always.

His mother was willing him to sleep and he was a good boy and he tried to do what she wanted. But after he closed his eyes the voices would go outside; hers mostly, rising and falling outside their cottage walls like a bitter wind.

. . . time to go to sleep.

So sad. So sad a song.

He lay on his back and stared up at the darkness. "What's happening to me?" he whispered.

For something moved inside of him. All his life he'd been leather-tough, stone patient, fierce as fire. He took pride in knowing every warp and grain of his own character. He thought he knew his heart like a house he'd made himself: the good and the bad together.

But something had changed.

He'd barely been scratched at the Red Keep, but he was bleeding to death inside. *T'awd Mark's dying, dying. It's like when you think you've woken in your own bed, but you're still asleep: everything you thought you knew is strange and witched wi' shadows.* The house he'd made of himself was full of long, empty passages he could not remember, and dark corners that had never seen the light. A wild, dark wind blew in his heart.

When had he forgotten that terrible lullaby? How long had he known that his mother was biting back her fury and willing him to sleep? How many years had wire been cutting into his heart?

How did you forget everything that mattered?

Lissa's blue eyes aglint with anger as she looked at Gail: *"You forget things."*

And all these things he thought, half-asleep with weariness and wine, while in the next room Gail and Lissa talked late, late into the night, and their womanvoices rose and fell, fell and rose, and still the long cloud stretched out from the Ghostwood like a weeping shadow.

A crisp rap on the wall woke him up.

"Rise and shine!" Gail cried. "Rise and—"

Mark groaned and thumped the wall with his fist.

Tucked under his blankets like a tubby brown-bearded cat, Valerian barely twitched.

Mark blinked and bleared. "Ower much wine, not enow . . . water!" *Ah! This is why Lissa ordered water for our rooms!* He stumbled over to the red clay basin and drank deep, then ran his wet hands over his face until his skin woke up.

Rise and shine, he thought, blinking. *Ugh.*

It took almost half an hour for him to dress, and he

needed some help from Valerian in managing the complicated lacings on his white shirt. "Oh, leave it," he grunted at
last. "A man in such a hat as this pink one o' mine can't
worry ower much on fashion." He plodded from the room,
leaving Val behind: *another hour to trim his beard and
brush his pants and polish his bum, no doubt. Now you
know what the rich people do instead of working,* he thought
sourly.

He knocked on the women's door.

"It's open," Gail yelled. "Fifty-seven."

"Val's to be a bit longer," Mark said, letting himself in.
"He still has his eyelashes to curl, and toes to powder. Are
the brace of you ready for breakfast?"

"Fifty-eight. Almost." Gail knelt on the bed with her back
to him, brushing Lissa's hair. Lissa sat looking out the
window at the grey sky. With her left hand Gail would
gather up a stream of golden hair, and then pull the brush
slowly through it with her right. The sight of his wife,
kneeling like a servant and slowly stroking Lissa's thick,
heavy golden hair, affected Mark strangely.

"Fifty-nine." The women did not look at him.

Mark gathered his wits together. "'Almost' as in soon, or
almost by Court time?"

"Forty more strokes," Gail said. "Sixty." She gathered
Lissa's golden hair and brushed it, serious as a nun at prayer.

You're not wanted.

She's my wife!

*You're not wanted all the same. This is private, here:
private to these two, and you've no business watching them.*

He left the women's chambers.

Downstairs the common room was empty. Carter's Kev
sat at one of the tables, head bowed. He did not rise as Mark
came down the stairs.

"Are we late for breakfast?"

"She's gone," the innkeeper said. He did not turn around.
"Pardon?"

"It weren't your fault. It were the dreams, I guess. Just
bad luck, that song." The innkeeper ran one long-fingered
hand through his greying hair. "She knows I can't pay
someone to wait tables. She'll be back."

Mark pulled out a chair and sat down.

Carter's Kev looked at him peevishly. "How can I pay
that, eh? We barely make ends meet doing all the work
ourselves. And the customers like her. They like to hear her
talk. People don't care to listen to me. I don't know what it
is, I try to please, but I don't have the gift." He shook his
head, and looked at Mark, as if remembering who he was.
"Very sorry about breakfast, sir. I don't like to disappoint
Quality. Betty will make up summat, I suppose. But Jane's
left, you see. Gone back to her people; makes it hard to run
things around here. Begging your pardon, sir, but you
oughtn't have sung that damn song. Not that, on top o' the
dreams."

"I . . . I'm sorry," Mary said. "I didn't know."

"She used to sing it to the baby, sir. Our Lily that was. All
the time singing, and after each verse she'd wet the rag and
wipe Lily's face, but it just weren't meant to be." Suddenly
the innkeeper looked straight up at Mark. "Tell me, sir: you
being a man who's seen a bit o' the world. Don't it seem that
doctors are a waste o' coin?"

Mark's heart thudded dully in his chest: once, twice, three
times. Slowly he nodded. "A waste of time," he said
carefully. "If someone's time is up, it's up. All the doctors in
the world can't change Fate."

Carter's Kev nodded vigorously. "Just what I always said
myself," he murmured. "You can always tell Quality, sir;
I've said it a thousand times and you're the living proof."

He rose slowly to his feet, as broken as a scarecrow, as lifeless. "Now: I'll get that breakfast on."

Mark tried to smile, but as soon as the innkeeper's back was turned he grimaced in pain. When the others came downstairs they found him blowing softly into his right hand, where a thin white line cut like frost across his palm.

7

Duke Richard

The scar was a door that let a cold wind blow into Mark. He tried to close it, thinking only happy things, looking only forward to the day's business, and further, to Duke Richard's keep at High Holt. Hoping for some healing there.

They left the Ram and walked west for High Holt. The flatlands began to gather their strength, cresting into long hills, each one higher than the last. At the bottom of each dale a rushing stream cut through the valley's green flesh and laid it open to its rocky grey bone.

Valerian produced another marvel: the copper tube he kept by his side was another one of his glass contraptions, one he called a "telescope." At the top of each ridge he passed it round. With it Mark could look back with hawk's eyes, and see the light flash and gleam from the glass windows of Swangard Palace.

Three mornings after leaving the Ram, they began the long climb south up High Holt's valley. Abandoned when the Ghost King's armies had overrun the kingdom in the Time of Troubles, Mark's Keep was five days ride to the north and west, between High Holt and the Ghostwood, where the forest crept down to the Border River's western bank. It was said Duke Aron had been the last man to pass through its gates, breaking the bridge behind him after driving the Ghost King's forces back into the Wood.

The High Holt loomed out from the mountainside above

them, jutting over the valley like a spur of rock. There were no wide glass windows as at Swangard, to let the sunlight in; only narrow slits through which an archer might fire upon his enemies. The mountain was the Holt's south wall; to the east and north it held up a shield of curving battlement. And on the western side a great Tower stood over the main gate; a stone spear with its butt sunk in the mountain and its head threatening the stars.

"Grim, is it not?" Lissa said with distaste. "All that granite."

"Brutal," Valerian said.

Mark grunted. "It's not a toy." There was a part of him that answered to the High Holt, as a soldier's heart leaps at the clash of steel. "It's a fright to you. But them as built it made a strong place, to stand against their enemies."

Gail grimaced. "I should worry about it falling on me, if I lived here."

"It's the Red Keep!" Mark said suddenly. "Only bigger: it's the stallion to the colt. Your Dad's palace has pretty little towers at each corner, but this and the Red Keep each have one giant Tower. Only here it's West, and there it's East."

"Facing one another," Valerian said.

"Exactly! I wonder if you could signal from one to t'other."

Valerian considered. "Perhaps, if the night were clear. An arrangement of lamps and mirrors. . . . It might also interest you to know," he added, blinking as if surprised by a rather beautiful idea, "the High Holt, like your Red Keep, is surrounded by a blush of cherry trees. They should be blooming even now."

"Now that's eerie," Gail said happily. Her narrow eyes glinted with satisfaction.

Mark flexed his right hand, feeling the seam of cold that ran across his palm where he had grabbed the black dagger from Queen Lerelil's son. "Was this where Duke Aron came from when he drove the spirits back?"

Valerian shook his head. "Aron came from Swangard."

"'Tis odd," Lissa said, frowning. "To think a Duke should linger in the capital, and with an army too! I cannot think the King would stand it. And more than this, where was the King himself, and why came he not to the darksome Wood at the head of his armies?"

Valerian shrugged. "Perhaps that King was lacking in resolve and strength for captaincy. After all, he could not stop the Time of Troubles, nor is his name preserved in any patronymic that I have ever seen."

Mark stopped, astonished. "You actually keep track of all those long names?"

Valerian raised his plump hands. "Only casually, and only for the major houses. Heraldry is a—"

"Hobby of yours," Mark sighed. "I know, I know."

Four hours later they had climbed through a garth of blooming cherry trees, and were trudging up the last incline below the main gate.

"My my, what a draggled clutch of singing birds we are," Gail chuckled. She was right. Dress boots were quickly wearing, stockings were spattered with mud, and their fine cloaks were streaked with grime. Gail, of course, had worn her proven walking boots and her travel-tested cloak.

"You'd be less smug if you had my blisters," Mark growled.

Lissa looked up at the towering gates, then down at her own dirty clothes. "If we slip in unobtrusively, we may just have time to dress for dinner."

"I wouldn't expect too warm a welcome," Gail warned Mark. "Richard's not a good loser. But I ducked him, just as

I told him I would. I heard the stories of what happened to his first wife when she didn't bear him children!"

"Gail! Those are gossip's whispers. It does not become a lady to repeat them."

"Well I still wish Malahat all the joy of him," Gail said, unabashed.

"The Countess Malahat conceived herself a rival with the Princess for Duke Richard's hand," Lissa explained. "Perhaps you noticed her at dinner on the night of your arrival?"

"Noticed her?" Gail snorted. "She was falling out of her bodice at him all night, the slut."

"Do you call the needle whore for clinging to the magnet?" Valerian mused. "I have always thought the Countess Malahat the victim of an irresistible attraction to powerful men."

"Among the ladies of the Court," Lissa observed, "the ailment is a common one."

The moat around the High Holt was narrow, and spanned by a wide stone bridge. "Well, what now?" Mark asked.

"Slip in the servants' entrance if we can," Lissa muttered.

It was not to be. As they stepped onto the bridge, four men in livery appeared on the battlements high above. Two held out banners; on one, the emblem of the King, a green shoot reaching for the sky. The other device was a gold shield crossed by a silver sword: Duke Richard's, Mark assumed. With a twirl and a flourish, two other men brought trumpets to their lips.

"Oh no," Lissa groaned.

The stirring trumpet fanfare was doubled and redoubled as two more trumpeters appeared on the wall, and four more again. "Come on!" Gail hissed, striding forward. "Don't just stand there like idiots!"

Mark trotted after her, cringing. *O lord this hideous hat!* Mercifully, rain had washed out the last of Gail's pink dye, but it was still an ungainly monster of quilted leather patches. *The Duke will take one look at you and yell "Good God! This man has a corset on his head!"*

So much for making an impression.

Damn.

What a crazy world it were, he thought grimly, *where the happily ever after is harder than the story part.*

As they walked forward the great double doors of High Holt swung outward to reveal an aisle of clapping dignitaries, down which they were obliged to walk. Mark blushed furiously. Glancing back he saw Valerian, blinking at the pomp and ceremony. His plump hands cringed at every trumpet blast. Lissa managed better, walking demurely with downcast eyes behind her mistress.

Gail was superb.

Looking every inch the Princess, she unbuckled her worn cloak and handed it to Lissa, revealing the royal black. A hush fell over the crowd.

And of course it don't show mud stains.

Her stride was firm, her poise unbroken; like an arrow thunking into a target Mark's heart was pierced by the memory of her first glance, that felled him across a crowded room. He was proud to have her, and lucky, and blessed.

The thought gave him strength. Turning calmly, he gave his hat and cloak to Valerian, and strode after his wife. *What's good for the goose is good for the gander; you'd better make a stab at being worthy of her, lad.*

When he reached Gail's side she squeezed his hand, grinned once for him alone, then let her face settle to a sovereign dignity. She swept a regal eye across the waiting crowd.

Duke Richard stood at the doors of the Holt's Great Hall, flanked by servants and administrators. He stepped forward and bowed deeply, first to Gail and then to Mark. "The citizens, the gentry, and the Lord of High Holt welcome you!" he announced in a firm, clear baritone that reached the corners of the courtyard.

Thunderous applause.

More quietly Duke Richard added, "You have journeyed far and must be weary. Come in! Cast off your travelling clothes. Knowing you would come before your baggage, I gave orders to my clothier; fresh garments now await you."

"For this welcome, Lord, much thanks," Gail said, graciously inclining her head.

Lissa curtsied. "My Lord."

Valerian bowed. "And how is your honoured father, sir?"

"Well, thank you, Valerian. His days are now engaged in spending that good leisure which the service of a lifetime earned. And the father your name honours I trust is also well?"

"Grieved by his delinquent son, but hale, my Lord."

Copying Valerian, Mark returned Duke Richard's bow with a deep one of his own, and tried the most eloquent phrase he could. "For this kind greeting are we deeply in your debt, your Grace."

Richard's eyes twinkled. "I have not yet been honoured with a Bishopric," he murmured. "Until that time you need not Grace me. We are equals now: plain 'Richard' will suffice."

At Mark's side, Gail grimaced. *Great. Now you've made her look like a fool for marrying a country Jack with his foot in his mouth and his thumb up his arse. God, she must cringe to see you side to side with Him: he's a man, and you're nowt but a boy.*

Richard of High Holt was tall, and strongly built. He was fifty, Gail had said, but he moved like a boss ram in the prime of his strength. Like Mark he wore red, but where Mark's doublet and breeches were a flaming scarlet, Richard's were a dull crimson, dark as venal blood. He had short, straight black hair, and a close-shaven black beard; a few streaks of grey, just below the corners of his mouth, were the only signs of age. His cheeks were strong and square, his mouth wide, with thick lips. Beneath strong brows, his grey eyes were the colour of stones.

A man beside a boy.

But Richard's smile was friendly. His hands, when he held them out to clasp Mark's, were warm and strong. "Come inside, Mark. The High Holt has a fearsome reputation back in Swangard, but a man like you must have some iron in him. I wager you will find the Holt more to your taste than Swangard's ball-gown world."

He turned inside and summoned servants to lead them to their quarters.

Mark glanced at his companions, trying to guess what lay behind Richard's words. Gail was regal, too aloof for Mark to read. Lissa looked more fiercely demure than ever. Only Valerian was visibly puzzled by Duke Richard's warm reception.

No need to worrit on a good crop. So far Richard was the first grand noble who hadn't treated Mark like a child, or a threat. *I'faith, I bet Duke Richard's like his house: too strong a brew to suit a Swangard tongue. Wouldn't it be funny if t'one man who's supposed to hate me turns out to be the only noble I respect?*

He followed Richard into his stronghold, and the boy within him marvelled at the soldiers in livery, and the weapons on the walls, and the sturdy stone beneath his feet, and thought with awe and bitter envy that here was a place indeed to be Somebody's Son.

Dinner at High Holt was simpler than at Court, but flavourful, solid, and deeply satisfying. Cheese to start, and a salad of shepherd's purse and dandelion leaves, followed by a hot, salty soup. Then roast venison, stuffed potatoes, hot fresh bread, good wine, and apple tarts for dessert.

They say he's a wick bastard, but he's got a free hand, Mark marvelled. They had arrived grubby and dirty at the end of day, bagless as beggars at the door. And yet Richard had prepared an elaborate reception and splendid banquet. The clothes he gave them were simple but elegant, and miraculously well-tailored; Mark's brown doublet and breeches fitted him exactly; the dull red cloak, he learned from his valet, had originally been meant for the Duke himself. *How to figure it? The King owes you his honour, and robs you. But you traipse in here as a thief, wi' what you stole from Richard hanging on your arm, and get gifts and soft words in return.*

Lissa, on the other hand, was not so impressed with the banquet Richard had prepared for them. She coughed and glanced with upraised eyebrows at the butler. "I know you do the best you can, but this simply will not do."

What the hell?

The butler cringed, darting a scared look from Lissa to his master. "Sorry, milady?"

"Common knowledge is it that the Princess does not care for vinaigrettes," Lissa said. "This salad is drenched in vinegar. No doubt a simple oversight, but not acceptable. Take it away, and return with something better suited to your royal guest."

Startled, Gail stared at her lady-in-waiting.

Mark was outraged. "Oh shite, Lissa! Leave it be! We're sitting in borrowed clothes in front of half the worthies in the valley and you're bickering about a salad?"

Only Val wasn't drop-jawed at Lissa's arrogance; he peered at her with a puzzled, thoughtful frown. *Of course he's sweet on her, God knows why. But if she opens that perfect mouth to complain again I'll stuff this fancy napkin down her throat.*

"Lissa!" Gail smiled anxiously at the butler. "Really, this is very good. Pray do not trouble yourself. Lissa, really, I don't mind vinegar at all," she said pleadingly.

Lissa raised her eyebrows at the Duke.

Slowly Richard nodded. "Take it away! We dine beside the Black; this is a Court occasion. The salad, like the rest of us, may only come to dinner rightly dressed."

Laughter went round the table as the servants collected the salad. The moment of tension was over, but no one chatted much with Lissa after that.

Gail and Mark talked to Richard mostly; or listened to him, rather, for he was a witty and entertaining host. He was just what Mark thought a Duke should be: strong, well-spoken, and courteous. His servants wore livery of charcoal and white: steady, tasteful colours that made Mark blush when he remembered how he had planned to gaud his troops in blue and silver.

"I was most distressed to miss your wedding," Richard said as the servants cleared away the remains of dessert. "I wanted very much to come, but was detained by whispers: my folk have told so many ghastly tales, at last they now believe them, and claim that ghosts and spectres walk the sunlit world."

"I knew there had to be a use for all these grim old battlements," Gail said. "Ghosts! I think it adds the perfect touch to High Holt."

"I wish I could agree with you. A prank, of course, but then peasants are so simply frightened. I fear *your* exploits," Duke Richard said, smiling at Mark, "have stirred up the common imagination. I have heard more talk of dreams and spirits this last month than in the last ten years together. Spectral sentries, oracular geese, cats that utter prophecy: every ear seems thirsty for such ale, and many tongues are self-licensed to dispense it. I was even forced against my

will to send my steward packing when last week he began
to babble of this Dreadful Figure on the battlements. I
wasted all my patience on him, and even did I sit up two
long nights watching for the spook, but nothing came.
Fermin pointed twice and cried out 'There he is!', but his
fingers marked out only shadows, sadly, and once a raven.
A pity," Richard said, shrugging. "His family have been
stewards of High Holt for many generations.

"So I must dismiss the old in favour of the new. My
mountain people are particularly given to these kind of
fancies: anything old, however worthless, is in the common
mind invested with a kind of awe. So in the valley I have
just spent weeks knocking down a town's worth of old
buildings, to throw up others new as spring and," his wide
mouth curved into a smile, "certifiably free of ghosts."

"Sorry will I be to see the ancient structures go," Valerian
sighed. "They have a history to them not found elsewhere in
the kingdom."

Duke Richard nodded. "Yes. Architecture is a hobby for
you, is it not?"

Gail threw Mark a look of such merriment that he grinned
broadly into his wine, hiding his smile behind his goblet.
Richard shook his head at Valerian. "No sir, history is a
plague upon my valley at the moment. I must put the past in
quarantine, and wipe it out before it spreads."

Mark nodded. "Where I grew up we had Deadman's
Howe. Nowt wrong with it for grazing, but the shepherds
stayed clear. They said the Ghosts had mustered on it, when
the war spilled across our land in the Time of Troubles. I
spent a few nights there getting used to being scared." He
grinned. "I figured it would be a good test for the Ghostwood: I reckoned I oughtn't mess wi' the bull if I couldn't
throw the calf."

Duke Richard laughed. "Gentlemen and ladies: here is a

man well used to getting what he wants! Do not underestimate him. His father may have given him a shield, but
perhaps one day he'll give his son a crown!"

Flattered, Mark tried to hide his pleasure. *By God I think
I could like this hard-handed Duke. . . .*

*Eh? Every face here smiling at those words but my
so-called friends. Gail's about as pleased as a cat i' the
rain. What could be wrong in what Duke Richard said?*

Lissa smiled and dabbed her napkin needlessly at her
mouth. "An excellent repast. I should like to see your
gardens, Duke. The garth of High Holt ever was my
favourite part."

"Of course. Terrina's Tam will guide you," Richard said,
summoning a servant.

Valerian rose hastily, offering his arm. "Would you
care . . . that is to say, if it would not trouble you, I too
would like a wander in the gardens. May I dare your
company?" Lissa nodded, and they left together.

*Gone, thank God. Good spot, gardens. Who knows,
maybe Val can find a way to thaw her out. . . . Warm
night, new moon, spring among the cherry blossoms: sly
dog. Good luck to him.*

He'll need it.

"Charming," Richard murmured, watching Lissa and
Valerian leave. "We are so blessed, to have a touch of true
Court style to grace our rough old backwater." He turned
back to Gail with a pleasant smile. "She was wearing Master
Civet's best, I think. Exquisite."

Uh oh.

Gail had the decency to blush.

The next morning dawned clear. Richard's plan was to
ride quickly to the Old Pension where his father lived, near
the duchy's western border. For two days they would "beat

the bounds," making sure they both agreed on where the boundaries were between the duchies of High Holt and Borders. "You say the King has sent his architect to restore your seat. I would be honoured should you stay in High Holt until the renovations at Borders are complete."

"Thank you," Mark said gratefully, "but I think I'll go on just the same. I hate to trust any man wi' my building. I mean to see it all, right down to the timber in my walls and the stones in my road."

Duke Richard laughed. "I admire a man who's not afraid to soil himself."

Mark's smile wavered. *Steady on, lad. He didn't mean it like that. Of course he didn't mean it like that.* In a moment he was sure of it, and laughed along with the Duke of High Holt, but for some reason the scar on his right palm began to ache fiercely. The pain did not ease for the length of their ride to the Old Pension.

The trip took longer than Richard had anticipated, for Mark had never ridden before. His balance was good and he wasn't afraid of falling, which helped, but he couldn't keep up any kind of speed without his horse jumping into a gallop.

Like a father teaching his son, Richard showed Mark how to sit a horse, how to direct it and control it. As many times as Mark thanked him, he graciously demurred. "We sit our beasts through no virtues native to ourselves, Mark. An accident of breeding only came between you and your horsemanship. Now, try you again, and see if we can get those knees in place. . . . You know, you are a natural. You are a gifted athlete, and a smart one, Mark; in very little time you will be able to impersonate a gentleman."

Mark shrugged. "You flatter me."

Richard waved his hand. "Not at all," he said, smiling easily. "I do not mean to flatter you at all."

Mark had always wanted to ride, and he liked learning, especially as Duke Richard said that he was good at it. His body didn't let him down. If he felt uncomfortable all day long, he told himself, it was only that he was too impatient. *There's a lot to learn, to be a Duke. That's what you bought into lad. It's what you asked for.*

But he was used to being good at things. He'd always been handy, clever, shrewd. But who cared that he could fix a threshing wheel with a wood peg and a length of wire? He could not quote from Aredwyth the Sage, as Valerian could. His tongue clogged like a wad of felt when he tried to imitate Lissa's polished sentences. Even Gail with her cherished bow was more use in a hunt than he, who'd hunted only turnips and tomatoes. He had been the terror of his county with a sword; but he would not last three heartbeats with Sir William.

You're like a mole in a world of foxes, Shielder's Mark: blind and slow and dirty.

He didn't like the feeling much.

He talked little, fearing the moment when Sir Richard would smile and gently correct him. Mark hated these times. "The way Gail winces: that's what gets me," he confided to Valerian.

It was afternoon on their second day out; they weren't far, Richard had assured them, from the Pension, and rest. The Duke rode ahead, talking merrily with Gail. Lissa rode just behind her mistress, and a little to the side.

"Do not let it worry you," Val said quietly. "The Princess is like a pond: her surface ruffles easily, but her deeps are steady."

"And what if she thinks to find another pond to ruffle around with?" Mark asked glumly. "Swans don't swim wi' ducks forever. I can't speak Court tongue, nor wear Court clothes, nor even ride a bloody horse." He clamped his knees around his placid grey mare; she slowed and eyed the grass beside the road.

"But Gail is sick of swans," Valerian said, pushing his spectacles back into place with one white-gloved finger. "Duke Richard's barbs are not such thorns as will make her balk."

"Barbs!" Mark spat. "You lot really have your knives out for him. But ever since we came, he's been a truer gentleman than the King ever was."

Valerian nodded unwillingly. "He certainly has shown us every attention." Ahead, Richard and Gail were laughing, riding so close together that their horses' shoulders almost touched. He was dressed in dull red; she in a gold cloak that touched fire in her eyes.

Pain stabbed through Mark's right hand. He clenched it into a fist. "Richard's hands have been open and his tongue soft: which is more than I could say for some."

Valerian peered at him suspiciously. "Lissa, you mean?"

"She's been acting like a flea-blown bitch for days."

"Don't judge what you don't understand, Mark."

"Stop telling me what I don't understand!" The grey mare jumped forward as Mark's knees dug into its side.

Valerian trotted up and grabbed Mark's reins, bringing both horses to a halt. "Lissa knows the political world as a swallow knows the sky. Do you? Duke Richard she has watched from the time that she was three. Have you? The King and Queen have sacrificed her life to the service of their daughter, Gail. This sacrifice she nobly made, but now her cross is twice as great, for now another witless babe is added to her charge: you. Lissa serves as best she can; but services too fine for country eyes to see, you reward with foul words and contempt."

"I see your tongue stands up for her as quickly as your dick," Mark snapped.

Valerian's breath went out in a hiss.

Mark's right hand ached with frost. "You think I'm so stupid, you Court bastards. But I'm not so deaf I can't hear a cock crow in your pants. Not that you'd ever dare to touch the ice queen. Or am I being common again?"

"Not common. Contemptible," Valerian said softly. "Anyone can be that, no matter who his father was, Shielder's Mark." He let go of Mark's reins. "No, I haven't touched her, Mark. Perhaps I am too great a coward. But in love am I the commoner, honoured Duke. I must work to woo my women. My wife will have to want to wed me: for unlike you, I cannot make her do it."

Mark's horse champed, shifted, fell still.

Bull's-eye.

The pain came stabbing into his palm again, like a needle of ice. "T'others will be wondering where we've been," he mumbled. Together they trotted forward, Mark swearing and holding onto the reins with his left hand.

"The same pain?"

"Mm."

". . . I'm sorry, Mark."

"No, I'm— . . . " Mark laughed, not pleasantly. "I think you're all too nice to know a man like me. I'm quick to anger and I play rough and I don't like losing."

"Then watch your temper like your sword!" Val snapped. "That much is your duty as a man. There are not so many hands that reach to help you, Mark. Be careful you don't lop them off."

". . . Aye."

After another time Valerian said, "Did you never stop to wonder that Duke Richard had prepared for us so noble a reception?"

Mark frowned.

"He could not know our coming, unless he had placed

sentries on the road," Val continued. His voice was soft and careful.

"Aye."

"So we must agree that he had time to give us any welcome that he chose. Why not let us slink within his gates with little fuss, and show us to his townspeople at dinner? Then would we in clean array appear, with our buckles bright and our cloaks agleam, fit objects for all ceremonial pomp."

"You'd make a kind man alm for greed, wi' this thinking."

"Why?" Valerian hurried on. "Because Richard knew that as a light is brighter in the darkness, so would the lustre of his generosity shine better on the backing of our filthiness. His wit is sharper as we are dull, his stride more youthful matched against our plodding, his dinner more delicious to our empty stomachs."

"He never called us ragged, or made jokes about us stinking," Mark said.

"Of course not. Richard is a shrewder man than you or I. He need not be petty. He knows that we are watching him for any sign of choler after Gail's surprising marriage, which struck a grievous blow to his ambitions at the Crown. He must remain in Astin's favour; the King owes him, and he will not game away that debt by careless incivility. Richard will not show his rage, *but that does not mean he doesn't feel it.* Do you understand? Lissa does not trust the man."

"She doesn't trust anybody," Mark objected. "I've known wasps wi' more charity."

"Suspicion is her duty, and in it she excels." Valerian sighed, nodding up at Gail. "Princesses need a deal of looking after, Mark. Gail may not even know it, but for many years the King and Queen have made Lissa know her life is serving Gail. Not befriending her, though friends they are, but serving her, at whatever cost.

"Try to see how this world works, Mark! The night that we arrived, why do you think that Lissa sent the salad back?"

"Bitchiness?"

"No, no! In that one stroke she changed the moral of Duke Richard's play. When Lissa sent the salad back, his every act thenceforth must be not special generosity, but only that obeisance that a subject owes the Crown. You and Gail were perfect, if a little rude: embarrassed for your servant, gracious, easily pleased, anxious that the little folk not feel chagrined. Your shadows Lissa drew upon herself, so Duke Mark and Princess Gail could walk more fully in the sun."

Mark flexed his hand and sighed, head buzzing. "Shite. . . . Well, maybe that were Lissa's thought, but can there be two such twisty folk? What if Richard was nowt but what he seemed?"

Valerian shrugged. "Perhaps. But he grew up in her world, Mark, not yours, and in that twisty world Duke Richard has excelled. If by his creatures you can judge a man, remember that Lord Peridot is High Holt's voice at Court."

Mark shuddered. "Peridot's good at his job, and you don't keep a watchdog to be friendly, after all. I'm sure the Duke's a nicer fellow than his lackey."

"You mean he shows to some advantage when you take the two together?" Valerian asked with a little smile. "As if Lord Peridot had drawn his master's shadow to himself?"

". . . Oh." Mark was rapidly getting a headache. "I'm feeling stupid again. I hate that."

"I know the feeling. Believe me, Mark: you alone have less aptitude for politics than I. I only ask you to be slower in your judgements. I think, where Lissa is concerned, you find it hard to value what you cannot understand."

"That's funny," Mark said. "I've thought the same thing about you not liking Richard."

Valerian laughed. "You may be right. I hope so."

For a time they trotted on in silence. The track they were on crested a ridge and began to slope down. On their left, lichen-covered rocks bulged from the steep hillside; a field of grass and blue-trimmed heather swept down upon their right. Far below, the road wound among a garth of apple trees, foaming with white blossoms. Beyond the orchard was the Pension; Mark could just see a stable-hand bringing a horse in from pasture. Overhead, clouds quarrelled with the sun, sending waves of shadow rushing across the vale.

Val brought out his telescope and looked around. The copper barrel lingered last upon the woman ahead of them, then slowly sank to his side. "She loved Gail, you know."

"Lissa?"

"Not just like . . . sisters, you know. Loved her like. . . . Was in love. With Gail."

Far down the track they were: Richard and Gail ahead; Lissa, as always, a little behind. Her hair was bound in a heavy yellow plait that swayed as her horse moved. Mark remembered it, hanging loose and thick over Gail's arm, their eyes turned away from him, sitting together on the bed, each long slow delicate brush stroke one of a thousand, a thousand thousand that had gone before, that were still to come. He remembered the looks that went between them, full with their two tangled lifetimes. He remembered his sure heart-knowing, that Lissa had touched things in Gail that he would never know.

So Lissa had loved her. Loved her. "I believe it," Mark said. He glanced at his friend. "That doesn't mean she won't love a lad too, you know."

"We were talking, in the garden at High Holt. I knew not what to say. I babbled on about the properties of licorice, and the seven kinds of elder. God, what magic is in women that simply sitting by them can turn a man into an ass?" He looked at Mark, all his wisdom fled, leaving his grey eyes baffled, blinking behind his spectacles. "You think she could love a man?"

"Mmm." Mark wisely let the grey mare pick her own way calmly down the slope. "I think so. Men look to cleave apart, women to cleave together. That's what Smith's George used to say."

Val blinked and sighed. "Who ever could imagine I might feel jealous of the Princess!"

Ahead of them, Gail laughed, a clear, ringing, merry laugh that carried faint and clean as far-off bells. Duke Richard had made a joke; Mark saw his dull red hat bend in mirth until it seemed to brush Gail's own. "O, I can imagine it. Feeling jealous of the Princess doesn't seem hard at all."

8

Grandfather Days

Ostlers were rubbing down the other horses by the time Mark and Val trotted through the Pension's high gate. Richard, Gail and Lissa were talking to a thin old man with hair and eyes the colour of steel. Richard presented them, saying, "This worthy is Valerian, Sir Owen's son, and this is Duke Mark, the storied hero of whom you must have heard."

"I hear no tales but what you send me," the old man said sharply. "How pray you could the world's news float up to my cell? Do you think the eagles whisper in my ear?" He turned, standing with his hands thrust deep into the pockets of his long grey tunic, and eyed Mark's clumsy dismount. "I am Gregor's Henry's Violet's Stargad's Deron's Marleth's Parker's Jervis—and of course my son's ghost until I die."

"My father," said Richard curtly. "He maintains an eccentric reputation, which, as you can see, it amuses him to reinforce at every opportunity."

For an instant their eyes met, father and son, steel on stone.

The old man's gaze dropped, and the moment passed. With a shrug he turned inside. "Well then follow me," he said. "You might as well be fed, and welcome."

Dinner was quickly served and swiftly eaten. Duke Richard and his father, sitting at each end of the table, both proved to be pleasing hosts, as long as they spoke only to their guests. When addressing one another, their words ranged from the coldly civil to the warmly rude: Mark could only guess what they would have been like without company present.

He was glad when it was time for bed. He bade their servant good night, closed the door behind Gail, and sighed with relief. They were alone.

At the same moment they saw there was only one bed.

"Ah," they said.

"Very well," Gail added, a moment after. "I'll take the far side and you can have the near."

"Would you like me to, uh. . . . Should I swear not to, to . . . ?"

Gail laughed. "Don't be stupid. I'd slap you if you tried anything." She flopped down on the edge of the bed and tugged at her shiny riding boots.

Mark gasped as he sat beside her.

"Feel like your butt's been caught in a mill-wheel?" Gail said sympathetically. "The second day of riding is always the worst. You learn fast, though! Richard's right about that."

"Is it true Lissa doesn't—ugh!—trust him?" Mark asked, pulling off his right boot.

"Lissa doesn't trust anybody."

"That's just what I said! Valerian said that was her job, and I should shut up and follow her lead."

Gail laughed and rolled over to the left side of the bed. She lay on her back and wiggled her black-stockinged toes.

God she's beautiful.

"You have to understand, Mark: stewards believe in, well, stewarding people. It's the way they see the world."

"What about—ugh!—you? Do you think Richard can be trusted?"

"Who cares?"

Eh?

Mark looked at her in such puzzlement that she burst out laughing. "If he's up to something devious, Lissa will deal with it. It pleases her to be suspicious of him, because it makes her more important. But every scheme involving me must come down to my actions, sooner or later: at which time I shall do just as I please. And nobody, not Richard or Lissa or his Majesty my father, can make me do otherwise."

"That's a pretty straight furrow," Mark said, frowning. "Lissa and Valerian make it sound much more . . . subtle."

Gail grinned. "One of the privileges of being a Princess is that you don't have to be subtle. In fact, even if you aren't a Princess you don't have to be subtle, unless you care about power." She turned on her side to face him so her body made an S, her head propped on her elbow, the line of her side sloping down to her waist, the swell of her hips. "Look: Richard meant to marry me in the hope I would be chosen Queen and the Crown would pass to (ugh!) our child. But what Richard doesn't know, and Father does, is that I wouldn't be Queen for all the reeds in Fenwold. Anyway, let's imagine Richard is angry and disappointed. Who cares? What can he do about it? Nothing."

"He could try to have our marriage annulled," Mark suggested.

"Father and I would tell him I would never be Queen, and that would be that."

"What if he were just a sore loser, and got the annulment and made your father give you to him?"

"I wouldn't marry him. I'd rather beg in the streets. If I had to, I could make a scene on our wedding day that would destroy his reputation forever." She smiled. "Isn't it simple? No matter how many schemes he has, and counter-schemes, he hasn't a hope, because *I don't mind settling for less than I've already got,* while he has to try to get more than he has.

At the very worst, my father could disinherit me: we'd be on our own, your life would be no worse than it ever was, and I would never have to wear a ball-gown again!" She closed her eyes and shivered. "Bliss!"

Mark turned to sit with his back to her, unrolling his stockings. "I hope you're right," he said doubtfully.

"Parker's Jervis is a character, isn't he? He used to terrify me when I was a child."

"Should I blow out the candles?"

"Mm."

Mark felt his way back to the bed in the dark. "You impressed me, in the High Holt. For a girl wh—"

"Woman!"

"Er, right. For a woman who says she can't stand Court life, you sounded like, like—"

"Like a real Princess?" In the darkness Gail giggled. "My sister Teris does it the best. Willan and I just parody her, but hardly anybody gets the joke. You have to see her sometime when she's really trying to be impressive. She oozes regal power, even now that she's pregnant. We think she'll be Queen. Father doesn't like Duke Gerald, though; says he can't be trusted. And he sweats too much."

Mark felt the bed rock as she swung her legs over the left edge. There was a sound of rustling cloth, and she pulled a dark shadow up over her head. He sat on the right edge, looking the other way, and pulled off his tunic.

"Lissa tells me I have a tendency to prattle," Gail said seriously. "If it bothers you, let me know, would you?"

"It doesn't bother me." The darkness loosed Mark's heart a little, he felt a rush of longing take him. "Don't stop talking. I . . . I like to hear your voice," he said, greatly daring.

Gail laughed. "I think you may be alone in that preference."

"Lucky I married you, then."

". . . I guess it is."

The bed bucked and her small feet slapped on the tiles. A moment later she shook back the coverlet, and he did the same on his side. They stood there for a moment, facing one another in a darkness barely paled by moon and starshine. A tension curled in Mark, like fear and yet not like, as if he was listening for Gail, listening with his ears and eyes and skin for any touch of her in the darkness, for the warmth of her body, the sound of her heartbeat.

Between any pair of lovers there come moments when the rules change, or are broken, and both know it, and let it happen. So it was then. They looked at one another, naked under their nightshirts, pretending the darkness was so dark that this moment was chaste, though both could taste of something wild in it, and sweet.

Gail stood before the window, across the bed from Mark, a shadow next to deeper shadows. The line of her neck showed against the window, topped by a tiny glimmer that might have been an earring, or a star. It was the sense of her that made Mark's heart drunk, her nearness in the darkness, how close she was, his wife. His feet were naked on the floor and he knew hers were too, and the coverlet hanging off the bed must brush her thighs as it brushed his.

She could see him as he saw her.

Don't go.

Mark stood still, tension stringing his gut like a bow. They were close, then; close as two drops of rain on a pane of glass, breathlessly waiting for the instant when they must touch and fuse and run down the window like a streak of wet lightning.

Don't

. . . go.

Gail took the coverlet and turned it down, her slender

wrists curiously slow, as sure as they had been stroking Lissa's hair.

Then, almost reluctantly, she climbed into bed, making the linen hiss and rustle where it touched her skin.

Damn.

The moment had passed.

Mark crawled in beside her. His muscles squeaked and gibbered as he tried to get comfortable. "I don't think I'll be going out tomorrow," he gasped.

"If you think you're sore now, wait until morning! We can beat the southern bounds tomorrow without you, and then you can come with us the day after to do the west and north. We'll have to decide where exactly the Border becomes ours. Fishing rights and so on."

"Great." Fishing rights.

The moment had passed. They were no longer lovers.

Mark's body fell asleep again, turned dull, no longer tense and waiting, but grumbling instead with bruises and sore muscles after two days of riding. His backside ached and his mind swam. Was Richard as kind as he seemed? If not, why not? Did it even matter, or could they ignore him as Gail seemed to think? And what should Mark do with his own castle and the Ghostwood, which made most of his duchy?

Why did his hand still hurt, six weeks after leaving the Red Keep? And what were ghosts doing on the battlement of the High Holt? If the ghosts weren't real, why were people suddenly talking about them? Why did the Red Keep seem so much like High Holt? What meant the serpent-charm Queen Lerelil had given him?

Husk's lean-to, rustling with squirrels, their quick dark eyes aglint with firelight. The past creeping in like black water through the boughs, making his fingers wet with memories; a day—so long ago!—when the moon fell like a cherry blossom onto a spire of red stone and the boy within him began to wake. . . .

"Mark?"

"Wh-wh-what? What?"

"Are you awake?"

"O God. Ugh. I am now."

"Sorry."

"Mark?"

"What? What!"

"Have you had any . . . dreams?"

"O God, Gail."

". . . I was just wondering. Ever since we talked to Janey at that inn, the Ram, I've been having the strangest dreams."

"What kind of dreams?"

"Oh, just . . . strange."

"What kind of dreams?" Mark asked again.

But Gail had drifted into sleep and did not answer.

For a long time Mark lay unfairly awake, staring up at the ceiling, cherishing a secret feeling in his heart, and breathing her faint scent, that stole from the pillow next to him.

Mark woke the next morning feeling as if his body were made of scorched planks and haywire. His hips ached and his hams burned and his butt was sore. He moaned and winced his way through breakfast. No one was surprised when he decided not to beat the southern bounds with them.

In truth, he could have gone. He hurt like hell, but then he was used to it: a man who gets up before the sun to make a warrior of himself, and then spends all day in the fields or before the forge or in the cooper's workshop is no stranger to sore muscles. Mark had been a long time 'prenticed to pain; he was pretty much a master of it now.

And he wanted to see his borders, dammit.

. . . But not enough to take another day with the gentlefolk. He could grit his teeth and bear the riding, but not another day of gaffes, quiet laughter, gentle corrections, shame.

Val offered to stay with him, but Mark shook his head. "I need a quick pair of eyes out there," he said. "And I'd like a voice there besides Gail's too."

Val didn't take much coaxing: not to ride a whole day with the Divine Lissa. Mark had to grin, watching them trot out through the big iron gate: *You may not have eyes quick for Court, Mark, but they're plenty keen for courting! Val's heart is about as hard to track as hoof-prints in snow.*

As they rode away he turned back to the Pension and felt a loosening in his chest, as if the wire around his heart had slipped out another notch, and he could breathe a little easier.

The Duke's father, Jervis, met him at the door. "She sits astraddle well enough."

"Eh?"

"Your wife. She rides well. Not a usual accomplishment in a lady of her rank."

Mark smiled. "I hear she's a dead eye shot too."

"She will find no lack of hunting by the Border, should she wish it: fowl as well as game. Are you a hunter?"

Mark shook his head. "Where I come from it's only work, not pleasure."

The old man nodded. "I have no time for hunting; a useless occupation unless stranded far from markets with an empty stomach. I warn you that for youth there is but little to amuse, here. Nor for age," he added, laughing drily as he turned to go inside. "To what there is, feel welcome. Our library perhaps will please; it is of all my failing years the sole accomplishment. You should find something in it to amuse yourself."

Mark stopped awkwardly in the passageway. "I don't think so," he said shortly.

"Oh." The old man looked back at him, steel eyes narrowing. "Oh, I see. That was thoughtless of me." He sighed, and his grim, seamed face seemed suddenly weary. "One danger of imprisonment is this: when you are your only company, it's easy to forget that not all men are like yourself."

"You're not by yourself," Mark said. "I've seen a village-worth of servants."

The old man paused. "Well—servants. Servants now are something different." He glanced sharply up at Mark. "You will learn that soon enough. For now, perhaps a walk among the trees? I have things I want to ask you, Shielder's Mark, if you can throw a grizzled dog a scrap of time. . . ."

"You are the man who brought our Sweetness back," Jervis said. "For this I thank you."

"Thank the King," Mark grunted. "I didn't give it up by choice. He threatened to set Sir William on me, and I figured better to be a live rat than a dead lion, as they say."

The old man laughed, dry as cork, bitter as wormwood. "Then will I feel a bandit's gratitude." They paced a winding path between crabbed apple trees with rough grey bark, all in blossom. "Knotty, gnarled, cranky things," Jervis said, laying a hand on an overhanging branch. "Like white-haired men with twisted backs. But in their autumn they bring forth a fruit, which old men seldom do, these days." The thought seemed to mean something profound to him; he paused and glanced sharply at Mark.

"I should dearly love to see the sword," he continued. "If Richard will not send it down, then must I crawl into the hills, and beg entrance at what was once my own damn door for the privilege of seeing it. Hah! That will make the young cock crow."

"It's worth seeing. And hearing," Mark added.

The old man's eyes sparkled. "So the legends then are true?" he asked hungrily. "The blade sings?"

Mark nodded, remembering the haunting song; a melody of loneliness, of empty places in the world, hollows in the heart. "It has a tune for every hand, I think: it sang a different song for Stargad than for me."

"Stargad, say you! You spoke with him?"

"Well, he broke my sword and I ran," Mark admitted. He didn't want to tell Jervis about seeing Stargad die.

The old man nodded. "Well you chose. He was a mighty man, by all accounts. Perhaps the greatest of my long-fathers."

"Your family has a better crop of fathers than mine," Mark said drily.

"Our line is old. And remember this: as he who broke the ancient curse, your name will stay forever in your line. But I have done no greatness: my name will die with my last breath. God-knows you will not hear it on my Richard's tongue." Jervis stopped to rest, leaning against the trunk of an ancient apple tree. "You know it used to bother that fool Astin that he had no sons? Hunh! But this is not a country for fathers, Duke Mark. Not any more." He started forward again, walking more quickly. "Upon a knoll there is a bench I like to sit sometimes, when the sun comes out, and let my old bones drink the light."

Mark followed Richard's father to the knoll at the orchard's edge and climbed up into the mid-morning sunshine.

"Here's a little riddle for you, Mark, locked within a name. Our family, you know, is ancient in this land. Since before Duke Aron's time the High Holt has been ours; our name is long. Now in my study is a book, perhaps the oldest in the kingdom, full of rules of etiquette. One chapter of this tome is given to Long Names: the rules by which the Sable must decide if Such-and-So, upon his death, shall have his name committed to the family patronymic. Imagine my surprise to see our line used as an example! But there, the name is different: *Nobody's Gregor's Henry's Coll* is how they styled our patronym." The old man looked up slyly, touching his tongue to his old grey lips. "We are *Nobody's* sons, my Richard and I; I wonder why."

Nobody's son.

The words ran down Mark's spine. How many times had he thought that about himself? Nobody's Son.

"Oh I should love to know just who that No One was," Jervis said, gasping as he climbed. "I wonder why our shield is plainer by far than that of any other family half so ancient as our own. There was more to it once than a single silver sword; I'd bet my life on it.

"Once sentenced to my dotage, history became my study, Shielder's Mark. An old man does not like to think about the future. Instead I gaze into the past, and wonder how this ever came to be." Reaching the top of the little knoll Jervis grasped the back of a wrought-iron bench and wheezed, showing grey teeth in a tight smile. "Would you like a seat?"

"God no!" Mark said. "After two days on horseback I doubt I'll ever sit again."

Jervis settled himself on the bench, and wrapped himself in his heavy cloak as if it were a blanket. "Old men had a job to do, back in grandfather days. Did you know that? Books tell us that in Aron's time both sexes had a mystery. The women's was of birth, of course: of life and the pain of life, and the joy of it. That mystery is still preserved, by our midwives and our mothers.

"But men had a mystery too, a mystery of death. It was the old man's job to teach the young men about death. . . . Everybody loves the spring: but fall and winter are seasons too, and they have been forgotten. They have been forgotten because we want to forget! Do you want to think about dying?" Jervis seized Mark's wrist, his old fingers dry and hard as bones. His steel eyes were cold, cold. Mark squirmed and looked away. "Of course you don't," Jervis said; and he let Mark's hand fall.

"We want to be young! We are all like my Richard. We want youth and beauty always, and the apple trees should always be in bloom; never should we have to see their branches bare. . . . But this is not life, Shielder's Mark. Every fall these apple trees let drop their crop of sin. The first frost kills their leaves, and then the snow flies: for a time they die and are dead."

Mark shivered. Trapped, he stood with his right hand on the cold iron back of the bench, trying not to meet the old man's bitter eyes. To his right he could see the track they had travelled the day before, climbing back into the hills, winding its way around outcrops of stone blotched with moss. Before Mark spread the great horse-runs that fell down to the Border River. Tiny gusts of wind ran through the tall grass like hidden animals, making it weave and shiver.

Close by, sheep grazed the hill's flank, and cows lazily cropped, bells tonking as they swung their heads. Farther off, a herd of horses, half-wild with so much freedom, galloped swiftly north.

"And maybe there is something more," Jervis said quietly. "A reason we old men have lost our way. After all, what should it matter if the young men do not wish to see? It should be our job to make them, to take our gift and stab them with it. But we have lost our wisdom: lost it back in Aron's time, and can't remember where we put it.

"The old books say—no, they demand! The ancient books demand that when a man has reached a certain time in life he put aside the playthings of this world, and this we still do. But the ancients do not say old men retreat to idleness, but to something else. We are to start upon our 'greater work'. . . ."

Jervis' grey eyes slid through Mark like steel pins through an insect. "Do you have the healer's touch, young man?"

Mark didn't know how to answer.

Jervis sighed. "I do not. All that I touch withers; for I am barren of life, and of death too. But History requires a healer's touch!" He grimaced in frustration. "So much past is jammed in this old head, and yet . . . . I can make its dead bones dance, but I cannot bring it back to life!" Jervis laughed his dry, unhappy laugh. "You have been to the Ghostwood, boy: tell me if these old bones can speak to you:

"If the Ghost King was real, then Aron must have laid his armies with a spell. *So where did the magic go?* Why has there been no magic in the land since then? Could Aron be the only man in history to wield it? Absurd. Of course he was not the only one: but it seems he was the last. Fifty generations since are buried in our graveyards; in all that weary time no other man has been a proven warlock. Why even the tales our granddams tell, of ghost and spook and Devil: even magic stories all run back before the Ghost King brought the Time of Troubles down on us.

"What did Aron know that no one knows today? I am compelled to wonder: were the old men pensioned off as I have been, back in grandfather days? Or did they have a gift to give back then, a 'greater work': an old man's magic brewed from contemplation, and steeped in years. . . ."

"But even if the magic died with Aron, surely that's no bad thing," Mark said slowly. "Who wants to live in a world of ghosts?"

"Who wants to get wet and catch a cold? Who wants the river to rise and sweep away their family in the flood?" Jervis replied. "And yet, I think we should miss the rain, if it ceased to fall. I wonder if magic isn't bigger than 'Good' or 'Bad', as the rain is."

A silence ran between them, chill as the north wind that whispered through the apple blossoms and swept over the fields. "Here's another question for you," Jervis said some time later. "What spectre walks the High Holt walls at midnight? You are startled I have heard the tale? Well well, I was lord of that place once. Even my Richard fears me still, when he thinks of it. . . ."

Jervis laughed again. A gust of wind rushed over the knoll, fluttering his steel grey hair, making him shiver within his cloak. "I had better get out of this damn wind. I do not know the old man's truth; I do not wish to die." And rising stiffly from the iron bench, he stared out across the plain, as if looking for his son. Then he turned and left that high place, heading for home.

"He was a fool, and a damn fool too, the king that first demanded every man must swear an oath to him alone." Jervis gestured with a crust of bread, then dipped it in his gravy.

Jervis seemed to be expecting some reply, so Mark mumbled an agreement, though he hadn't been paying much attention to the old man's words. *Summat bitter about this manor-house,* Mark thought. *There's emptiness in every corner. T'awd man's half a ghost himself, haunting the place.* Half a dozen times that day Mark had looked up suddenly to find Jervis watching him from a doorway, or a window.

A servant announced that Richard's party had been seen heading for the Pension. Mark leapt quickly to his feet, babbling something about meeting his wife. Jervis left orders for a second meal to be laid.

Together they walked out into the twilight, waiting in the courtyard before the gates. "It was better in grandfather days," the old man continued. "All of us to swear allegiance to the King! Who can be loyal to a man he does not know?"

"Mm," Mark said. He did not care about kings tonight: he just wanted to see Val's friendly baffled face, and hear Gail's laughter as she climbed into the big double bed with him.

But something was wrong.

Richard seemed in excellent spirits, jumping easily down from his bay, and Lissa was inscrutable, of course. But seeing Mark, Gail scowled and looked away. Even Valerian's round face was troubled by a frown.

"But kings are greedy men, with little wit or foresight. In ancient days, when each swore fealty to the man above him, five men only had the king to watch for treason: five men kept close at hand. Now are we a commonwealth of traitors; and doubt must gnaw the king's suspicious heart because he cannot keep us all in view."

"Droning on, I see, in your usual delightful vein," Richard said cheerfully.

"You look like a wet cat," Mark said, smiling at Gail. "Summat wrong?"

"Nothing's wrong," Gail snapped, swinging herself off her horse. She tossed the reins to a stable boy and stood looking angrily at Mark. *Oh shite, here it comes—she's got some words stuck in her throat she'll spit out in a moment.*

But she only growled, "For God's sake—take off that stupid hat," and stalked past him into the house.

• • •

That evening was unpleasant; everyone was crabby and out of joint. *Like the wheels on a cart with bent axles,* Mark thought, *no one running true to anybody else.* Apparently Richard had put a foot wrong, making a few chance comments that had nettled Gail considerably, but when Mark asked her, she didn't want to talk about it.

Even the next morning Gail seemed strained, Val awkward, Lissa subdued. Duke Richard alone was in excellent spirits. His witty jests and pleasing conversation carried the day as they beat the northern bounds.

And yet, when Richard swept off his hat in a final bow, turned his horse for home and left them standing on the plain, Mark's heart felt suddenly lighter, as if an unnoticed cloud had finally drifted away, and he could feel the sun again at last.

9

Borders

As Richard galloped away Gail grabbed Mark's reins and turned the grey mare's head around. "And all this," she said with a grin and a wide sweep of her riding crop, "belongs to you!"

It was a fair country of tangled grass and wildflowers and a scattering of heather. A few smallish trees jutted from the plain, mountain ash and poplar. They were standing on the old North Way, at a place where long ago it had forked. The east branch ran toward Fenwold, the province ruled by Sir Deron's horse-faced aunt. The other arm led down to Borders, but it had been long abandoned. All that now remained was a raised dike, a wrinkle snaking northwest through the meadows and down to the river valley.

Mark dismounted and knelt on the ground, thinking how this had been a road once, leading to a place men called home. Strings of shepherd's purse tangled with the long grass on the sloping dike. Cleavers grew there too, and plantains, whose leaves stretched like taffy when you pulled on them. Smith's George's wife made an ointment out of plantain and elder leaves to put on cuts and burns and bruises, Mark remembered. He wished he had a pot to slather on his backside.

He reached beneath a plantain's leaves and let his hand rest on the cool ground. Where he had grabbed the cold black dagger his right palm tingled; he imagined roots sinking down from it, running into the earth.

Roots; or rain; or blood. As if his blood went flowing out of him, hot and rich into the earth to wake it after long winter, draining from his body into the thirsty ground.

He pulled back his hand, feeling faint and weak. The frost-white scar on his palm had grown. What had Stargad said? 'Stay the dagger must, or the heart will bleed.'

The heart will bleed.

The grassy plain stretched out around him, tinged red with sunset and his blood.

"Good country." Gail brushed back her straight bangs and smiled. "And now it belongs to you."

Slowly Mark stood up, shaking his head. "I belong to it," he said.

They ambled along the top of the broad dike, gilded by the westering sun. Shadow hooves flashed and flickered behind them, and they were pursued by shadowy riders, bent by the slope of the dike, who drifted like dark clouds over the grasslands.

They set camp in the early evening. Soon the old road would turn to the north and run along the river valley.

"I'm off to fetch some game for dinner," Gail announced, brandishing her short bow stave and fetching a waxed string from her pocket. "Who wants to come with me?"

Lissa smiled politely. "I would rather be eaten by wild dogs," she observed, shaking out a tarp.

Valerian looked at Mark. "Er, perhaps the Duke would—"

"Don't know nowt about hunting," Mark said briskly. "And I'm not getting back on a horse today for any money."

"But—"

"Great!" Gail clapped Val stoutly on the shoulder. "You can use that spy-glass of yours to spot our game. I'll send you to beat the bushes." She considered the thickets of the river valley. "Ought to be some good stuff in there: deer, maybe, or wild boar."

Valerian's arched eyebrows flapped up like scared owls. Then, seeing Lissa's eye on him, he stiffened, turning his elegant hat slowly in his plump white hands, and smiled with the best grace he could muster. "Your servant, Princess. However I can serve the Crown. . . ." Gail grinned, strapped a quiver on her back, and stumped off toward the river. Val swung himself back on his mount and ambled after her, casting Mark a look of mild reproach.

Oh. Shite. You just cocked up his chance to be alone wi' Lissa, you stupid bugger.

Too late now. Mark winced his apology to Val, and waved goodbye.

"I had an uncle once, wounded in the hunt," Lissa said, tightlipped. She was unpacking their saddlebags, taking out food and kit and oilcloths with brisk, angry motions.

What the hell is she mad about?

"I'm sorry to hear it," Mark said, confused. *But this isn't about your uncle, is it? That would be too simple.*

Lissa continued unpacking in silence. Duke Richard had been lavish in his gifts. Smoked meat they had, and bread, cheese and wine and a clutch of cherry tarts. They even had a stoppered flask of oil, and a lamp to use it in; they could cook over its flame, if firewood was scarce. Mark unbuckled the saddlebags on his grey mare.

"It won't be long to twilight," Lissa snapped.

Mark turned as if stung. Lissa rarely spoke to him unless she had to, and never in such an angry tone. "Look you, if you've summat to say, spit it out."

Lissa turned, and raked him with a glance of cold contempt. "I am not some village wench for you to push around, cousin. Do not tell *me* what to do!"

Mark spat deliberately and stood with his hands on his

hips. "Now I've tried wi' you, Lissa. I know you are no village wench. You're a lady-in-waiting from a noble family," he said slowly. "But I am your bloody Duke.

"You are my servant, Lissa. By forge or farm I've been a free man all my life, though there's been dirt beneath my fingernails. But you are a servant. You serve me now, me and mine. And when I give you an order, by God you'll do it! Do I make myself clear—girl?"

Lissa's face went white with rage.

It was the "girl" that capped it, Mark decided. After weeks of saying "coz" and "cousin" like they did at Court, he'd called her as they called the chamber-maids.

That felt just as nice as hitting her.

Good.

God it feels good to be angry. "That galls you, doesn't it Lissa? You grew up wi' Gail, but now you've got to call her mistress. She doesn't give you orders; you've got your own funny bargain struck between you. But I'm not in the bargain, Lissa. I'm your Duke and I can order you around any time I like. So get this, and get it good. I'm tired of your bullshit. You're the only servant I've got and I *need* you. You know things I won't ever learn. So when you've got something to say to me that matters, you say it straight. That's your job. Understand?"

Hell, Mark decided in the ensuing silence, *looks a lot like a pair of blue eyes.*

"My lord, I understand."

Mark waited.

"I will never forget this."

Mark shrugged. "I like a lass you don't have to tell twice."

"I should not have to say these things. You should not make me," Lissa said, voice shaking with anger. "Very well, my lord. As servant to my mistress and to you, I ask you to

consider what it is you let Gail do. Dark is falling fast and there she goes, with no one to protect her. What if bandits come upon her, or that boar of which she spoke?"

Mark's anger dwindled. "Val's with her, isn't he?"

"Is Valerian a hero?"

"He's a noble."

"Gail does not need a noble here!" Lissa yelled. "She needs a sword-arm, not a spy-glass at her side! Worse than useless are you to the Princess at Court. To compound this by leading her into the wild and leaving her! Incredible!

"Gail is daughter to the King! Her husband should be a shield for her, not a walking target. Who will keep her from the poison sting of intrigue—you? Who will run her house—you? Have you provided for her carriages and costume, picked her out a clothier, cook, a chamber-maid? A steward, almoner, chaplain or physician? What if she falls ill of fever—who then will you call? I am no friend of Richard's, but at least the Duke had offered us a civil refuge until your household was complete.

"I thought her lucky to escape his hand; little did I know she would be sold to one who loved her less than carpentry!

"Gail is not a piece of trash for you to use and throw away! She deserves a husband who will place above all things her honour and her safety and her happiness, who strives to make her glad in every hour of the day and does not ask for thanks, but feels blessed to warm himself beside the fire of her soul."

Falling silent at last, Lissa stood with her fine head tilted proudly.

"Someone like you," Mark said.

Lissa shuddered, drawing a deep breath, then looked away and wiped her eyes unladylike, with the palm of her hand.

Mark thought he saw a flash from near the river valley; it

might have been the sunset glinting on Val's copper spy-glass. Gail he could not see. "You win. I feel like shite."

Lissa laughed raggedly. "I never yet knew happiness to follow from plain speaking."

"Not in the short run," Mark agreed. "But I still fancy it. I heard a little bit of the real Lissa there; I liked her better than the fake one. Even if she didn't like me."

"I will endeavour to express myself more gently, lord."

"No 'my lords'! No 'honours' or 'cousins' either: we're not family, you and I."

"No more 'girls,' then."

Mark nodded. "No more 'girls'. Just Mark and Lissa."

"That will not do in Swangard. Honour is another form of power in this land. For Gail's sake I cannot let you fritter yours away: it is a shield against malice and envy."

Mark shrugged. "Do as you think best, then. But when we're just by ourselves, Mark will do. Gail too: no more 'my mistress'."

Lissa winced. "That is your sovereign will?"

"Aye."

"To such familiarity it will be hard to school my tongue—or Gail's ear."

Mark snickered. "It'll be good for her." He gazed again toward the river valley. What if Lissa was right? What if some great-whiskered boar lay waiting in the bushes for Valerian and Gail?

Lissa must have seen his look. "My fear spoke louder than my reason. I doubt there is much danger; Valerian is no great flusher of game. If I were you, I would prepare to eat what Richard sent with us."

"And is the Princess no great shot after all?"

"This I never said: few men I know can shoot a shaft so fair. Gail has killed her share of game, and skinned it too."

Taking a tent peg from Mark, Lissa knelt to plant it without quite touching the ground.

Doesn't want to dirty her walking skirt, Mark realized. *And all that anger, run back into hiding like a stream under ice. What kind of woman is she, anyway? Not just the faceless lady she makes out to be. A stream under ice: slick and cold up top, but down below all fierce current and swirling stones. . . .*

Lissa glanced slyly at him. "Gail does not always realize how much . . . preparation goes into a hunting expedition. Game perhaps is scarcer when the land has not been worked by, say, ten of Astin's finest gamekeepers for hours before the Princess in her glory treads the field."

"Ten!"

"The reflection always pained me, that Gail might have her day ruined by so small a thing as lack of game. I found ten keepers, more or less, sufficient to be sure she would not come home empty-handed."

"Ten good men to scare up a bunny for a spoiled Princess! And she never knew?"

Lissa shrugged. "My duty is to smooth her way: discreetly, if I can. I like to think I do it well."

Mark spat, impressed.

Sharp as a knife and quiet as the grave, this Waiting Lady is. Mark loved good tools, and he was beginning to realize that Lissa could be the best tool he'd ever have for dealing with the world of the Court. *If you can learn to handle her right, lad.*

"Uh, Lissa, I've a question for you. What happened yesterday, while you were out beating the bounds? Polecats get kinder looks than I got from Gail when you all came back."

Lissa put up the tent poles. Carefully, she said, "The Duke spoke nothing ill of you, and much that might be good. He admired the speed with which you learned to ride. He expressed his heartfelt pleasure that, aside from trivialities of speech, your breeding barely showed. Gail, he thought, could not have come off better . . . given that she had no choice in wedding, but was forced to take a man to bed she never met before, and him a commoner as well." Lissa's fine, curved brows rose. "Do you understand? This was the burden of Duke Richard's song: that in time you well might do a fine impersonation of a gentleman."

"Is that how you all feel?" Mark said bitterly.

Lissa tilted her head to one side. "Why no, Mark. I cannot think that you will ever be a gentleman at all. What's more," she added quickly, "Gail would loathe you if you were."

"But then why—"

"See through her eyes," Lissa said impatiently. "Gail knows she wants some other life than balls and gowns and palaces; a husband who is more than braid and epaulets. She cannot flee farther from the Court than to your arms, God knows. But even though she did not crave her jewelled life, it is the only one she knows. However fine your qualities, you must lack virtues she heard always called important."

"I'm Nobody's Son, you mean."

Lissa shrugged.

Soon they had the tent set up, a spacious beauty panelled inside with silk. Tonight Mark would sleep with his back on his land; and somehow that made it easier to be Nobody's Son.

So you weren't born a noble, to be given your land and wealth and title. You did summat better: you earned it, wi' strength and courage and cunning. Here on this land, under these stars, you're as great as any primping Jack in the country.

Squatting in front of the tent, he grinned at Lissa, feeling joy and triumph welling from the ground. His ground.

"You're a deft hand at tent-setting. I wouldn't have guessed it."

Lissa studied her immaculate blue tail-coat, still unstained. "Gail has always been an ardent camper. When the weather warmed we used to sleep outside, in the Palace gardens," she continued softly. "We pitched our tent behind the Laughing Fountain. There was a big magnolia there; on summer nights the blossoms glowed with moonlight; the breeze would make them sway like lanterns held by dancing angels." Lissa sat down then, folding her legs beneath her. Sunset licked red flame onto the western clouds. "We stayed up late, of course, and went sneaking through the garden in the dark. Three times we found coy Teris with her lovers. Gail would snarl and snuffle like a wild thing, trying to scare them. Once from behind a shrub she reached and nipped one on the ankle. Half fox she was back then, and the other half less girl than goblin. . . ."

"And nowt's changed since." Mark squatted beside her with his chin on his knee. A flock of startled birds rose from the river valley and hung, circling, in the twilight sky. "You remember a lot of things."

Lissa nodded. "Many things. And ever more, of late. Remember what the woman said, our hostess at the Ram? Dreams. . . . Strange dreams." There was something new in Lissa's quiet voice now, something like fear. "I may yet believe in magic," she said, trying to smile. "I saw the ghost, Mark. At the High Holt. *I saw him.*"

"What! Did you tell Richard?"

Lissa shook her head. "It was late on our first night. There was something in the air; the wind; and something bedded too in all that dreadful stone. I was frightened, too frightened to sleep."

Mark stared at Lissa in surprise. "You! I thought you used to scare Gail half to death wi' stories."

"I paid a higher price for them than she. She ran to Mother's bed and fell asleep: I always stayed behind, and stayed awake. Gail enjoys being scared; to her it is exciting, like wind or wine." Lissa shook her head and shuddered. "I am frightened all the time, and I hate it, Shielder's Mark. I hate it.

"But enough of this. I could not sleep. Sometime after midnight I rose and wandered to my window. Then I saw him.

"When Janey told us of the High Holt's ghost, I conjured up a sentry in my mind, pacing his damned watch across the battlements and back, pike resting on his shoulder, dripping supernatural gore; an arrow, perhaps, transfixing his breast, its shaft jerking with each step and breath and heartbeat."

She swallowed. "The real ghost was different. He was an old man, a terrible old man. He turned around, as if he felt me watching him, and looked at me with such hate. His eyes! Those eyes were cold and hard as iron. They had known such horrible things. Had seen horrors done on his command."

Softly, Mark asked, "You're sure it wasn't a real person?"

"There was something wrong about him, Mark. *Wrong* that he should be there; I half believed the Ghost King walked again. O God, there was a richness to that terrible man. As music is to talking was he to the world. As red wine is to water.

"And . . . and I saw myself dying in his eyes, Mark. I saw myself with a lump in my throat as big as an egg and I was withered and in pain, dying in a splendid room, alone. Dying alone. . . ." She faltered, staring at the ground. "You cannot believe me, can you?"

Mark grunted. "I've been to a place where the same day happened for a thousand years, and I've hefted a singing sword. I carry a scar on my hand that hurts worse the farther west I go. I'll not call the kettle black. Even Gail's had witchy dreams. Does she know you saw the Ghost?"

Lissa shook her head.

"Why not?"

"It is difficult, sometimes, believing anything can matter that happens to me, and not to her. Besides," Lissa said with a smile, "are you not the hero, Shielder's Mark? You must be the expert when it comes to breaking spells."

"Hunh! Then we're knee-deep in the pig-shite for sure." Dark was falling around them. "Hope they bring back firewood," Mark muttered. What had Jérvis said, about old men's magic? Was there such a thing once?

Old men. An old man on the battlement with death in his iron eyes.

And another at the Red Keep, who sat before his fire and stared at some dreadful mystery, drawing in the ashes.

It was full dark by the time Gail and Valerian trudged back empty-handed. "Tragically, there was no game to be found," Val said, grinning with relief.

"Nor firewood neither, eh?"

"Oops! Sorry."

Mark spat, considering a cold night in the tent.

Gail shook her head in frustration. "It was the queerest thing! I used to hunt around the castle all the time. But you know, we barely saw a damn thing all the time we were out there! It's . . . harder than I thought," she said with a frown.

Ten men! Mark fought to keep from laughing. "Bad luck!" He glanced at Lissa, sitting beside their large oil lamp. She met his gaze with her usual polished polite smile, but he thought he caught a gleam of merriment in her eye. And just this once, the joke wasn't on him.

The river had cut three broad steps into the plain on its eastern side, each perhaps two hundred paces wide. Borders, or what remained of it, sat on the lowest terrace. An arch of stone, still standing by a miracle, faced east toward the road, marking where the main gate must have been. When they reached it, Mark sent Val and Lissa to deal with the King's architect, who awaited them in a tent encampment just upriver from the Keep; this allowed him and Gail to walk through Borders alone. "Buy me a little time to look ower my new home," he said. "I want to know what it feels like here, before I go changing it."

Borders was a crumbled ruin, its grey bones cancered with moss and ivy. Mark and Gail walked down corridors now open to the sky. *Nowt left here of folk or life. Time has cracked the stone walls open and the spirit's fled,* Mark thought, sombre. *A dead body wi' soul gone.*

A hundred paces farther on came the riverbank itself, a willow-lined bank six feet high. There the first span of a shattered stone bridge hung above the water. *This must be the one Aron broke behind him when he penned the Ghost King in the Wood,* Mark mused. *A lot of mystery in those crumbled stones.*

They had come in the late afternoon. Here the river was shallow and rocky. The Borders chattered with cold; splinters of sunlight broke like ice on its back and went whirling downstream.

The far bank was a steep, sandy bluff, pitted with small caves that housed otters, minks, stoats: maybe a fox and a badger or two. Streams cut the cliff-side, running swiftly to the river. The bluff was crowned with darkness: the Ghostwood, a dark cloud of cedar, fir and pine. This Wood, cupped in a circle of hills that started north of the High Holt and did not come down to the Borders' edge again for a hundred miles, formed the great bulk of Mark's territory.

Great. Duke of a haunted wood. Well, you'll find summat to use it for.

The thin strip of land allowed him on the Borders' eastern side, seventy miles long and never more than five miles wide, formed the useful part of his duchy: land so far west of anything, Astin could grant it to him without offending his neighbours in High Holt and Fenwold.

Mark stepped cautiously on the bridge. It held. He stood a long time there, with one foot on that broken span, while a melancholy filled him, sweet and sad and grieving. Once he had felt like a machine, driven toward his destiny. But in the Ghostwood, part of the machine had broken, some chain around his heart. Now he felt loose as cloud inside; changing shape with every wind of feeling. He wondered if he were about to cry.

What the hell? You never wept, before the Ghostwood got you. A shadow slipped into you there, lad: you've gone weak and funny inside.

And yet it felt . . . it felt almost good. *I'm alive,* he thought, remembering the rush of feeling, standing next to Gail in the dark, or lying in the Ram, hearing his mother's lullaby. *I'm alive at last. And I've been dead so long.*

Things go so far, and no further. A boy grows up, but doesn't become a man; the men grow old, but they can't find their wisdom.

A man gets married but can't even come into his wife's bed. They live together for a while, then one day the love is gone. The husband leaves, leaves his wife and child behind. What's begun is never finished: and the man that starts across this bridge will never reach t'other side.

Come into his own at last, with the rush of the river in his ears and his heart, Mark knew then that he needed, that he must have a son.

He had to have a son.

• • •

"The workmen will be wondering where we are," Gail said gently. "Lissa and Val won't satisfy them long. They want to see the Duke."

"And the Princess."

Gail shook her head. "I was a princess in another life. While I am here, I am the Duchess first. Well, Gail first," she said with a grin. "Then the Duchess, and the Princess last of all. But now Gail and Mark have had a chance to see their playground: it's time for the Duke and Duchess to get to work."

Mark held up his hands. "All right, all right! I surrender!" He settled his clumsy leather hat more firmly on his head and strode back for the Keep.

His Keep.

A copse of chestnut trees stood south of the ruins, their smooth, blossom-coated branches reaching out like fingers gloved in lace. "That must have been the orchard," Mark guessed. "Like the cherry trees at High Holt and the Red Keep."

"Or the apple trees at Jervis' Pension," Gail said.

Beyond this grove the workmen had burned a clearing out of the brush and brambles. They stood before a fleet of canvas tents, chatting together and staring curiously at Mark and Gail. Before them, Valerian and Lissa were listening to a small, thin, superior man who clutched a sheaf of drawings.

Lissa, seeing Gail and Mark approach, turned with eyes downcast and gave her most deferential bow. Mark was about to bow back with Gail dug her strong fingers into his forearm. He settled for a gracious inclination of his head.

Valerian bowed. "Er, um, Master Orrin, architect in chief to his Majesty," he mumbled, indicating the dapper man with the drawings.

"Very good," Mark said. "Um, so, Master Orrin. How does your honoured father?"

"Ooh! Fine, fine! Tip top!" From the way the man coloured and fussed with his sketches and glanced at his feet, Mark guessed that he'd let slip a sign of great favour. Gail's hand quivered on his arm. *Trying not to laugh, the minx.*

"Well then, Orrin, how goes the work?"

"Of course we haven't been here long, your Lordship, and many of the masons haven't yet arrived, but even so I have been able to get a feeling from the land, a feeling for the possibilities, and I have some ideas I really think you'll find intriguing.

"Just here, behind the tents, I see something really nice. Something light, something airy: with that southern face we should get lots of sun, and any stinginess of Nature we can rectify with windows, if they be but broad and deep enough. Oak and marble, don't you think? For that stately, classic feel: a little paradise set in a wooded river valley. Rustically charming!" Looking up from his sketches, his eyes fell on Valerian's emerald ring, and Lissa's fashionable swallow-tailed coat. "Yet, sophisticated!"

"This looks nice," Mark said, studying Master Orrin's drawings. "Very neat. I can see you're good at your job, Master Orrin, and we'll build this someday. But I want Borders just as it were five hundred years ago."

Master Orrin's jaw dropped. "But, but . . . but your Lordship! This is impossible! No one can tell what the old place looked like! . . . Besides," he wheedled, "between you and me, those old keeps were nasty places. Have you seen the High Holt? Dark. Damp. Dusty. Full of bats. Bats, your Lordship! You can't want bats in your Ladyship's hair."

Gail squashed a snigger down into a sneeze.

Mark clasped the architect's shoulder. "Harder to bring t'awd place back than press wine from cherry stones, Orrin. I know it. That's why you're t'only man for the job. But we can't just cart the stones away and blot Borders from the earth. We're by the Ghostwood here; the past must have its say." Mark knew this heartwise. Nobody's Son needed roots, and the roots of Borders dug deep.

"But your Lordship! Half the walls have fallen, nor can we trust the ones still left. To do what you require we would be forced to tear them down and build again on the selfsame spot!"

Mark clapped him on the shoulder. "Good thinking, Orrin. I knew you were the right man for the job."

Val blinked, eyes shining with enthusiasm. "Think of it! A chance to delve into the past, to crawl into a builder's mind now fifty generations dust. Any architect can make buildings from his fancy, Master Orrin: but you will be producing something quite unique, a manor that the fickle wind of fashion never can erode. No lesser task than resurrection has the Duke of Borders given you, to give life not to corpses, but to the grave itself."

"And you'll get your fair free hand," Mark promised. "Too much is lost for you to lean on simple imitation. You'll have to crawl into t'awd builder's head like a mouse into a wine bottle."

"Oh, really," Orrin said. A flicker of hope came to his eyes and he glanced beseechingly at Gail. "Your Highness—"

"The Duke is master of his house," Gail said briskly. "Your business is to indulge his whims, however mad."

The architect's shoulders sagged. He looked back through the ragged rows of chestnut trees. "We could start on the Great Hall first," he mumbled. "Once that's done we can move inside. Kitchens too, of course, to feed the lads. . . ." His eyes narrowed, flicking down to the broken bridge, up the river valley to where the road would run, along the skyline. "Would have grown up around the ford, I suppose. Not really defensible; from what's left of the walls I should guess they didn't try."

"Not such a fortress as the High Holt," Valerian murmured.

Orrin shook his head. "No, not at all. The chestnuts, now . . . shade, of course, in the summer. Which means there were probably gardens outside the south wall: a lawn at least, for walking or playing. That runs the road back behind the north wall and down to the bridge. . . ." He fumbled for a piece of charcoal and flipped over one of his drawings to begin sketching on the back.

Gail grinned quickly at Mark.

Master Orrin was rapidly forgetting that the Duke existed. Suddenly his fingers stopped. "Wind!" he cried, starting to draw again more feverishly. "That's the second reason for the trees: the valley must funnel the wind down from the south. That's why chestnuts instead of apple trees or cherries," he said, blinking as if surprised to find Mark still there. "Taller, stronger, with broader leaves. Shade from the south sun if you need it, and a windbreak too. Which must mean that the first builder didn't want the place to be damp and drafty, of course! What good builder would? What could I have been thinking?" he cried, and forgetting to take his leave of the Duke, he hurried over to his foreman.

"If you do not need me lord, I would like to follow him," Valerian said. "Your challenge excites my imagination; and too, I have always had the strongest fascination for the art of landscaping. It's a, a—"

"A hobby of yours?" Lissa enquired, one eyebrow raised.

"Well, it is," Val said defensively; and with a quick bow he hurried over to Orrin before he missed any more of the plans.

• • •

The next few weeks passed by in a whirl of activity. Mark and Gail stunned Orrin and his men by joining in the work: scrambling over fallen walls, digging for old foundation lines, even hauling stones. Mark's body fell into the comfortable rhythm of hard work it expected as April dried into May and May warmed into June. Spring waxed slowly into summer, and Gail hopped around the Keep like a goblin, getting ever browner and stronger, loving every day she spent outside. Valerian was ecstatic, and spent countless hours doodling visions of what Borders might have been.

The idea of the Old Borders began to exert a weird hold on everyone, not just Mark. Orrin's masons marvelled at how well the old blocks had been cut, and how cleverly they had been joined, particularly in the making of arches, like that at the Main Gate. Orrin's carpenter looked longingly at the stands of cedar across the river, his hand itching on his adze. Even the cook, as it turned out, had a passion for chestnuts; he could hardly wait for the fall crop.

As for Orrin, the architect was a man possessed. He had spent his working life in the flatlands, building elegant mansions for clients who craved light and space and air. These were good things, and he did not mean to abandon them. Clearly much at Borders had been made from cedar timber, a wood he knew well and for which he felt great affection.

But here at Borders Master Orrin fell in love with stone. Its solidity. Its permanence. Its *substance*, as he said many times each day, running his hand along a smooth granite block. "You think of it as dull, until you look! Then you see white and grey and flecks of red smouldering within the rock. Leave it rough on the outer walls, of course. But imagine it polished, facing into a room with broad windows and a high ceiling! And so little risk of fire!" And so on.

As workmen pieced the old stones together, so Orrin and Valerian laboured to reconstruct the mind that had built Borders in the first place. They called him the Maker, and admired him beyond reason: his deep knowledge, his keen vision, his profound wisdom. Whenever Orrin would suggest, for example, some way in which the west window of the Great Hall must have been positioned so as to catch perfectly the afternoon light, then he and Val would stare at one another, and shake their heads, and express their amazement at the way the Maker thought of everything.

"Of course he was a genius," Lissa observed to Mark one day as they watched Val and Orrin at work. "The Maker never can look dull, when he is given credit for all of Orrin's shrewdest thoughts, and all Valerian's insight!"

Lissa too was busy, though Mark wasn't exactly sure what she was doing.

Finally, one day at the beginning of June, she approached Gail and Mark as they watched the doorway of the Great Hall go up. "My lord—"

"Mark!"

Lissa curtsied. "Ahem. Mark, you told me once that when I spoke to you as servant I was to make my speaking plain. Very well: bear with my attempt.

"I have tried to stave this moment off as fiercely as I could, but the crisis comes upon us soon. You two have work to do, and you must do it."

Mark looked at her, mystified. "You may be speaking plain, but I'm not understanding you. I'm working every day, as hard as any other man, right down to humping blocks of stone or chopping firewood."

"That is play, my lord. Not work."

"Play! You try it for an afternoon!"

"Boys sweat when they play ball," Lissa said tartly. "It does not excuse them from lessons. You are Duke of

Borders now. The duty of a Duke does not reside in hauling rocks or stoking fires: his obligation is to rule."

Mark looked at Gail. "I take it from that guilty face you think she's right. Very well then: order folk about? I can do that."

Lissa smiled. *Looks like a cat watching a mouse creep from its hole.* "I am so glad you feel that way—my lord."

As it turned out, there was much ruling to be done.

Without Mark really noticing, the camp in the river valley had swollen greatly since they first arrived at April's end. Many newcomers were workmen, of course, sent by Astin to build Gail's home. But soon other folk were drifting in as well. Merchants and peddlers, adventurers, tinkers, pilgrims. High-spirited youths who came because they thought it fine to serve the man who broke the Ghostwood's spell. People so poor and desperate they were willing to leave everything behind and head west in the hope of a better life.

Most of these pilgrims came with tents, food, and money, but some did not. Master Orrin wanted them sent packing before they interfered with his work, but Mark wouldn't hear of it. He was a Duke now: a father to the people on his land. It was his job to find them food, and shelter, and hope. His job to protect them.

"You can't protect them from everything," Gail said. "No ruler can do that."

But Mark said, "He must try."

At first he asked Valerian for advice. "Come on, Val: you're Somebody's Son. Tell me about laws and taxes and armies, mayors and tithes and town councils and common land."

". . . Er, well, this is rather embarrassing," Val mumbled, "but I really, em, don't know anything about all that."

"Goat's piss. You know everything. Lord Peridot said it himself."

"Lord Peridot, may I remind you, is not famous for his truthfulness." Valerian squirmed and stroked his beard and blinked. *He's ashamed,* Mark realized. *Shite and swanpiece.* "You see, my lord,—"

"Mark!"

"Mark, yes. The issue is I never did . . . I was not very good at, at all that sort of thing: at governance. It was my father's shame and cross." Val forced out a little laugh. "My interests were somehow ever of another star, or in the sky, or growing in the earth. I collected beetles more than taxes, gave out alms more easily than justice. I might perhaps compel myself to think on, on land disputes or fishing rights, but then by imperceptible degrees my thought would shift to the invention of a water-wheel that could lie flat, for instance, instead of standing vertical. . . ." His eyes brightened. "Which reminds me! What a thought I have for Orrin! I saw a perfect place upstream for such a wheel. You see, one need only cut a semi-circle in the bank, thusly—"

"Val, I've two villages worth of souls to care for here, and more coming every day."

Valerian stroked his soft beard and fluttered one plump hand. "W-well, you will need a water-wheel eventually," he said meekly. "This design of mine not only will mill grain, but will drive a bellows too, if executed properly."

"Shite." Mark gave Val a long, hard stare. "So you grew up without a day's work in your life, and t'only thing you didn't learn was—"

"My duty," Val said softly. "Yes, you have it right. I cannot stand to give an order, force a point, tell another what to do."

Mark looked at him with wonder and exasperation and pity all mingled together. For the first time he had an inkling of how Val's father must have felt.

But he's your friend, and you've no right to shame him for not knowing what you don't know either, he thought, clapping Val on the back and leaving him to his water-wheels.

It's a pain in the arse, though, and no mistake.

Well, it isn't as if you can't find it in you to order folk around.

It was thinking of sensible orders to give that was the problem. Lissa was invaluable, of course, but she was used to managing a Princess, not an estate. She too was learning as they went along.

Mark found he liked ruling. He had always been handy, had always prided himself on being a man who got things done. Though building his duchy from the ground up was a bastard, and each night found him battered into the ground, each morning he woke glad to fight again.

He sent messengers out into neighbouring counties to announce that he had land to lease. He set the rents low, but with the catch that for the first five years they must be paid in goods or service, not in coin. "We need their backs and arms and crops. Coin's not much good until the road's fixed up and we've steady trade through here," he argued, and even Lissa admitted that his plan was sound.

Lissa was most impressed by how Mark dealt with the Vagabonds, as she called the many young men who had run away from the farming life, and arrived at Borders with nothing but their pride. "You see that?" Mark would ask each lad, waving at his Keep, now busy as an anthill. "Today this place is crawling wi' masons and glaziers and cabinet-makers and shinglers and who knows what else. The King has lent us a clothier, a dyer, a tanner, four seam-stresses, a huntsman, a chef, a tent-maker—even a per-fumer, I think." Here he would meet the young man's eyes, and make him feel he was being given a special duty. "I want you to help one o' these men. Stick to him like a leech and suck him dry. Learn everything he'll teach and spy out what he doesn't tell you. By Christmas he'll be back in Swangard, and we'll have to dye our own cloth, or tan our own leather, or hunt for our own game: and you'll be in charge of it."

It nearly always worked.

The craftsmen didn't like it much: 'prentices take more time than they're worth, as Orrin said, and nobody liked giving out his trade secrets.

But Mark was the Duke. *Which means you have the hammer,* he thought with satisfaction. *Orrin and his clan can bark and snap, but you hawd the leash and they know it.*

"You are a natural leader," Gail said simply. "I knew that from the first moment I saw you."

"The Princess was quite eloquent that night," Lissa said. "'Like a hawk among the songbirds.' Those were her words."

Mark shot a wicked grin at Gail. "And she a fox among hens."

It was a fair morning in the middle of June when Deron came trotting down the track toward Borders on a fine white stallion.

Mark walked up to meet him. "Good God lad, welcome! Any man that hits Lord Peridot is a friend of mine." *He rides easy: good. Wasn't hurt too bad, then.* Though Mark was sure Sir William had gone easy on the lad, Deron had fought long and well, refusing to surrender until his collarbone was broken. *Looks like it healed up well.*

Gravely Deron inclined his head. "My Lord of Borders, thank you for your courtesy. I hope I may redeem it with a minted coin of loyalty, and swear to you my fealty, if your household can withstand the tarnish which a young and unaccomplished knight must bring."

Mark smiled. "You'll tarnish nowt but my pride, Deron: I think I always wanted to be just like you. Get off this bloody beast before he kicks me, will you?"

"How could you, the hero of the Ghostwood, ever long to be like me?" Deron said, startled.

"You've a quick sword an' you smell nice," Mark laughed. "Get down!"

Deron dismounted and Mark looked him over. *Grow out that short blond hair a bit and he could be Lissa's cousin. About the same age as me; about the same most ways. Except for him being taller, and prettier, and finer, and better able to read and dance and sing: except for those things, you mean?*

Shite.

"So—what brings you to t'outhouse of the kingdom?"

Deron blushed, beautifully of course. "I must have great regard for the man who broke the Ghostwood's spell, my lord. And . . . and more than this, I cannot help but love the lord who chose to play Janseni's music at his nuptials, and throw the gauntlet of a ripe disdain between Lord Peridot's teeth. I am third of my father's sons; I have no purpose on our estate. Even if I did, our seat is on Duke Richard's land: a demesne I cannot bear to frequent."

Envy twisted in Mark's gut. *Oh aye he's a gracious son of a bitch. A fighter and a dancer too. Look at him, Shielder's Mark: you could have been that, if you'd been Somebody's Son.*

Deron's blush grew deeper. "And Swangard for me is haunted by unhappy memories."

Janseni. Must be. Like snow melting in the sun, Mark's envy turned to pity. *He's not some young knighted God; just another luckless corked-up whelp running from a broken heart. He loved Janseni and she couldn't tell him from polecat piss. The same awd story. Poor bugger.*

A shadow crossed Mark's heart. *You might not always feel so superior, Shielder's Mark. Not if Gail gets tired of her ploughboy and trades you in for summat more her style. If she leaves you it'll be for just so soft a tongue, for hands just so white.*

"Come on," Mark growled, feeling like Deron was his friend and enemy and younger brother at once. "Get your beast to Ostler's Bill, and then we'll talk."

"Deron says we rank just after gall to your father's taste, and just before goatshit," Mark said later that night.

He and Gail had slipped away from the camp, leaving Lissa and Valerian to see about finding Deron a place to sleep. The night was dark, but warm. They sat at the edge of the old bridge, with their feet dangling over the rushing water.

"There is something magic in a midsummer moon," Gail said. "Look at it! Hanging over the Ghostwood: so bright it almost hurts your eyes. Ghost clouds too, up there, drifting in a dark purple sky."

"He wasn't fond of me to start with, I guess, but the Janseni business didn't help, Deron says."

"Have you ever noticed how clouds move? Especially on moonlit nights like this. They seem so purposeful, sliding to a destination in another world, always changing shape, and you're sure what the next shape will be, only it never turns out like you expect, and you think you know where they're going, but you don't."

A snatch of laughter and a bit of song carried to them from the camp. "And then there's the bloody ghost. Walks about t' High Holt in broad daylight these days, Deron says. Tradesmen won't come up no more. Not that I blame them.

The Ghost King's come back and I brung him: that's what they say in Swangard now." Mark took out the black iron dagger and slapped it anxiously against his thigh. The blade was cold.

Old men on battlements, or staring into ashes.

Old men's magic.

"This mad quest to wake the darkness. . . ."

"The same moonlight we see here is glinting on the mere around the Red Keep," Gail whispered. "And beneath the water, something feels the light, and sinks yet farther into darkness."

"It's all dried up," Mark said shortly. "I told you that. Nowt but a ditch I walked across to get Sweetness." His mind fell swiftly back to plans, worries, calculations. "Our last night in pavilions; tomorrow the Hall."

"O God. Don't remind me."

Eh? "What was that?"

"This is our last night!' Gail grabbed his arm. "Don't you understand? After tonight we are trapped inside that mausoleum. The Duke and Duchess of Ghostwood, with valets and footmen and ladies-in-waiting. Then it will be ten times harder to walk alone by the river on a June night, and smell the moonlight in the air. God, Mark, you don't even see how beautiful this is. This was my fairy tale: my prince and I alone in the summer night, under the stars. I don't want to give it up."

Her grip loosened from his arm.

He reached to hold her hand. "I'm sorry, Gail. I just got to thinking. . . ."

"Not about me, that's certain."

"What do you mean by that?" *Steady on, lad. Ease up.* "There's been a lot of work to do. And it's not so easy to think about your wife, when she isn't really. . . ."

"Can't you just think of me as a friend?"

"Well, no," Mark said.

Shite. Get out of here. It's no good talking love at her. Damned if you end up like Deron. If you babble out your feelings you'll only make a bad thing worse.

"I'm in love wi' you," he snapped.

O, great. Very subtle.

He loved her.

He had tried to forget that, tried to lose himself in his duchy. But as he spoke the words he suddenly saw how true they were, as if the moonlight showed him a corner of his heart the sunlight never reached. "I loved you the first time I saw you, with a dagger in your belt and laughing like a fox." *Marvellous. That's it you silly bastard. Pull out your heart and put it in her hand.* "I thought we were a story," he stammered. "I thought we were meant to be. And after I knew you better, I loved you more. But by then I'd found out we weren't to be a story after all."

"Is that what you found out?" Gail said quietly. "Is that what I said when I kissed you on our wedding day?"

Moonlight fell like mist over the world. Willows crouched beside them on the bank, their trailing leaves the hair of hunchbacked old women, hiding their faces, their secret eyes. Beneath Mark's feet the river bubbled over stone; moonfoam trailed around each rock, glimmering glinting vanishing gone: swallowed by the sweep of shadow.

The moonlight witched their clasping hands from friends' hands into lovers'. They were touching now, in the darkness; the thought crawled up Mark's wrist like a spider and scuttled into his heart. Against his thick arm her slender one; one of her woman's slim pale fingers between each of his.

Then pulling, shifting, her flank pressing against him as she turned, her lips on his like moth wings. "We are," she whispered. "We are a story."

She kissed him then. A shock ran deep into him, into his

groin, his heart, the hollow of his body: a shock at the press of her breasts against his side, her thin lips now soft and opening for him, against him.

The blood shimmered under his skin; his sex was like an iron bar, enchanted by her nearness.

I'm alive.

His whole body had been dead, or sleeping; now it woke, blessed into life by her warmth, her mouth opening under his, the smell of her hair, the wild near stroke and smell of her hair, beautiful beyond all singing. He slid his hand up the back of her neck, holding her. From her ears dangled hoops of gold, bumping and swinging against his hand, each touch filling him with unbearable desire, made sweeter still because he knew, he knew now that he would have her. The smell of her hair, the warmth of her back against his arm, her lips open under his: these things eternal as the stars, as true.

"Oh God," Gail whispered.

"Hmmm. M'hmm. Do . . . d'you think—?"

"Yes." Gail nodded. She stared at Mark with naked eyes. "Definitely yes."

O boy o boy o boy. "Let's get off this bridge. I don't want to fall off it while, um—"

"Yes." Gail leaned forward and kissed him again. "You know," she murmured into his neck, "I'm sure that there's a way to make love right here. The Maker would have foreseen that this span would be left—"

"And that we would come here. . . ." Mark giggled.

"And that I would want to take off this button here," Gail whispered.

"We're in the bloody open, Gail!"

". . . and this one here. . . ."

"Gail?"

"Mmm?"

"Just this once, if you don't mind, I think I'll take off this bonny hat you gave me."

She laughed into his neck and they rolled over into the grass together. "Never!" she whispered.

10

The Broken Bridge

O sweet devils! Mark thought some hours later, flushed and alive. *You're not going to sleep again this night!* A warm wind blew in his blood. He left Gail snoozing in their ducal tent, dressed and crept out into the June moonlight.

He picked his way into the Keep and entered the Great Hall, a dark cavern smelling of cedar beams and sawdust. The stone flags had all been washed and strewn with rushes gathered from a fenny spot a few miles down the river. A flood of moonlight welled in from tall mullioned windows, dappling the floor with diamonds. *Orrin's making damn quick work of it. Two windows each side he said, ready in a week. But here are three each side, already fitted! Must have been inspired.*

A door had been hung in an archway at the back of the hall. Intrigued, Mark walked through it. Tomorrow he would be hungry for sleep, but he didn't regret being up now. Throughout Mark's life this hour, the last before dawn, had always been the time of his secret mastery. Now it was good to be alive in the night, tasting his happiness.

It was also good to see how Master Orrin was getting on; the business of governance was taking up most of Mark's attention these days. *Lay some of that on Deron? Surely he would have learned to be a gentleman.*

Oh, right. Third sons are warriors: they do death, not taxes. Damn.

The door led to a corridor, the corridor to other passages. Mark was impressed. The corridor ended in a flight of stairs. Mark went up, testing each one: he didn't want to step off into space if the flight was only half built. Stepping through a door at the top, he found himself in open air, on the western battlements. "By the Devil's thumb, that's quick work," he muttered, grinning like a fool. *Lerelil's Son came through a door just like this before you thwacked him and pinched his dagger, remember?*

The memory drove a nail of ice through Mark's palm and he gasped with pain. He felt the dagger too, like an icicle belted at his hip.

The door behind Mark opened and a figure stepped lightly through, then stopped. "Dost a right, mate?"

Must be one of the workers. Mountain stock, to judge by the accent. Mark nodded; the pain was fading to pins and needles, as if his hand had fallen asleep and were just now waking. "Nowt but an awd scratch. Gets me sometimes."

The newcomer nodded sympathetically. "I've one in me shoulder. Devil's brach when the weather turns. Fletcher's Bill, hight I."

"Out late or up early?" Mark asked, deciding not to let on who he was. If Bill didn't recognize the Duke, so much the better.

His companion laughed softly in the gloom. "Early, sure. A damn sight too early, I wis. But I promised lad I'd shew him a tiff o' sword-play. Is nae time on duty, and his mother's agin it, so an it be fine, we meet afore cock-crew." The stranger yawned hugely; Mark could just see his teeth and his sleepy smile.

"Damn good of you," Mark said softly. "It's a lot of trouble."

Bill shrugged. "Well, it's my son, isn't it?" Suddenly he winced. "Shite."

"What's bit you?"

"Damn. I thought to get loaned a second sword, but I baint memorized to. And nowt's bloody stirred at ilka hour."

Swiftly Mark unbuckled Harvest.

"O, no call, friend! Simon'll last well enow one day wi'out—"

"Take it," Mark said. "Don't make your son wait, not even a day. Please, take it. I don't use the damn thing anyway. Not any more."

"Mercy, master," Bill said slowly. "I'll oath to bring it back by cock-crew."

"Oh no you don't! I mean to be sleeping! I'll collect it from you. Fletcher's Bill, right?"

The other man took the sword and put out his hand. "Certes. And who mun I mak Simon courtsey to?"

". . . Mark. Just Mark."

The two men shook hands, and then Bill hurried away; Mark listened to his footsteps patter softly into the darkness. Then all was quiet again, save for the sound of the river.

Simon, eh? Another boy up before the dawn to learn his swordplay.

Only Simon wasn't alone, lunging and thrusting and stumbling over molehills. He had a father to be there with him.

A grief grew in Mark, but did not make his happiness less. More strongly than ever he felt his feelings come alive, like roots stirring at the touch of spring rain. The joy he'd felt with Gail, for one; the heart-knowing that they were meant for one another. *You'd given up on that a time or two. You've got summat to look forward to, all right.*

Yet even as he thought this he was looking back, turning to face a shadow that had followed him from the Ghost-wood: the shadow of a little cottage where a mother sang her boy to sleep, and an angry father rummaged for his things, about to leave. About to leave again.

Mark stood upon the western wall and wept while the eastern sky paled, pink at last as the inside of a rabbit's ear. He cried steadily and silently, spilling into the morning, weeping for what he had found, and what he had lost. Once by chance he raised his right hand and wiped away his tears; they stung on his scar like salt on an open wound.

At last the rain stopped streaming from the cloud within his breast. He left the Keep, and lay down beside Gail just as the sun was rising.

"Mark?"

Val.

Ugh. "G'way. I'm dead."

"Milord, I think you would do well to rouse yourself."

Something in Val's voice drove away sleep. Mark blinked and shook his head. Gail had risen and was nowhere to be seen. *Bright. Must be well into morning.* "What is it?" Mark mumbled, pulling on a pair of pants.

"I think you would do better looking for yourself," Valerian said nervously.

Great. All I need in life is a valet who loves surprises. He buckled on his belt and frowned: *where's the damn sw— Oh, right. Fletcher's Bill. Hat, hat: oops. Down by the river, in that little grassy place where. . . . Must look for her earring before someone finds it in the tall grass shite. . . .*

"Well?" he said, stepping out and squinting in the sunshine. "Hey!" he said, frowning. "Where's the west wall?"

Master Orrin and Valerian exchanged startled glances. "We can't possibly begin work on the west wall this year," Orrin said.

"But—!" Something writhed and twisted in Mark's gut.

Of course the west wall wasn't up. None of the walls were up. "But I was there," he whispered. "I'd swear I was there last night." He shivered. "Must have been a dream. . . ."

"Perhaps you dreamt, but I doubt it." Valerian gestured at one of the workers. "We resurrected this from underneath the rubble of the western wall," he said grimly.

Mark leaned forward, and felt an icy fist close slowly around his heart. The workman held a sheet of canvas between his hands. Harvest lay upon it. The beautiful blade was now in three pieces, and so pitted with rust he could barely make out its pattern of vines. The silver wire around the haft had tarnished into nothing and the gem in the pommel had fallen out. Lying next to the pitted steel were a few rags of what might once have been red leather.

"From the condition and the placement of these frag-ments, I would guess your sword has been lying in the rubble for many centuries." Valerian's high brows arched as he met Mark's eyes. "I find that very curious. Don't you?"

Leaving Orrin to manage affairs, Valerian, Mark, Gail and Lissa withdrew to a shady spot behind the ruined northern walls. It was a hot day, but the moss-covered stones on which they sat were cool.

Gail shuddered. "Ghosts!"

Lissa smiled in her cool, ironic way. "Now consensus is complete: first two, now four among our merry band believe in ghosts."

"Wonderful! I knew you'd come around. Nobody could tell stories like you did and not believe in magic. But what made you change your mind?"

Swiftly Lissa told Gail and Val about seeing the terrible Ghost on the battlements of the High Holt.

"And think on this," Mark added, as his mind turned to the mysterious events at the Holt, and its equally mysterious past. "Jervis says their family name used to be one titch longer: it began wi' *Nobody's,* back in grandfather days. They used to have a tricked-up coat of arms too, but somewhen all but the silver sword were blanked out."

"Nobody's son? Their shield blanked and stripped of charges? We must infer some great humiliation in the line, some terrible disgrace," Valerian mused. "Even those accused of treason do not have their charges censured so."

"Well, summat must have caused the Time of Troubles," Mark said slowly. "Why did Duke Aron have to lay the ghosts and their horrible King? Were they always abroad, or did summat wake 'em from their graves?"

"Clearly something happened, and it happened at the dreadful crimson Keep whose challenge you alone have met," Val said excitedly. "It must be so. Duke Aron drove the darkness to the Ghostwood, this we know, and so the direful time was closed. Now, what did he do? By your tale we know 'twas always the same day at the scarlet Keep. My guess is that Duke Aron cast a spell to trap the Red Keep in time, to never let it go past the day the spectres first arose. He spread his magic like a bandage on the wound through which the spirits bled; no consequences from that day could spring, trapped in a coil of eternity. Until. . . ." He looked up at Mark, eyes widening.

"Until *I broke the spell,*" Mark whispered. "Like pulling out the keystone from a dam. That's what Stargad meant when he said that without the dagger the heart must bleed." He remembered how he had felt, sitting on the bank looking at the Red Keep with his boyhood stirring in his breast, the wash of miracles rushing by him into the world. "When the spell was broken, time started running again from in the Red Keep, and all the magic and all the ghosts bottled there so long started spilling out!" Mark stared at Gail. "Oh shite, your father was right! All this really was my fault!"

"We cannot say for sure," Lissa said. "And even were it true, there was no way you could know."

"I wonder if the Ghost King will return?" Valerian mused.

Mark looked desperately from one face to another. "Why? Why the bloody decree, that the King should grant one wish to the man who broke the Ghostwood's curse, if that curse was all that kept the Time of Troubles back?"

Valerian winced. "My guess is, they forgot."

"Forgot!"

"Duke Aron has been dead nigh on a thousand years," Val murmured. "More than enough time for people to forget what exactly waited in the Wood. And in time no one believed in spectres any more. No one believed in ghosts, and the Wood was just a place of menace, and finally no more than an inconvenience."

"Is bravery cowardice too? Is light dark? What else do I have wrong?" Sitting in the shadow of Borders' crumbled northern wall, Mark felt the past rising like a flood within his breast.

You were a fly in spiderwebs at Court, boy, but this is worse, far worse. Court you can dodge: but the past is everywhere. "Nobody" has a son who has a son and so on for fifty generations, and even now every bloody thing Duke Richard does is framed by things a thousand years old he doesn't know a thing about. His life touches yours, yours Gail's, Gail's Lissa's and so it goes, everyone thinking they're on solid ground, but really just floating on the river of the past.

Mark felt empty as an eggshell, as brittle; his hollow insides swirled with diamonds of moonlight and the scent of Gail's hair, rotted red leather and the sound of a dead man teaching sword-play to his son. *Father and son now both dust. They might be sticking to your boots, or blown against this very rock you're squatting on.*

Mark swore and jumped to his feet.

"The Ghostwood was a dark place: that was at the root of things." Valerian's voice was soft with wonder. "Duke Aron's magic perished with him, and with it all enchantment else. Perhaps the end of magic was the price they paid to chain the ghosts within the Wood. One mighty spell, one terrible sacrifice: a dam, Duke Aron built, that trapped not just ghosts but all magic else behind it. When Aron died, and his line faltered, the secret of the Ghostwood faltered with it. It was a dark place, a blot upon the kingdom.

"If my memory serves, Jasper II it was who offered first a princely sum to any hero who could free the kingdom from the pall that crept o'er it from the west. This is twenty generations later, understand. Duke Aron's line was long gone into dust, and its secrets lost. Jasper blamed the evils of his day upon the wood. An easy gesture. Probably he never thought to pay, for who could do what mighty Aron left undone?"

"What a stroke of genius!" Lissa said admiringly. "Thus did he the Crown absolve by making of the Wood a wellspring for all woes: a scapegoat that need never suffer persecution, yet would never go away. Add to this that many charismatic knights of proven worth—the sort of men who otherwise might challenge for the throne—would undertake the Ghostwood Quest instead. Very neat."

"How do you know so much about these ancient proclamations?" Gail muttered. "Don't tell me history is another one of your hobbies."

"Er,—well, um, actually. . . ." Val fumbled with his spectacles, and avoided answering. "Im—, er, imagine if you will what happened after Fletcher's Bill returned from practice with his son. No doubt he asked around for Mark; but no man did he find who could claim such a name, and such a blade." He pointed at Harvest's rusted bones. "He thinks, *I must have seen a ghost!*" Valerian's brown eyes looked far into the past. He was almost chanting now. "From time to time as his life passed, Fletcher's Bill would draw a pint and tell a new acquaintance of his meeting on the wall. Did he think you walked unquiet without your blade in hand? Or did he fear he had been cozened, tripped up by the Devil into unholy bargain when he took the fancy weapon from its hellish master? Perhaps as he lay dying he bade his son to lay the blade beneath the wall where you had met, in hopes to end his bargain with his life."

"Stop it. You're scaring me," Gail said sharply.

"You are right to be afraid. I am. I wonder at the scar that pains your husband's hand; I wonder at his cold black knife. That iron dagger at his hip was buried in this kingdom's heart; and when he drew it forth, blood gushed from the wound."

"What blood?" Gail demanded. "What gushes from the Red Keep?"

Valerian shrugged. "Poetry."

"Magic," Lissa added.

But Mark said, "The past."

He drew in a long breath. A dark tide was running into him, a strange flood of old griefs and ancient sorrows. He felt it each time his right palm ached. *That wound's a chink through which the draughty past comes creeping in.*

And yet. . . .

And yet the sun was shining overhead, the sky was blue, the summer day was warm and full of life. The air rang with shouts and orders, the chink of hammers, horses whiffling as they cropped the grass; farther off, the river's hiss and chatter. Larks sang amongst the chestnut trees. On a stone nearby a grey thrush hopped, glancing at them warily, hunting for beetles.

Mark looked at his friends: Valerian enchanted by the

strangeness of things, Lissa inscrutable, Gail frowning and determined and a little scared. "You know," he sighed at last, "for the life of me I just can't seem to hang on to my damn swords."

Lissa laughed. "Good thing they took dead Stargad's weapon from you! The King would not be pleased, to see Sweetness gone so sour," she said, pointing at the heap of rust that had once been Harvest.

"Father won't be happy as it is," Gail said glumly. "And that was your wedding present too."

"When I was a lad," Mark said dreamily, "I wanted to be a famous hero and have a sword with a name. For a long time it was to be a great two-handed blade named *Head-Slicer*."

Gail and Lissa burst out laughing. "Head-slicer?"

"I was young. When I got older, I changed the name to *Decapitator*; it sounded more grown up."

"Oh, infinitely more adult," Val said.

"Then I went through a noble period. Longswords, mostly: a knight rode through town wearing one that moved me greatly. *Justice* was a favourite, and *Defender*." Mark was smiling now, looking back over so many years. These were his secret boy's thoughts; and silly as they seemed, they had flowered into the man he was today.

"*Thief, Sweetness, Harvest,*" Valerian mused. "It seems to be the kiss of death when you name your swords, Mark. What will you call the next one? May I suggest *The Sword That Has No Name?*"

"How about '*Spear*'?" Lissa suggested. "A cunning name to baffle your misfortune."

" '*Overcoat*'!" Gail cried. "The garment that keeps off death!" She toppled off her stone seat, whooping, and even Lissa cackled with glee. Mark wiped tears of laughter from his cheeks. "Mebbe I'd better do wi' nowt for awhile. Giving me a sword's a waste of good steel."

Master Orrin came hurrying around the side of the building. "Ah. Enjoying yourselves, are you," he said, pursing his lips. "I'm glad you can take this morning's events so lightly. Pray, do me the honour of coming around to the Main Gate. I think I can give you yet more cause for hilarity."

There was something in his pinched face that stilled the laughter on their lips.

"I sent one of your Vagabonds to clean the arch," Orrin explained when they had assembled, along with the rest of the men, in front of the main gate. Master Orrin pointed up to the centre stone at the top of the archway. "And that's what he found."

The old arch had been cleared of ivy, and the moss scraped from its stones. There, clearly carved to hang above the gate, a symbol now appeared: a large, coiling serpent, with its tail in its mouth, and dark sockets where once garnets might have flashed for eyes. It was the same design as on Husk's wooden charm, the same as on the amulet Queen Lerelil had given Mark; only here it was graven into stone.

Valerian whistled. "Steady now. The answer to this mystery is not hard to find: Queen Lerelil must have come from Borders, and come into the Red Keep's clan by marriage."

"But her husband wasn't at the Red Keep," Mark objected. "Leastwise, she never mentioned him. I'd swear her son was cock-o'-the-walk there." Mark spat and sighed. There was so much he didn't know: the past was lurking under everything he touched these days, like bass in a deep pool. From time to time he caught a glimpse of tail, a flash of fin: Lerelil's bracelet or Duke Richard's family name.

Ancient signs that made the present shiver as they darted to snap the surface, and then were gone.

Only you're the fly, he thought glumly. *Buzzing ower that water wi' nowt to keep you from the jaws of the past.*

It was a bad day. The past hung heavy on Mark's back. Gail grew troubled and irritable, worried that she might have gotten pregnant when they made love. They fought before going to bed.

That night Mark dreamt a terrible dream. In it, he woke in his own bed in the finished Borders. It was night, and dark; the taper on the wall had burned down to the nub.

A shadow fell over his soul.

something

Like black water running into a foundering ship, dread filled his feet, his legs, his groin. It rose into his chest; touched his heart; and he was lost. It struck down his soul and everything alive in him could only lay face down, grovelling, and wait for the coming horror.

in the house.

A long time later he breathed. Dread had crushed his heart to a hard cold thing, a pebble rattling in his ribs. Slowly he got out of bed. He reached for his sword and walked around the room to reassure himself.

something

He saw nothing, heard nothing: but still the dread grew, heavier and heavier, rising up from the floor, pressing down from the darkness overhead.

something in the house.

The words whispered in his heart.

Something that should be *outside*, that should never be allowed in. Something dark and evil had crept into his walls, his home, his heart.

Evil. He'd never known what the word meant before now.

Evil. Like a wild animal, evil had come, drawn by the light of his fire.

Evil was in the house. He couldn't keep it out. He couldn't resist it. If it came on him, on his wife and friends and family, he would lie coward in the dirt and pray it did not see him. Shielder's Mark, the great hero, soldier, Duke, would fall on the floor and weep and cower. He would sell them all rather than see its face. They would cry to him for help and he would fail.

Val, he thought suddenly. *Val will know what to do.*

He belted a robe around his waist and hurried down to Valerian's room. *You despised him, didn't you? You thought him a dreamer, a tinkerer, a clever clown who'd never amount to much. Nowt compared to a soldier hero Duke. Kept him around because he made you feel superior, didn't you?*

Bloody idiot. This, this is the real test. Who stands and who falls, when the horror comes.

Val will know.

Valerian looked up from a black book with gold lettering. Mark gasped out his terror, begging for help.

Valerian nodded, and took his hand; Mark drew strength from his friend's profound strength. Val's gray eyes were grave and deep and wise as centuries behind his spectacles. Owlwise, firm as mountains, he held Mark's trembling hands and said, "These things must you do. . . ."

Mark woke up. Dread still clung to him.

Shite.

What a nightmare. The worst of his life, though it had no monster, no scene of madness: a dream of pure emotion, a dread that stabbed like spears. The echo of it, lingering in his heart, still froze his breath in his chest. His right hand was ice.

Panic gripped him. He turned over quickly and stared at Gail, sure she was dead.

Life flooded back into him as she breathed. Her eyelids fluttered open and she looked at him, staring at her. They closed again, and she was asleep.

. . . *So.*

It wasn't Gail.

It was their first night inside his Keep; a thick curtain closed off this end of the Great Hall from the main area where his people slept. Still shaking with fear Mark rolled slowly out of bed and pulled on his pants and shirt. *No sword, damn it!* He drew out the iron dagger instead, though it felt like frost in his hand.

Twitching aside the curtain he stepped into the great hall. Two rushlights burned on each of the long stone walls. A double line of pallets stretched beneath them. Slowly Mark walked down the corridor of sleeping men. His friends. His people.

They've put their faith in you: but you're a cracked pot and you can't hold it.

Row on row of sleeping faces, slack jaws, nerveless fingers. *A half-step from death, every one. How fragile they are. A child of two could draw the black dagger across each throat. Some will drown, or die of drink, or fever like Ma. Some will go mad with age, like George's dad, t'awd Smith: railing at the darkness in every heart until his own gave way.*

You're soft, Shielder's Mark. Once you were hard as steel and leather tough, headed for your Greatness. But summat at the Red Keep cracked your heart and let a wet draught in, swirling and swirling. Summat rusted out your iron soul: there's nowt in you but emptiness now, and darkness, and wind.

That damn Old Man, staring into ashes, ashes, ashes.

Shite.

Every hard thing squeezes tears from you like juice from a grape. And now this dream has come and slit you open.

So many things were clear. Terrible things.

He lingered by a pallet just under one of the rushlights. A mason sprawled there under a scrap of blanket. His big man's life beat in his throat; *cut if off as easy as stamp a spider under your boot.*

All your life you fought to protect. To build a place where you'd be safe. You whipped yourself into the Ghostwood and broke it open, and soon you'll have a fine Keep wi' walls of stone and men in livery to walk 'em.

It means nowt. You might as well have built the wall wi' lace and armed your men wi' flowers. It means nowt because you're useless. You'll not stand against the horror when it comes. You can't protect a damn of what you made or stole or won. You can't defend one friend, nor Gail, nor the child you mean to get on her. The thought twisted his heart. *What kind of father, what worthless piece of shite couldn't even look after his little boy?*

Mark rose, and walked among his people with dread heavy on his heart. His life was cracked clay around an empty place. His dreams were ashes.

"I found God," he said.

It was early the next morning and he was walking with Valerian down by the river. "Or at least I found why people look for Him." Mark stopped and stared out over the water, shaking his head. "I always thought that religion was about whether or not you believed in God. You know: is there a great bloody shepherd watching you even when you wash your private parts? But that isn't it at all. God's about what you do when the horror comes." And he told Valerian his dream.

Val took out his spy-glass and peered across the river with it. "It has often seemed to me that whether you believe in God is a matter of small moment, where religion is concerned. I have not had much luck explaining this, before today."

"It was so . . . *brutal*," Mark said, shaking. Where had the warrior in him gone? He felt like a leaf twisting in the wind. "It was so *wicked*, Val. . . . Something so horrible it shouldn't be allowed to exist."

Valerian took down his spy-glass. "'Faith is a candle where Reason is the sun; no one needs a candle: until darkness falls.'"

"Until darkness falls," Mark murmured. He brushed aside a curtain of willow wands and sat down with his back against the tree's rough trunk. The old willow's gnarled roots clung to the riverbank like miser's fingers. The yellow fronds overhung an eddy, small but deep, studded with grey stones. *Bass under there. Must come back some day wi' rod and line, if there's ever rest from Duking*

"I've got to find God," he said. He glanced at the black dagger at his hip. "When I was younger, I didn't care. But I've a wife now, and friends, and subjects. It's just lazy not to have religion, Val. A boy can go without, but a man has responsibilities. Folk count on me. They deserve a Duke who can face the darkness for them. And I can't do that without help."

Valerian settled down beside him. "Nobody can."

"Belief isn't the question any more," Mark said grimly. "I need a, a *shield-mate*, for when the horror comes." He poked Val in the ribs with his elbow, and gave a faint smile. "So? Tell me! Where can I find this God friend of yours?"

Valerian laughed and shrugged. "You are not the first person to ask!" He held up his spy-glass. "Look. Listen. If you look hard enough, you will see something; if you listen closely enough, you'll hear. After all," he said wryly, "God is everywhere in everything. Women, now: women are elusive."

"But what does God sound like? Astin's herald, with a voice like a well? Will he shout at me from behind a bush some day?"

"Look for Joy: that's God's echo, and his footprint. Happiness . . . happiness and wittiness and cleverness do not count for much when darkness falls. Joy is tougher. And in the dark you need that candle."

Slowly Mark nodded. *Better find your God in a hurry, lad: especially if a second Time of Troubles is sweeping out of the Wood. You're running out of time.*

Lord, wouldn't that be good? To run out of Time, and into some other place. No more day after weary day of Duking, struggling, building, fearing. To run out of Time like a deer leaping from under the forest eaves and into sunshine.

"Water," he said, some time later. "God's in running water for me. And in wind."

"Music," Val said. "Definitely music. Remember Janseni's wedding melodies?" His eyes widened and he shivered, like a fluffing bird. "Those were angels' songs for skipping rope, and seraph's lullabies."

Finding a twig in the grass, Mark tossed it into the river. It spun slowly past him, then slid downstream, picking up speed until it was swallowed by the rapids. "How's Deron? Out here nursing a broken heart, is he?"

"Badly fractured," Val agreed. To Mark's surprise Val's face, so serene when he talked of God, was now awkward with confusion and shame. "I tell you, Mark, sometimes I do not comprehend the female sex. Consider Deron: handsome, brave, clever, and devoted, yet Janseni will have nought to do with him. Can you explain it?" He turned his hand-glass over and over between his fingers. "You can fill your heart with courtesy and throw it at a woman's feet, and it doesn't matter."

Mark spat and shook his head. "Life is so hard, Val. Janseni knows it. They all know it." *Don't mention Lissa, whatever you do!* "A—worshipper isn't much of a lover. No one wants a mate who only offers weakness. When the darkness comes for Janseni, she's going to need someone with steel in his back. She wants a husband, not a subject or a son. She wants someone to stand back to back with her, swords drawn, when the wolves come in."

Valerian smiled faintly. "A shield-mate." Slowly he pulled up a strand of grass and nibbled the white stem. "That's what you see in Gail, I think, and she in you. You are persuasive, Mark. Almost you convince me that women are not mad. But your words hold little hope for me." He opened his plump hands and waved down at his soft body. "There's lead in me, and wind, but not much steel."

"You were t'only man I knew who could stand against the darkness," Mark said softly. "That counts."

"It is not darkness I must stand against," Val said gloomily, "but blue eyes and perfume. O God, Mark, that scent she wears! Warm rain falling on the roots of my heart."

"Good mope."

"Can you blame a knee for bending, if it pass before an altar?"

"Just don't let the altar see you at it! Not yet, anyway. If there's one thing Lissa *doesn't* need, it's another person to take care of on top of Gail."

"And you."

Mark scowled. "Thanks."

"The woman is so . . . elegant," Valerian sighed. "The way she looks, the way she acts. The way she *thinks*; her mind spies round corners. I am very vague. Abstract.

Puttery. I putter," he said with disgust. "But Lissa's world is a shifting field of people in play, ambitions, dreams, desires. . . . Each time we talk she opens my eyes to undiscovered continents of character."

"Now that's a good line for a wedding night," Mark said. "Romantic, flattering, heartfelt. But if you start wi' such stuff—"

"Down my hopes will topple before a scythe of scorn, and lie stricken on the field of love."

"Dead as a drowned rat," Mark agreed.

"So how do I let the lady know I live and breathe, if I cannot give my heart a tongue?"

"You can tell a lass you fancy her without spreading like a cowpie at her feet, Val! What about the knowing smile, the quick wit, the gallant flirting? I thought the gentry were good at that."

"Not this gentle," Val grumbled.

Mark spread his hands. "So you're shy."

"So I am a *eunuch*."

"This isn't getting us anywhere," Mark said firmly. He grasped Val's shoulder and turned him around. "If you want to court a woman, you've got to be a man, Val. You respect her strength; you've got to show her yours. That doesn't mean brawling and swearing and acting the lout: it means showing the strength you have, here," (tapping Val's head), "and here," (tapping his heart). "If I can go looking for God, you can at least cast around for a little extra. . . ."

"Manhood."

Mark slowly nodded.

Val stood and brushed off his pants, then walked out from under the willow. "I wonder if the ladies too have talks like this. Are they confused and hapless when it comes to matters of emotion? Could it be our loved ones struggle also as we do, through the dim obscurities of the heart?"

Val and Mark stared at one another.

"Nah," they said.

You're changing, Mark thought as the days went by. Looking back, he saw his whole life had been driven by the terrible pressure to protect, to hold. When at last he realized he would never be truly safe, he was an older man: freer than he had ever been, but cold too, and afraid. It was the freedom that a beggar knows, cast out into a dangerous world.

It was slow and it was hard, but he figured he was becoming a man.

As June wore into July, and July smouldered into August, finding God seemed more and more important. Terrible rumours came one upon the other. Ghost stories came with the steady stream of refugees that trickled into Borders, mostly from the High Holt. Men said the Time of Troubles had returned, and darkness was loosed in the land. The pilgrims came because they thought Shielder's Mark, the mighty Hero, could save them from peril, if anybody could.

Poor bastards.

Their trust galled Mark. It made his search for God—for a shield-mate—ever more desperate.

But what Mark needed was time, time to sort through his life, time to listen for the joy that Val said was God's echo.

Time was what he didn't have.

His people were confused and afraid. As their numbers swelled he had to spend ever-longer hours comforting them, setting tasks, organizing work parties, farming parties, hunting parties. They built two mills. The second, downstream, lay on its side, according to Valerian's plan. To Mark's surprise it worked.

Then building got harder as the skilled workmen Astin had sent fled back to the capital, uneasy under the shadow of the Ghostwood. More refugees streamed in every day. Soon it would be autumn; winter would follow fast behind.

And it wasn't only Mark's duchy that gave him problems. After he made love to Gail on Mid-summer night he had expected they would grow together. Instead, they drifted apart. Gail was furious with herself for giving in to a moment of passion, and at Mark for taking advantage of her.

Bitch.

She prowled around the Keep, pale and venomous, until Lissa was the only one who dared to speak to her. *You'd have thought she had dodged Death when the blood finally came. That's how glad she was to know she wasn't carrying any brat of yours.*

The thought grew between them like a cancer.

The few moments Mark had to himself he meant to look for God, but somehow he ended up daydreaming instead. He saw his castle finished, his children playing on the grass, saw himself walking with Gail by the river, listening gravely to Sir William explain some affair of state. More and more of his dreams involved Sir William, that wise gentle hardy man with greyshot beard and strong hands. Mark dreamt of William fixing medals to his chest as a young boy dreams of his first kiss.

So the search Mark meant to make for God was put off from one sunrise to the next. The Hall was finished, the east wing and the kitchen started. They would be lucky to get to any of the walls before winter. Master Orrin stayed after most of his men had left, obsessed with his plans. He said the towers would have to wait at least two summers; it might be three years before the broken bridge could be made whole again.

They would just make one crop of rye and a selection of fall vegetables: pumpkins, squash, carrots and maybe some potatoes. Mark knew it would be touch and go to feed his people. *Hope they like chestnuts,* he thought grimly.

Summer burned up into fall, and every day sunk into night. Ghosts walked out of the shadows after sunset, and darkness was running into more hearts than just Mark's own.

His right palm ached constantly and never warmed. He stopped shaking hands.

One other thing remained from his night upon the battlements with Fletcher's Bill. All that long summer the sun beat down upon Borders; on their breaks the men threw themselves gratefully under the shady chestnut trees. But Mark stayed by the Keep through the long afternoons; as the sun sank into the west, the day seemed cool to him, cooler than it did to others. Then the light dimmed.

By August Mark began to guess what it meant. By September he was sure.

There was a shadow over the Keep that only he could feel, a shadow that grew sharper as the days went by. It crept out from the rubble just after noon, and lengthened until evening. It was the shadow of a western wall, thirty feet high, that only Mark could see.

The first frost came in mid-October, and brought Duke Richard with it. "The farmers now foretell a bitter winter," he remarked, a splendid guest at their meagre board. "Grieved I am to hear it. I do not care for cold. If I were God I would declare it summer all year round, that men might sun themselves in January and eat peaches through December. Tragically, such is our degenerate age that even Dukes may never make the weather what they please." He sighed and winked, provoking laughter from the table.

"How thoughtless of God," Valerian said blandly.

"By the devil, yes I say! What say you Mark: we are two

men of substance in the world. Shall we try to reason with this God, or shall we simply order his dismissal?" Richard sat at the head table with Mark and Gail, Lissa and Valerian, and Master Orrin. Orrin looked uncomfortable at the honour. Fitly, the place should have gone to Sir Deron, but he had begged off, saying that he had enjoyed Duke Richard's company more than enough before now.

Richard looked well. Frost had crept a little further into his beard, but his straight hair was still coal-black, his face quick and lively when he spoke, his hand still strong and sure when he cut his meat.

"And to what do we owe the honour of this visit?" Gail inquired. Tension sat behind her eyes. *Shamed,* Mark thought. *Embarrassed to greet her father's greatest vassal in a half-made house wi' rubble for walls.*

Richard's face grew sombre. "There you touch upon a tragic tale," he said at last. "I have come out of my way to give you warning. My visit here will be but brief; I am on an urgent course to Swangard, where I seek succour for my people." He lowered his voice, that he might not be heard beyond the head table. "I spoke too rashly in the spring when I declared there could not be such things as ghosts."

"You have seen the old man?" Lissa asked uneasily.

Slowly Richard nodded. "At last I saw him for myself. Four days since he burst into my Hall of Audience, a ghastly ancient with haggard brow and dreadful eye." Duke Richard leaned back and shrugged. "I sent my new steward Berol to inquire into the apparition's needs and send it on its way. In this I freely call myself at fault, for Berol I had judged a man of courage. But he blanched and quaked, and when at last he challenged the spectre his knees knocked and his tongue stammered on his teeth. The Ghost reached out and touched him on the chest, and then my steward fell dead in the centre of the room, stricken by pure fright."

Duke Richard shook his head. "You can imagine the panic that ensued. However well a common man performs his duties, he will not keep his wits when faced by such a spectacle. What people were left in my Keep were mad with fear, shrieking and falling over one another in their haste to flee. Seeing that my house was on the edge of rout, I seized the bell of audience and declared the session over. We then withdrew and left the Ghost to his own damnable devices. Immediately I sent for horses, gathered those trifles you saw when I arrived, and set out. My meaning was to warn you of this evil, then make for Swangard by the straightest route. There I trust the King and I and Bishop Cirdon may consult with Cabinet on how to baffle this Ghost."

Lissa frowned, her face a mask of polite puzzlement. "But who will rule in High Holt if the Duke is gone and the steward dead?"

"I assure you I was not remiss in statecraft. I named a second steward as I left, and sent a messenger to Father, bidding him return from his retreat," Richard said smoothly. "It is a pity to disturb his well-earned rest with care, but the people still recall him, and in a time of crisis will rally to a member of the blood."

Lissa nodded, as if she understood the arrangements all too well. "Much do I admire the family bond between you, to trust your father with the handling of so grave a threat to properties you swore an oath ever to defend."

Richard's eyes narrowed. "My father is a capable man," he said tersely. "I suggest that Borders had better concern itself with its own business. This place is nice enough," he said, waving a hand at the building Master Orrin's men had worked so hard to resurrect. "The view in truth is very pretty: but it is nothing like defensible, is it?"

"It wasn't meant to be a fortress—" Orrin objected.

Duke Richard's eyebrows rose. "Excuse me," he said

pleasantly. "Have we met before, Master . . . Orrin, was it? I think we have. I was at your daughter's wedding, two summers back. She married that extremely worthy glazier: a good catch, I thought." He smiled politely. *Orrin wants to stuff a chisel up his arse,* Mark thought. *Look at his fingers twisting in the tablecloth.* "You are Astin's architect." Richard glanced around at the old-fashioned stone floors, the mullioned windows glazed with horn, the sawdust coating every beam. "I must remind myself to tell him all about the job you're doing here."

Orrin's pinched face paled.

"I asked Master Orrin to remake Borders as it was a thousand years ago," Mark said. "He's done miracles here. I hope that's what you'll tell the King, milord."

"You need not 'milord' me," Richard said easily. "Astin will be jealous. You are not my vassal, my dear Mark: we are equals, now. And you may trust that my report will grace Orrin with all the credit he deserves."

"And anyway I don't see what being defensible has to do with owt," Mark snapped. "This is not a toy. I can protect my own. We aren't talking about an invading army."

"Mark." Under the table Gail dug her fingers into his, trying to hush him up.

It only made him angrier. "We're talking ghosts in the graveyard, spectres on the battlement. No weight of stone will change that."

"Very likely not," Richard said urbanely. "But soon you may contend with more than ghosts. When the common people panic, they will flock to Borders, Mark, to the Hero of the Ghostwood. You clearly cannot house them, but with your present forces and position you cannot hope to throw them back. So what then will you do?"

"I don't know." Under the table Gail pinched harder; across it, Lissa eyed him sharply. *That's it, that's it: pet me into place. Don't let the nasty commoner foul our pleasant little chat.* "I don't know what I'll do," he said distinctly. "But I don't think, if my people were in danger, that I'd tuck tail between my legs and fly for the King's skirts, leaving my father to face the danger."

There was a long, shocked silence, broken at last when Duke Richard pushed back his plate, smiled coldly at Mark, and said, "But here you have the vantage of me, Mark. Perhaps we all would be so brave, if we had no fathers either."

I'll kill him.

Wiping his mouth with his napkin Duke Richard rose from the table. "I think tempers are a little short. With your permission, I would like to take a look around your place while dinner settles." With that he bowed to the others at the table, Gail last of all, and turned to leave the room.

"When are you going to grow up?" Gail demanded that night as she and Mark prepared for bed. Angrily she took off an earring and hurled it into her jewelry box. "For the first few years here we must depend on my father to survive, Mark. Do you think insulting his friend and greatest subject is going to help?"

"You were a cat to his kitten," Mark said contemptuously. "Rushing out to tour him round the place. I'm sure he liked having his fur licked."

Gail whirled and slapped him, hard. "I hate that man," she yelled. "I should never, never have been forced to trail behind and listen to his loathsome compliments. You should have been there, Mark. You should have been there. You're my husband, damn it."

Mark grabbed her wrists, burning with anger. But the bitterness, the terrible unhappiness in her voice brought him up short.

Good God. You were just about to hit her.

Mark's angry hands clenched around her wrists. "If you hate Richard, why are you so mad wi' me for shitting on him? What the hell did the prick say? You've got to learn not to let bastards like that get to you."

Gail stood suddenly still, as if stabbed. "What did he say?" she whispered. Tears of rage beaded in her eyes. "Here we sit in this heap of rock while the dead walk around us and the frost closes in and all you can do is antagonize the most powerful man in the land. Are you trying to make the things they say come true?"

"'They'? Who is They? People like Richard? Like Lissa? Court songbirds in scent and satin? Is that who we're trying to impress?"

"Oh yes we hate them, don't we," Gail said, narrow eyes murderous. "That insufferable King with his simpering courtiers and his pampered bitch daughters. We *really* are too good for trash like that." She turned away, shaking her head. "God I'm lucky to have married up in the world, that's all I can say. At least my whelps will be born into a better class of family, eh?"

"That's what all this is about, isn't it?" Mark said, voice dead. "That's why you won't let me touch you. You don't think I'd be a father for your children, do you? You think I'll do what my dad did and cut out. Or stay in: which would be worse?"

"At times like tonight, Mark, it's so hard to choose."

Mark sat down heavily on the edge of the bed.

How, from where we started, did it ever come to this?

His dreams, his quest, his title, his love: all dead. Frost on his palm, the taste of ashes on his tongue. "Don't let's be like this," he said. "We were meant for one another Gail. Don't let's be like this."

"Right now," Gail said, "I can't see any other way for us to be."

The harvest moon was full that night, but Mark's heart was empty. His duchy was in ruins, his people would go hungry. Evil stalked the countryside and he had no way to stop it. His friends were ashamed of him, his wife despised him. Everything he wanted, he had gotten: and all of it was ashes.

Empty, he rose from their bed, leaving Gail lying stiffly in the dark, pretending to sleep. Empty, he dressed and buckled the black dagger to his hip, his right hand ice. Empty he left his Keep through the gate in the tall west wall. Empty he walked down to the river, and crossed the bridge, and passed into the Ghostwood, where the moonlight failed.

11

Ashes

It was dark and Mark was alone. He had turned to water, black water, running down, down, down to find its lowest level. Down through his fight with Gail, down through his ruined dreams of love for her. Down through the cares of his duchy, the bitter fruit of his pride and ambition. He had demanded love and gotten grief, demanded power and gotten care in its place. With his sweat and his drive and his relentless will he had built up this thing, this Shielder's Mark: soldier, lover, Duke, Hero. Now Shielder's Mark was crumbling around him.

He walked like a wraith from the ruins, into the woods, alone.

At first the dread was on him, the dread from his dream. Around him tall trees groped into the sky with hidden hands; an evil mist crept along the ground. The air was dank and cold as the side of an open grave.

In his dream, there had been *something in the house*, some wickedness seeping between the stones, inside his strong walls, inside his loving circle of friends, sinking into his flesh.

But now he was outside. He had come to it, come to where the evil lived. He remembered turning to Gail as they walked away from Swangard, her fox-face dim in the twilight and spattered with rain. "Take down your hood, and hear how big the darkness is." *The evil scares you less*

231

because you've become its creature, Mark. You too are a thing of darkness.

You thought you knew loneliness the first time you came here. That was nowt. You were a boy then, hung about wi' hopes and dreams.

Now his dreams were dead, for they had all come true, and were turned to ashes. He could imagine no tomorrow, nothing ahead but trees and darkness, and the sad smell of cedar. He was black water, creeping to a low place.

But with each step forward into darkness, the past behind got brighter and brighter.

He remembered the smell of dirt, and bracelets of dew cold around his wrists, doing push-ups in the Commons before dawn, one for every syllable of the sheep-counting rhyme, six verses, seven verses, eight. . . . And for what.

So his mind went back, touching each point of pain, each grief, each wound: unsparing, relentless as February rain. Back to the beginning, back to the lullaby day, his father standing over an open trunk with his back turned.

With his back turned.

And there Mark's memory stopped and pooled, turning slowly around and around on itself, gathering tears. And his father was always bending down, picking up his shield, his stiff back was always leaving, the door was closing, he was walking away and Mark knew, had known even then that his father was going away and would never, ever come back. He was leaving, leaving, leaving.

He was gone.

And he never came back.

No matter how hard Mark worked, he didn't come back. No matter how many chores he did. No matter how handy he was, how good, how clever, how charming. He was nice to other children and his father didn't come back. He swept the steps and lit the fire and his father didn't come back. He took care of his mother and tried to fill her grief, but he failed there too. He grew stronger, tougher, faster, smarter: got up before dawn and pushed himself until he dropped, a little more each day nine verses ten verses twelve verses, *and he never came back.* He took for himself a sword as his father had, and when his mother died he left her as his father had and he left the village as his father had and he went into the dark Wood and he came to the Red Keep and he broke the ancient spell and he made the King do his bidding and he married a beautiful princess and he became a mighty man and he lived in a great stone house and still it wasn't enough it wasn't enough he had done everything he could do and the tight voice had called in anger and the stiff back had left the cottage door and he had gone, he had gone, he had gone.

And he wasn't ever coming back. He wasn't ever, ever, ever coming back.

And he would never come to the great main gate of Mark's fine new house and say, "It was enough." And the tight voice would never say he had been wrong to leave. And the door would never open, and the stiff back would never turn, and Mark would never see the face that he could not remember o god he could not even remember his father's face, his god damn face.

He walked along the darkling path, out of sight, and time, eyes blind with tears.

It was dark when he came to the Keep. It was always dark in the Wood, now. Sometimes it was twilight, the wind the dying day's last breath, full of regret, passing, remorse. Other times it was midnight, black with a blackness that choked out the stars, and he had to feel for the path with each careful step, reaching ahead with his hands, splashing suddenly into unseen pools.

When he came to the Keep it was the paler darkness of the last hour before dawn. How well he knew the night-blue sky, the indifferent stars, the grass cold with dew! This was the hour least known. The workman did not know it, waiting for the sun to start his day. Neither did the reveller, who staggered home in the smaller hours. Few people know that time, when dawn can't be seen, but only smelled on the wind. It is the loneliest hour of the day, and you cannot touch its heart in company. You cannot feel it from a carriage, you cannot get its scent beside a fire. Only outside, in the darkness, alone, can you touch that time and know it for what it is.

Mark knew it well.

The cherry trees were bare. No scent of them lingered in the air; dead leaves, damp with dew, sank beneath Mark's feet as he walked through the barren orchard.

The mere was gone and in its place a ditch. He stumbled through margins rank with skullcap. Underfoot long grass tangled around bits of bone and metal, rusted swords, rotten shields, stilled hands, tongues long silenced by a drink of black water.

Mark crossed the ditch. Once he felt something give beneath his foot with a wet crunch, felt it splay and drag across his ankle. It could have been a twig.

The Red Keep was empty. No sentries walked its crumbled battlements, no guards looked down from atop its rusting gate. Inside, no horses clopped slowly home to rest, no voices chattered and sang from within the great hall. All the busy life was gone, and even the ghosts had fled. Where once the Keep had been thick with memories, there now lay only dust.

How old it is, how terribly old. Men lived here once, and married and fathered children and died here too, genera-tions of them, and now they're nowt but dust beneath your feet. All their proud voices quiet now, dark their eyes, cold their hearts that laughed once and loved and struggled through their lives. Gone, gone, down into dust and ashes.

O God O God the world's a slaughterhouse. Every cobble in the street could be pressed from human bones; every pot on the fire could be made of human clay.

In the kitchen a little fire still burned, sunk almost into embers. Before it sat the Old Man, stirring in the ashes with a blackthorn staff.

Mark watched him for an hour, or a day, or a week, before at last he spoke. "Where are they?" he said. "There were princes here and lovers; grooms, soldiers, clothiers, dyers, cooks, scullions, chambermaids, ostlers, maidens. Little boys. Where have they all gone?"

The Old Man turned then. His skull bore a long white scar, his face was hard and white as bone: his eyes were black. "That was long ago," he said. "Now even their ghosts have grown old and died."

Mark asked, "Who are you?"

The Old Man turned back to the fire. "I am Nobody," he said. "My name is dead." He stirred the ashes with his stick, staring at the patterns he made as if they revealed some deep and terrible mystery. "And dost tha cum to give back what tha stole?"

Mark's hand strayed to his hip where the dagger lay. "It was you!" he whispered. "Your awd scar: that's where I clubbed you when I took the dagger! You were the Prince."

"Am still," the Old Man said, with a spasm of hatred. "Hedrod my father taught me nought of ruling: I could not hold what I had taken. Even in death he must be King."

Slowly Mark drew the black dagger and held it out to the Old Man, who took it, laughing with a sound like bone splintering. "And wherefore cum tha, whelp?"

"I do not know."

"Then tha must learn."

"Yes."

"I warn tha, 'tis nae always easy for boys to learn what old men teach. It will go hard for tha."

"I can learn," Mark said. Gently, fearfully as a lover, he approached the Old Man's turned back. "I promise I can learn your teaching."

Suddenly the staff whipped back and caught Mark a staggering blow on the side of his head. "Tha mewls," the Old Man said. "Tha'rt soft."

Mark's head rang, yet he barely felt the blow. "Aye. Aye, I'm grown too soft," he whispered, feeling himself like a pool of black water, a teardrop, barely able to hold his shape, breaking around the blackthorn staff, lapping around the pain in his head, his hand.

And he thought suddenly that evil was the same as emptiness, and the dread that lay upon the Wood was made of darkness, wind and water. It was emptiness that crept through the stones of his fine house, emptiness that ran into him through the wound in his hand.

And a great fear came over him, that he would be empty forever. He craved filling as he once craved light and air. He had lost his edges in the darkness and he had to have a shape. "I am too soft," he said. And he wanted to beg the Old Man to fill him up, to give him shape, to teach him how to be a man.

He had never had that. Never had a man to show him what a man should be. Never worked at his father's side, never rambled in the woods with him. Never learned to ride and shoot and hunt with Duke Richard, never learned swordplay from Sir William.

He'd taught himself as much as he could, but something had gone wrong, terribly wrong: now his dreams were dust and his love was ashes and his fine castle lay abandoned

behind him. But he dared not beg the Old Man for his
teaching, for fear of showing how soft he was.

At last the Old Man said, "Cum then: look into my fire
and tell me aught you see."

Weeping tears of gratitude Mark drew near, and crouched
beside the Old Man's stool, and stared into the fire. "I see
nowt," he said at last.

The Old Man beat Mark with his staff, beat him with an
old man's wiry strength, and Mark did not resist. Then he
bade Mark lie amongst the cinders, beside the fire, and go to
sleep. And this he did.

Another day passed this way, and then another. Each
morning, just before dawn, the Old Man would ask Mark to
stare into the fire and tell him what he saw; when Mark said
he saw nothing, the Old Man beat him and would not speak
to him again. The day would break and the shadows would
fade from the room. Sometime in the morning he would point
outside and Mark would go to gather firewood, and then
return. Shafts of sunlight crept across the floor, now slender,
swelling, now long and wide, now slanting, narrower, gone. At
twilight the Old Man would pull a chestnut from the fire and
crack it open with his teeth, and give it to Mark to eat. Mark
was never hungry, but he ate what he was given, though the
nuts were often rotten, or burned and hard.

As time went by his mind grew hungry. He looked for
firewood everywhere: in the stables, the Hall, the palace. He
peered through every window and opened every doorway:
all except the door to the Tower, which the Old Man forbade
him ever to pass. Soon he knew the whole ruined Keep by
heart, every passage and every room, every tree in its
orchard, every skeleton in the ditch around its walls. At last,
when he had explored the buildings and the grounds and the
woods around, he gave up his journeys. He gathered a great

store of brush into the main courtyard, and did not leave the castle any more.

He dreamt of the morning he would see something in the fire, and the Old Man would be glad, and speak words of praise to him, and begin his teaching. But as the days wore on Mark grew more desperate, feeling the Old Man must soon weary of his stupidity, his ignorance. At last in desperation he lied, and claimed to see a crown of flame hidden in the fire.

The Old Man beat him, but no worse than usual.

Mark began to think that with luck he would guess what the Old Man wanted him to see. He spent each day absorbed in speculation, imagining and discarding one possibility after another, testing each out in his mind, sneaking glances at the Old Man, trying to guess what he was waiting for.

At first he tried simple things: after the crown a throne, a sword, a goblet, a maiden, a white charger, a castle, an army with banners. Soon his imagination grew: he saw dragons, devils, horrors out of nightmare, elfin feasts, scenes of the past and future. He told elaborate stories that grew from one day to the next, thinking that perhaps the Old Man was looking for a tale, an image, a legend of long ago. He made up songs and claimed to hear them in the hissing flames, the popping embers.

One night, heart almost stopping, he saw Gail in the flames.

The Old Man beat him, as always.

He saw Valerian then, and Lissa, and Sir William and Duke Richard and Deron and Astin and Vultemar and Anujel and Lord Peridot and his mother and so on through all the people of his life; and as he saw each one, they seemed to drop from his memory, consumed like moths by the fire.

Finally he could see no more. In three days he had moved

only to bring in brush for the fire; when the Old Man beat him he lay in his spot by the grate and did not flinch. "Cum," the Old Man said, with a voice like a coal popping, "look into my fire and tell me aught you see."

Mark stared dully, unmoving, from his place by the grate. "Ashes," he said.

The silence lengthened and no blow fell. A wild hope flared in Mark's heart that he had passed the test at last, that his days (weeks? months?) of stupidity would be forgiven.

The Old Man turned his back on Mark. "Cum," he said coldly. "Tha hast work to do."

The Old Man led him to a forge. "Tha hast worked a smith before. Here be fire and water, an anvil and iron. Each day tha'lt cum here and light the fire until it blazons. Then shalt tha beat oncet on the iron. An I hear a second stroke, I'll heave tha from hence and teach tha nought."

"What am I making?" Mark asked.

The Old Man's voice was hard as December. "A sword."

"One stroke a day! How can I ever—"

The blackthorn staff leaped out and struck him in the stomach, so hard it made tears spring to his eyes. He could not speak for days; he carried the ache much longer, like a rat that gnawed his belly.

Each day he came to the forge and lit the fire. Then he pulled upon the great bellows until the flames roared and the iron began to glow, like a red serpent in black skin. And each day he hammered down a single stroke.

The days passed very slowly. The fire's heat toughened his skin, and his broad shoulders grew broader from pumping the great bellows.

And each day, as he woke in the darkness before dawn, he

saw his father again, bending, leaving, gone. And the Old Man kept his back turned, and he never spoke.

Until one day he said, "Art tha yet eager to 'prentice on me? Dost tha wish to be more swift about thy making?"

Mark spoke the truth, waiting to be beaten. "Aye."

"Fair enow. Now mayst tha strike the iron thrice each day; but tha must never step out o' doors. From now will I gather wood."

And though many days (weeks? months?) had passed since Mark had felt the world's wind on his cheek, it galled him that the Old Man should take away his right to go outside. But the dark drive to make his sword was greater than his thirst for light and air. From that day forth he never felt the wind; but his anger rolled from him like sweat as he pumped the bellows and struck his iron. Slowly, slowly, the iron's shape began to change, but Mark knew it would never be a sword within his lifetime.

Then one day the Old Man said, "How goes thy making? Wouldst tha crave to go more swiftly still?"

"How much swifter?" Mark replied bitterly. "Five strokes? Ten?"

"Tha mayst labour at forge as tha will—an tha oath to never see the sun. Tha'lt sleep here, aface of forge, waking ony in darkness, walking ony in shadow: no light to thine eye but embers and hot iron."

A sudden fierce desire blazed up in Mark to see sunshine, hear birdsong, smell grass wet with dew. If he agreed to the Old Man's terms, his world would hold only darkness and fire, iron and ashes. He knew he could not live like that.

Yet hunger drove him. "I'll do it," he said.

From that day forth he woke at night and slept through the day. He closed the forge door; there were no windows. He woke without knowing morning: slept without seeing sunset. His world was the stink of hot iron; the roar of flame; sweat; the taste of ashes. He knew no more than what the iron knew, felt nothing but what it felt. He worked fiercely, day after day; his chest deepened and his strong arms grew stronger still from hammering. And with every stroke he beat hate into the iron: hate for the Old Man who kept him penned in a lightless prison. When he woke, he burned with rage: when he slept, he dreamt of murder.

He made the pommel first. When it was almost done he put it in the flames until it began to smoulder with a dull red glow. With tongs he swiftly plucked it out, and scored it all around with the black dagger, leaving a single line spiralling from the butt up to the pommel's top. This was the grip, the striving of his life, circling ever upward without rest.

Then he made the hilts, a plain iron bar to keep his hands from sliding up the blade, and keep a foe's weapon from sliding down. Grimly he laughed at the joke: he was Shielder's Mark; yet his father had left him no shield. The hilts on his sword would be all his protection.

The blade he fashioned last, long and straight and black. When he was done he smashed it against the anvil and it shattered. He picked up the pieces, and began again. The next time the blade was stronger, and did not break against the anvil, but the black dagger cut his sword in half as if cutting cheese. A third time he fashioned the blade; and this time the dagger could not mar it.

Then he worked to give the blade an edge. When he was done, he tore a strip from his shirt. It only took the lightest pressure against the edge to make the cloth split, but Mark was not satisfied, and went to work again. The next time he merely dropped the strip of cloth onto the upturned blade. It fell cleanly into two pieces and fluttered to the ground. Still it was not enough. The third time he dropped a strip of cloth upon the blade it fell in one piece to the floor. Only when

Mark squatted to pull on one edge with a finger could he tell it was in two halves.

He fitted the blade in the pommel, the hilts across them both, and joined all parts together. Then he called the Old Man, and said that he was done.

"Give me the dagger," the Old Man said. "Now name thy blade."

Mark held the weapon into his hand: a thing of darkness, made of iron, sweat, and bitter hate; the cruel hiss of coals, the bellows' dragon-breath. "Its name is Ashes," Mark said, for this was the teaching the Old Man had given him.

The Old Man plucked Ashes from his hand, and dropped it with a clatter to the floor. "It's not enough," he said, turning for the door.

Mark boiled with rage. Ashes was his child, his life for an endless term of hell. It was all his darkness: pure as rage, strong as hate, sharp as grief.

The next thing he knew he was standing with Ashes in his hand, its point at the Old Man's bald head, just where the white scar seamed his ancient scalp. "It is enow," Mark hissed.

"I say it is not." The Old Man's words were dry as bones.

"It is enow!" Mark screamed. "Turn around. *Turn around and look at me!* Or by God I'll kill you where you stand."

He felt Ashes, cold and heavy in his hand.

How simple, how simple it would be. All he had to do was kill the Old Man and walk away. He could know sunshine again, and open air, and sky.

He hated the Old Man; hated his dry voice, his hard bones, his blackthorn staff, his walk, his cruel laugh. The Old Man was evil and his touch was unclean. "You *robbed* me," Mark hissed. "I had a world to look at and you made me see ashes."

The Old Man said, "All there is, is ashes."

At that moment Mark hated the Old Man selflessly, entirely, utterly.

He hated him almost as much as he hated his father.

"I gave you *everything,*" he cried.

The Old Man said, "Tha'rt nae worth loving. An thy own father could not love tha, how could I?"

A great shudder ran through Mark's body. The shock of pain was so great he thought he would die.

But in that instant, before he knew he was still alive and began to swing his sword to crack the Old Man's skull, some part of the old Mark, a part that had never quite died, held his hand, trembling, for one fraction of a moment. *Why? Why is t'Awd Man so cruel? What does he want from you?*

He wants to die.

He wants to die.

T'Awd Man is trying every way he knows to make you kill him. And it isn't hard, because you've hated him for weeks (months? years?). He's beaten you, stroke by stroke, into a long black weapon wi' blade as sharp as grief.

"I can kill," Mark said slowly. "You've taught me that." Slowly he dropped his arms, until his swordpoint scraped against the stone floor. "But I won't do it for any man's bidding but my own."

The Old Man turned, eyes bright with fury. "It is the ony way! Hast tha learnt nought after all? Tell me, what dost tha see i' the fire?"

"Ashes."

"Ashes!" the Old Man cried.

". . . But there are also faces in the flames," Mark said softly.

What was it Val said? *Look for joy. That must be your candle, when the darkness falls.*

God was in running water, you said to him, and wind. He thought of the river behind his Keep, racing through rapids, or pooling under willow-wands. Each fishing hole a cup of shadows. He remembered the hissing rain on the road from Swangard, their sudden booming footsteps as they crossed a plankboard bridge; farm windows in the distance, lamplit yellow squares of human hope.

He thought of Gail for the first time in what seemed like years. Remembered her, flushed and quivering and ready to punch him if he laughed, giving him that monstrous pink hat. Remembered her too as he'd seen her first, standing by the throne with her vixen's face and narrow laughing eyes. He held her like a match before his eyes, her and Val and Lissa too, and the wind that had billowed up behind him when he broke the Ghostwood's spell, and the infinite blue and empty hawk-specked sky over Borders. His home.

"There are faces in the fire, Old Man, and crowns and swords and elfin feasts. If you listen, you can hear their songs. There is more to life than ashes: I don't think yours is all the wisdom there is."

"Perhaps not," the Old Man replied, his gaunt face raised. "But it is wisdom I have earned." He gazed at Mark, frail and unimaginably old. "Tha buys wisdom not only from the sins tha suffer, boy, but from the sins tha commit."

Bitter then was the voice of Hedrod's Son. "An endless time I waited for my sons to cum and tak my teaching from mé, but they did not. Tha'rt the ony son I am ever like to have, Shielder's Mark. Ashes is the ony wisdom I am master of; I taught it all to tha."

"It's what you had to give," Mark said. "I won't turn it down."

"I thought it would change all, when tha stole the black

blade Aron used to dam Hedrod my father and all magic else. The spell would be broke and he would be loose again, and he would cum for me at last, in hate or love, and free me from this cursed Keep. But he did not cum. He chose to raise his armies, reclaim his crown, rip tribute from the living: but he did not cum." The Old Man's eyes glittered with hate and fear. "Glad I am I murthered him! That I'll not repent! How can a son absolve his father for not loving him?"

Hedrod, Mark thought. *That must be the Ghost King! And this Old Man must be Hedrod's son; the Prince who murdered him all those years ago.* Mark's mind was racing, trying to make sense of the Old Man's words. What was that about raising armies? It must have been Hedrod who appeared before Duke Richard, to lay claim to his ancient territories.

The Old Man backed toward a door that led into the heart of the Keep. His lips twitched, and the black dagger in his hand swayed and trembled. "A thousand years have I burned my eyes on ashes, held by Aron's spell. Waiting, waiting. But now I wait no longer!" he cried. And turning, he fled within the Keep. Mark started after him.

At that moment came a sound so utterly strange that for the longest time Mark could not recognize it. Only gradually, like dawn finally coming up out of the blue darkness before morning, did he realize it was another human voice. And it was calling his name.

Swiftly he turned and flung open the other smithy door, the one that opened onto the courtyard. Outside it was the last hour before dawn. The night was cool and unimaginably fresh after a lifetime before the forge.

Mark halted, stunned by the touch of open air. Overhead, morning stars blinked in a paling sky.

"Mark? Is that you?" Val stood fumbling for a weapon at his side, eyes blinking with fear.

"Good God!" Mark cried. "Next pigs will turn to peacocks! Valerian is wearing a sword!"

"Not to much purpose," Val gasped, letting his scabbard dangle.

A thin figure went hurrying across the eastern wall and disappeared into the Tower. "There he goes!" Mark cried.

"Wha—?"

"Come on!" Mark yelled, and they were off, pelting across the courtyard. "T'Awd Man means some devilment."

The oaken door at the base of the Tower was a lattice of rotting boards held in place by iron bands and a great iron padlock on a chain. Mark raised Ashes above his head and burst the bands asunder with a single terrific stroke. He kicked the door open. Piles of rubble lay inside, spattered with bat droppings, dead leaves and smashed glass. The air was thick with the smell of death and decay. A coil of stairs rose up inside the wall like a stone serpent: overhead, the sound of a tapping staff dwindled into the darkness.

Mark glanced at his friend, who stood on the edge of that desolation, pale and blinking. Valerian's sword wavered like a feather in his hand. "You don't have to come, Val. This isn't scholar's business."

"This isn't *anyone's* business," Val gulped. "But I didn't come into the Ghostwood to let you go up those stairs alone."

Gravely Mark nodded.

Together they plunged into the darkness. Mark took the stairs three at a time, holding Ashes in his right hand while with his left he felt for the wall.

The footsteps above him stopped. A bolt drew back and a door creaked open. Sounds pelted down like hail: glass smashing, tiles bursting, iron chopping against wood or bone, the Old Man's shrieks.

Mark charged into the topmost chamber of the Scarlet Tower, then stood, watching the Old Man in amazement. "Here I am!" cried Hedrod's Son. "I will hide no longer!"

Once this had been a chamber of dark knowledge. Now books lay scattered along the floor, their covers slashed and rotted. "Cum, cum tha bastard, tha King of Kings! Drop a cloak of flesh around thy black heart and cum to me!" The Old Man swept a row of glass jars from a table: dark pulpy bodies oozed from them, stinking horribly, and quivered on the floor.

The mummified corpse of a young boy drooped from a pillar where it had been tied. A web of black rags hung around its shoulders. The Old Man danced among the rubble, slashing wildly at the corpse. At its feet crouched a wide copper basin, spattered with dried blood. "Listen to me!" the Old Man howled. "Listen to me!"

A voice grim and low said, "I hear."

"Oh shite," Mark said weakly.

A shadow took shape at the far end of the room, behind the pillar where the sacrifice was bound. The air seemed to thicken, the stink of death to weave itself into a form, a tall man, old and terrible. Fear clung to him. The scar on Mark's right palm opened like a door and magic whirled through it like a cold, damp wind: he felt his skin creep with dread.

something in the house

O god he wanted to throw himself back down the stairs, jump from the window, do anything but meet its face, anything but look beneath its crown into its terrible eyes.

The fingernails of the Ghost's left hand clicked against the pommel of a long grey sword. His right hand rested on the dead boy's thin shoulder. "Who dares call?"

The Old Man stood still at last, his thin chest heaving, the black dagger shaking in his hand. His eyes flicked quickly at Mark. "Hast tha cum to learn another lesson then?" he said, with a queer, cackling gasp, half mad with fear. "Allow me to present my honoured father."

The Ghost King's mail clinked and muttered. "Son."

The Old Man seemed now so frail, so empty, as if his father's presence struck the life from him and left but a shell behind. But when he looked up at his father, his eyes glittered with fear and hate.

Hedrod's left hand reached to touch his own chest, above his heart, then fell away. "Tha!" he whispered. "It was tha. I should have known that even so base a deed was not beneath tha."

A great shudder rocked the Old Man's body. "I would have died and gladly, to prove my true son's love, but tha never graunted me the chance. Tha penned me with tutors, that tha need not speak with me thyself; tha graunted me this castle so my shade would never cross thy own. Tha shewed me no trust, and gave me no teaching."

Hedrod shook his head impatiently. "A son must take some weight on his own shoulders. He cannot seek for plaints in every err his father makes. Tha wert always weak; tha could not be trusted. Time hath shown me right, for with black art tha murthered me."

"He murdered you," Mark said. The bitterness between them took his breath away. "Hedrod, look upon your son. Blow by blow you made your son an enemy, hard as hate and sharp as grief."

"Thruff the heart," the Old Man murmured, fingering the black dagger. "I slid it thruff the heart of an orphan-boy, swaddled in thy old cloak; I watched thy blood stream from him, felt him twitching root and boughs with thy death-throes."

Through the heart of an orphan boy, Mark thought. The

frail body hung between the two terrible old men, unheeded. *Through the heart of an orphan boy.*

He heard Val stagger into the room behind him, panting and gasping. *Steady, Mark. Got to hold on. Poor Val shaking like a willow wand but here beside me, and his eyes are steady because he can face the darkness.* Mark forced himself to look upon Hedrod's Ghost and said, "Bless him, ancient King."

"He hath no bless to give," Hedrod's Son said bitterly.

"Oh, I can bless," the old King murmured. "I can give you your death." Dread pooled around him, thick as midnight, cold as the grave. The Old Ghost's eyes were black and hard as iron. Lissa said she had seen her death in the Ghost's eyes. Now, horrified, Mark saw himself there, lying on a black-draped bed. The smell of sickness came foully to him. Valerian, his soft beard almost white, dipped a cloth in a bowl of rosewater and washed his brow. The wire in his chest clenched, cutting into his heart, and

Stop!

Don't think. O God. Move fast. "You may not take my life, awd King."

Hedrod's heavy shadow grew to lap against Mark's feet. "Nobody commands me."

Mark laughed unsteadily. "As it happens, I'm Nobody's Son," he said. "And what I tell you, you must do."

Where's Gail? Why isn't she there if I'm sick? Val's there but Gail, Gail. . . .

Don't think.

Keep your steel about you just a little longer, Shielder's Mark. You've got to shift the ground on this Ghost somehow. That's what you've always done, lad. When you answered awd Husk's riddle, when you stole the dagger from Hedrod's Son, when you claimed King Astin's daughter: each

time the trick was shifting the ground from their strength to yours.

Well what was the Ghost's strength? Fear, of course. Fear and dread. *But what does a ghost fear?*

And then, with a start, he knew.

From his side the Ghost King drew a rune-carved sword, grey as dead men's flesh. "Tha be but a fool in a leather hat and muddy breeches. Tha'rt nought. Tha hast no power."

Quick as thought Mark whirled with Ashes. Hedrod's sword leaped to block a cut—

But Mark did not swing at him. Instead he laid his long black blade against the Old Man's throat. "An you so much as blink an eye I'll kill your son," Mark said, sick with dread.

No matter how hard he tried, he could not tear his eyes away from the Ghost King's deadly gaze. His body shook with fever; the smell of stale sheets and rosewater clogged his throat. He was dizzy, no longer sure if he stood, or lay upon a feather bed. He heard women crying.

Hedrod's iron eyes narrowed. "Feel the turn?" Mark gasped, moving one step closer to the terrible Ghost. "Feel the floor start to slip beneath your feet? Here stands your son. Your killer. If you be ghost, and I kill him, you are avenged. And what then holds you to this second life?"

What must a ghost fear?

Death, of course.

Slowly Hedrod lowered his sword. "Tha wouldst not. Tha hast not the belly for it, to slay a weak old man with thy blood as cold as snow."

Mark tried to spit but his mouth was dry. "Try me," he said.

He felt sick and fevered and half in dream, as if he lay already on that black-draped bed while his life burned away.

But cutting through the fever Mark felt Ashes in his hand, cold and heavy with darkness.

He had seen faces in the fire, and heard their song. But he had learned another lesson in the Red Keep; mastered it before his forge.

He too was a thing of darkness. He knew the taste of ashes.

If Hedrod stirred, Mark would slay his son. Not with joy and not with pleasure: but he would kill the Old Man, quickly and forever

The Old Man laughed his laugh of breaking stone. "So tha didst learn, after all." Turning to his father he said, "He will do as he says."

And o god life was sweet, was sweet.

Gail?

But you will die, whether Hedrod's vision were truth or but illusion. You will die of fever or some other thing.

Working at the Red Keep's forge, he had let the taste of ashes fill his mouth: once he had let the fear of death and failure rob his life of sweetness.

Never again. I swear it.

"Will it be enow?" Mark said steadily. "To send you back to your grave? I don't know. But I don't think you can take the risk."

Hedrod looked at him through narrow eyes. "And if I were to slay tha now, with but a glance?"

"Your son would fall before Mark hit the floor," Gail said, voice shaking but clear.

Gail?

In the pale morning light just creeping into the Tower, Mark whirled to see her dimly in the doorway, wrapped in her beloved brown travelling cloak. She was wearing the shooting glove Lissa had given her; she had an arrow nocked and drawn back to her ear, aimed at the middle of the Old Man's back. "If I want my husband killed," she said, "I'll do it myself."

"Shite, Gail, what the—" Mark looked at Val, at Gail and Lissa coming up behind her. The sight of them, his closest friends, miraculously here with him in the midst of darkness, filled him with joy, and awe. He remembered how he had felt that day in the Spring Room, meeting Gail for the first time, with his life strong within him, brave and fresh as rainbows. He stepped forward another pace, to stand directly before the Ghost King as once he stood before Astin the Munificent. "We are stretches of the same river, you and I, awd King. I am fated to destroy you. I knocked the Red Keep down, and I hold Borders now. It was I who last saw your wife Queen Lerelil alive. Though I did not mean to, I killed her when I broke the Ghostwood's spell." Reaching around his neck, Mark lifted up the Queen's talisman, let it dangle for a moment in the weak red light, then dropped it clattering to the floor. "Everything you are is in my power, and you can't beat me ever, because deep down you're held here by only hate and fear. You're a great man with a great line. But I'm just Nobody's Son, wi' nowt to lose, and you can go spit."

An endless silence spun out then, while he and Hedrod looked deeply into one another; he felt steel shiver as their looks crossed, and knew that the ancient King saw his death too, deep within Mark's eyes.

At last Hedrod sighed and looked away, and with that breath he seemed to dwindle. "Thy father was lucky not to know tha, Nobody's Son. Of all things i' th' world, be there nought so troublesome as a child." He looked from Mark to Gail with something almost like amusement. "I hope tha's cursed with a pack of them. For myself, King of Kings, I found one to be too many." He stared at his son; in his eyes Mark saw rage and bafflement, deep frustration, and wonder, and something, far behind, almost like hurt. "Murthered me, eh?" Hedrod shook his head, and sheathed his long grey sword. "Do not kill my boy, Nobody's Son."

And Mark started to relax, and the fear began to drain from him, for it seemed that father and son might after all be reconciled.

But the Old Man, eyes glittering with hatred, said, "Too long have I been stirring all my ashes. Let the fire blaze, or go out!" And raising up the iron dagger he lunged with all his strength toward his father.

Mark dropped Ashes and dove, but he missed the Old Man's wrist, and his hand closed on the dagger's blade instead, a hair's breadth from Hedrod's heart. But though the white scar on his right palm screamed with agony, the blade did not lay him open to the bone. Only a few drops of blood squeezed out between his fingers, drying instantly upon the blade to patches like red rust.

Mark rose slowly to his feet to stand between the two of them, father and son. The Old Man snarled at him in fury, but his frail struggles were like a child's against Mark's strength. Emptiness filled Mark's heart. Too much had gone through him today. Too much grief, too much pain. He knew a kind of darkness would be a part of him forever.

Suddenly he hungered for sunlight. He wanted to feel the wind on his cheek, the kiss of rain on his brow. He looked upon the Old Man, and sighed, and said, "There's other things than ashes."

And then, with his aching right hand, brown and veined and hard, he crushed the black blade like a withered leaf within his fist, and let the fragments clatter to the ground.

The Tower shook, and the Old Man shrieked, and Hedrod his father roared like a peal of thunder that explodes overhead and then goes howling, rumbling, fading, dwindling into silence, and darkness; and his hands withered, and his chain shirt slid clinking to the floor, falling from a shadow that held its shape for a single heartbeat and then was gone, like mist blown away by the wind.

The Ghost King was gone.

Where his son had stood, a black robe settled gently to the floor, and was still.

12

Goodbye

Mark and Val and Gail and Lissa sat on blocks of red granite fallen from the Red Keep's walls, glad of the pale October sun. The black limbs of the cherry trees were bare, and the path that led from the Ghostwood was carpeted in dull red leaves.

Gail stripped off her shooting glove. "Valerian. How good to see you," she said, in a tone of low menace. "And of course hello to you, Husband."

Lissa winced. Hat in hand, Valerian glanced at Mark and bit his lip in silent sympathy.

Mark had gone down into darkness and come out again. He had faced down the Old Man; there was new heaviness in his hands, a weight of iron in his belly.

All this iron seemed to melt before the flame in Gail's eyes. *That's happily ever after for you.*

Gail stalked over to Mark, grabbed his collar and yanked his face down to hers. Fiercely, she kissed him. "I'm glad you're not dead."

Mark blinked. "Me too."

"But if you ever walk out on me again I'll hunt you down and murder you myself," Gail finished.

Oh boy.

Jerk. "Do you believe me?" Shake.

"You bet," Mark squeaked. Gail's eyes carried absolute conviction. "I swear I didn't mean—"

"How could you do this?" Gail yelled, rage and hurt

pouring through her shaking hands. "How could you leave me alone with ghosts everywhere and that horrible man in the house? How could you desert me? What kind of man are you, you, you *idiot!*"

"A stupid one." Mark took Gail in his arms and held her. Her body was stiff with fear and anger. "But getting smarter, I hope. I'll not leave you again."

"Better not," Gail swore. Her arms softened, and one great sob wrenched her body. "Here I am, taking care of you again," she muttered fiercely. "Can't be trusted to tie your own damn bootlaces." Pushing herself away she took a deep breath, and bent to unstring her bow.

Mark winced. "It's good to see you all."

"It's good to see *anyone*," Valerian muttered, gazing nervously around at the ruins of the Red Keep. "That must have been the Ghost that came to High Holt. Richard's servants say he declared himself King again, and demanded tribute from the living."

Gail laughed. "I don't think we'll have to pay up now."

Val nodded. "The dagger—and the hate between them— was all that held those two to life, I think. Perhaps that was all that remained of Duke Aron's spell."

Lissa studied Mark without enthusiasm. "I never thought I'd see you looking wilder than you did that first day you strode into Swangard, but that sooty face! That beard! That shaggy hair! How did you grow it all in three days?"

"Three days! But it seemed like months, Years!"

Valerian looked at him curiously. At last he shook his head. "Well, there's magic in the world again, I guess." He turned back to the women, baffled. "What I want to know is how you came to be here. I meant to slip out unobserved."

Offended, Lissa's immaculate eyebrows rose a fraction of an inch: you think rain is dry? you think ice is hot? "You thought you could commandeer a brace of carpenters without me finding out?"

Mark blinked. "Carpenters?"

Valerian shivered. "When we found you gone, I guessed that you were headed for the Keep. I asked the carpenters to slap me up a boat: not a fancy craft, just good enough to cross the Border once and back. I launched below the rapids and pulled across. The boat is knotted to a cedar bough upon this side. Great heroes may ford icy rivers in October in the dark, but even by the light of day I could not swim the Border, thank you. I am very glad to let you use the boat returning, unless a mighty hero scoffs at such conveniences, and you would rather swim across again."

"Actually, I didn't ford the river," Mark said blandly, with a sly glance at his friend. "I walked ower the bridge."

"You walked over the . . . bridge?" Val sighed. "I foresee a rare few weeks of weaseling to ferret all your stories out." Valerian blinked and slid down off his stone to stand, studying Mark as if examining him through a scrying glass. "You are different, Shielder's Mark. Heavier. I can hear the paving stones crack beneath your feet. I see cold iron in your eyes." Slowly Val unbuckled his belt and drew his sword. Tossing it on the ground, he held the belt and scabbard out to Mark. "I wonder at that coal-black blade you carry in your hand."

Gravely Mark took the scabbard Valerian offered him, buckled it around his waist, and sheathed Ashes in it. "A scabbard's the best place for this blade of mine. And nowt could keep it better than a gift from you."

Val blinked, and, charmingly, blushed a little.

Gail laughed. "I think at last you've got a sword you will not lose. But tell me, you bastard, why did you run off into the Ghostwood anyway?"

"I was looking for God."

Gail blinked, nonplussed. Val said, "What did you find?"

"Ashes." Startled, Valerian cast an anxious glance at Mark. "Ashes first, anyway. Only at t'end did I remember my wise friend's words and think to look for joy." They looked at one another, a flash of understanding. *Two souls shaking hands.* "Thanks," Mark said. And then he told his story, from the time he had left Borders until Gail and Lissa had found him with Val atop the Scarlet Tower.

When he was done Val frowned and rubbed his glasses on his tunic hem, mulling over the tale. "So royal patricide then was the crime so great that Nobody's name was forgotten and his shield blanked."

Lissa nodded. "And High Holt was once the capital. This explains much."

But Mark was feeling the wind against his cheek, and the stone cool and real beneath him, thinking about other things. "And you know, my father's probably in a bar somewhere, and drinking. Getting awd to be a soldier now, bitched knees, maybe, and a sore back all the time. Thinks about me sometimes: Ma always said I had his hands, his eyes. Still guilty after all this time for running out on me."

"He knows he failed," Val said softly. "He knows he is a coward, and wonders why his father did not make *him* a better man."

And even if he came to you right now and held out his hand, what would it help, Shielder's Mark? It wouldn't change the loneliness that cankered in you at four and ten and sixteen. It could never heal that four-year-old boy who still sits inside you, abandoned and betrayed. Your father and that four-year-old: those two ghosts made you what you are, and for better or for worser, that's what you'll stay.

"All those years I worked and waited for my dad to come back. And he didn't. So I looked for someone else to do his job, looked for awd men like a schoolboy lusting after girls.

Damn near anything wi' beard would do: Sir William, Duke Richard. No matter what you or Lissa told me about Richard I just ached for him to shake my hand and say, 'Good work, lad: I'm proud of you,' and so I swallowed down every shovelful of shite he tossed my way."

"Richard can give you a pretty steady diet of that stuff," Gail observed.

Mark laughed. And as a sharp stroke upon an old black bell will ring off the rust, so that laughter, deep and real and rooted in his belly, shook the last self-pity from his soul. He felt his black iron sword heavy in his hand; felt too the weight of the earth underneath his feet, the jolly kiss of sunshine, the breeze bearing up his heart like the wind under a hawk's wing. He was strong, strong as he had never been before.

Mark spat for the sheer pleasure of it, a long carpenter's spit. "But come, let's start for home: I want to see what Orrin's done while I've been gone." They slid from their stones and began the long trek, and it was good to Mark, to be walking away from the Red Keep with his dearest friends, treading a forest path in fall, kicking through drifts of oak and cherry leaves, the sky overhead that certain clear blue that foretells a frosty morrow. "And I still want to know how came my wife to be here. Aren't you supposed to be back at Borders, minding the place like a good Duchess should?"

Lissa scowled. "Precisely what I told her—"

"—All the way here!" Gail laughed. "She must have said it a hundred times. But I left Deron in charge. I don't see what's so wrong with. . . ." She faltered before Val's astonishment and Lissa's frank disapproval. She turned beseechingly to Mark. "He seems like a nice young man."

Lissa rolled her eyes.

Mark barely suppressed a laugh. "And once you knew Val

had gone, how did you manage to follow him? Those keen hunter's eyes, I guess?"

Gail blushed. "Well, not exactly. . . ."

"Ten gamekeepers," Lissa said succinctly. "They're waiting down the path. They were only too happy when Gail told them they didn't have to come to the Red Keep proper."

This time Mark couldn't help himself. "Ten g-g-gamekeepers!" he roared, gasping with laughter. He slid whooping to the grass. Lissa shot him a quick glance, her blue eyes alight with merriment.

"What?" Gail said, smiling and confused. "What's so funny?"

Lissa blanched and swiftly turned the conversation. "I think the Duke should be aware of Richard's scheme."

Gail's eyes grew hard and narrow with remembered anger. "Scheme?" Mark asked.

Gail burst a drift of cherry leaves with a vicious kick. "He's going to my father, you see. I could have stopped him, but there are some things I won't do, not for you or any man."

"Stop! Whoah! Slow down," Mark pleaded. "Explain, please."

Gail scowled. "That night after dinner, when you stormed off to our room and I had to show Richard around Borders: he told me if I didn't agree to be his mistress, he would have my father fix you with the blame for summoning these ghosts and order you hanged."

Mark's heart turned slowly to ice at the thought of Richard touching Gail, peeling back her clothing as a man might pull the petals off a flower. "And you said . . . ?"

Gail snorted. "I told him to swive himself, of course."

"Of course." Mark laughed out loud. "I didn't think they taught young ladies to talk that way."

"The Princess speaks that particular language fluently," Lissa observed.

Gail glanced over her shoulder at Mark, almost embarrassed, the ghost of a smile on her thin lips. "Actually, I think I taught Richard a good few phrases of that tongue in a very short time. Then I kicked him in the leg. Then he left."

She blew out a little breath and stumped forward, battered brown cloak flapping at her knees. "So you see, my father's troops will be coming to string you up."

"My life wasn't worth your honour, eh?"

Gail shrugged. "No, it wasn't that exactly. In the first place, I didn't want to sleep with that toad, and as I told you once, I am accustomed to getting what I want. In the second place, I didn't think you'd want to be married to a woman tangled up in something that . . . base. I would have been miserable, and made you a miserable wife."

"When Gail suffers," Lissa reflected, "everybody suffers."

Val bit his lip and fiercely polished his spectacles.

"But why?" Mark asked. "Even if you were his mistress he could never come at the Crown. I always thought he wanted your power, not your body."

"Revenge," Lissa said simply. "If Gail gave in, then he was in part revenged on you: especially if he could get a child on her. If she chose to resist, then he could get Astin to hang you and would once more be in line to wed the Princess. I warned you that the Duke was not a gracious loser."

Walking beside Gail, Mark reached to take her hand. It was small and hard; not the hand of a Princess at all. "You are the cantiest, bravest, boldest woman in the world," he said softly. "And I'm the luckiest man to have you."

"From time to time you seem to forget this," Gail said drily.

"I won't again, I promise." He gave her hand a squeeze. Down the path one of Mark's Vagabonds had spotted them, and raised a cry. Mark waved back and grinned. "But I think we'd better make a trip to see your honoured father."

The Winter Room of Swangard Palace was intended to be cozy. An enormous fireplace took up most of one wall; beside it stood a long trestle laden with hot punch.

Hoop skirts, Mark noted, were no longer the fashion. The women now wore long gowns that fell in tiers down to their ankles. The ankles themselves were cleverly exposed by cutting a circle out of all the ladies' shoes.

Liked the butter churns better.

"But Mark," Duke Richard said, "What you say is very well, but does not change the fact that you loosed a darkness on the kingdom. Our people still are troubled by terrifying dreams, and other wraiths now walk the night beside this ghostly King you claim to have destroyed."

"Things are now as once they were in grandfather days," Valerian said impatiently. "Duke Aron dammed a stream; when Mark pulled out the keystone, of course there was a wash of magic through the land. That will settle, but it will not drain entirely away, nor should it. There is magic in our world and in our past. We only hurt ourselves when we deny it."

"You are as ever free with your opinions," Duke Richard snapped, "But let the Duke defend himself."

Val quivered indignantly but Mark held up his hand. "Duke Richard's right. I will speak for myself." He looked slowly around the room, until every eye was locked upon him. "I, Shielder's Mark, Duke of the Ghostwood, Lord of

Borders, do here before this witness and the Crown call Richard, Lord of High Holt, a villain base, and traitor."

The room was shocked into silence.

Well, so much for the prepared bit he'd worked on with Lissa. He began to speak more plainly, in a clear voice that carried to the back of the room. "When I came from the Ghostwood I was new to Court. I didn't understand the rules by which my sword was taken from me, or know why a brilliant young musician could be shamed without someone crying foul. I still don't understand the rules; but now I know I don't have to play the game."

Shift the ground, shift the ground.

Satisfaction was building in Mark like a thunderhead, tall and fierce and fraught with lightning. He felt like laughing. "When the ghosts came, Duke of High Holt, you ran. You sent your own steward to his death to cover your escape. Then, while your people went half-mad with fear, you had no thought but scheming and plotting. You came under my roof, and told my wife you'd have me killed unless she slept wi' you. Said you'd set the King against me."

Richard blanched, his gaze flicking around the room. Every eye was fixed on him. "These are lies! Patent, gross and palpable untruths!"

A shiver of pure gladness ran down Mark's spine. "You're welcome to prove that on my body," he purred. "I b'lieve that's grounds for a challenge, ain't it? Or do I need to tell a few more truths about you?"

Richard stopped, jaw working, then whirled to face the King. "This peasant knows he cannot best me any way but with a knife. You saw him try to goad me to a duel. Let him catch the tiger by the tail! As Duke of High Holt, to whom you swore to give your youngest daughter, I demand the service of your champion!"

"Eh now, this is a matter of honour," Mark said. "Besides,

you haven't got Lord Peridot's excuse. You're plenty fit, from all I hear." *In fact, you could probably carve me like a Christmas cake, but you don't know that. The question is, do you have the stomach to put your precious body on the line?*

"I will not dispute on duelling technicalities," Richard said coldly. "The Crown knows it is unthinkable for the Duke of High Holt to soil himself by crossing swords with you. I demand what is my right: support from my sovereign and friend against invidious calumny."

Mark blinked. "Against what?"

Astin fretted. At last he glanced unhappily at his champion. "William?"

Sir William scratched his beard and sighed. "The years are growing on me, sire. I think I shall retire soon." The old knight looked steadily down at Richard; there was little love in his eyes. "Very soon. Perhaps today. I pray you to look elsewhere for a champion."

"What, William? You too? Is everyone afraid of this, this Nobody?" Richard cried.

Sir William's gaze abruptly lost its weariness. "Did I just hear you call me coward, Duke?" His right hand fell to the pommel of his sword. "I do not think your *honour* would be hurt if you crossed swords with me, cousin. *Nobody's* Jervis' Richard, I ask again: did I just hear you call me coward?"

Fear and fury chased each other across Richard's face. The room held its breath.

At last the Duke of High Holt's eye, drawn as if by magnet, fell to the sword beneath Sir William's hand, and stuck there. "No," he said at last. "Of course I meant nothing of the kind."

"I thought not," Sir William said. "That would be— *ungentlemanly.*"

"Dick, you're yellow as goat's-piss," Mark said pleasantly. "Let me tell you one other thing. If you ever trouble me or mine again, in public or private, by hidden slight or open insult, I'll not answer in the Court." *Don't fight a spider wi' webs.* "I'll find you and I'll break you. Got it?"

Richard's hands twitched with fury. "I will not stay to savour the treachery of those whose honour is in debt to me," he hissed at Astin, and turning on his heel he strode from the room.

"The thing about roaches," Val remarked, his quiet words large in the silence, "is that they cannot abide the light."

"Beautifully done," Lissa said afterwards, sipping a tumbler of punch. Brilliantly coloured courtiers hummed and buzzed around them like a hive of wasps, all contentedly sinking their stings into the helpless Duke Richard, who had stormed from Swangard and was headed back to the High Holt. "You will be quite a diplomat, my Lord of Borders."

Mark's jaw dropped open like a trap door.

"Your timing was exquisite," she continued imperturbably, "and you chose well when you gambled on Sir William. Really, Mark, you are becoming subtle in your old age. I begin to hope we shall make a Duke of you yet."

Gail laughed. "That was subtle?"

Lissa shrugged. "As Valerian remarked, a schemer cannot stand the light. It does not matter if the Court believes the things that Mark just said: they know now that Richard is a coward and a plotter. The power of a man like our dear departed Duke is at heart a subtle thing: it rests on his ability to sway the minds and hearts of others. Mark has stripped away his credibility; his influence at Court will rapidly decrease. A man with so much land and wealth cannot vanish overnight, but Richard does not have the knack of using his brute force. I should not be surprised to hear of his retirement.

"Which reminds me," she said more quietly. "A thing I meant to speak to you before, my lord. We are in Court now: my advice is that you wire Ashes in its sheath, or better, leave it in your room."

Mark looked at her, mystified. "No other man has to leave his sword at home, so long as he doesn't wave it at the King."

"No other sword is bladed in the royal black," Lissa murmured.

"Aaah!—I never thought of that!"

Lissa allowed herself a small sardonic smile. "Evidently." She shook her head. "Valerian brave and Duke Mark subtle! The world indeed is strange these days: there must be magic in the air."

Valerian blinked. "Brave?"

"Oh come on!" Gail cried merrily. "It's all very well for my husband to go leaping over rivers and slaying ghosts and shambling hither and yon performing heroic deeds generally. But for a scholar to belt on his sword and dare the Ghostwood! Now that is bravery. Lissa and I were both very impressed," she added slyly.

"Uh: well. I—" Val gulped and gasped and seemed to be praying for a merciful pit to open in the earth and swallow him. "Er, um . . . Ow!!"

"Oh, sorry about that," Mark said blithely. "Didn't mean to step on your foot there, Val."

"You left a bruise," Valerian complained later, peering at his foot as he prepared to lead his horse out of the King's stables.

Mark shrugged. "You'll be riding, won't you? You won't even notice." The big bay stood calmly outside his stall, shaking his head and whiffling as Val closed the door and led him outside.

Mark tossed a coin to the stable boy and followed his friend into the courtyard. It was a crisp, cool day, bright with pale November sunshine. "So you're really going back?"

"Yes," Val tinkered with girth, reins, saddlebags. "I should have known I could not come into the Ghostwood and expect to leave unchanged." He pushed his spectacles higher up his nose and glanced at Mark, smiling but serious. "It was . . . important to me, Mark. To belt on a sword and walk into that Wood. I never imagined doing such a thing; it was not part of anything I was. But looking back I think I made myself smaller than I had to be, in the hope I might be ignored, forgotten, left to go about my business. I made myself so small my father must despair of me.

"But the Ghostwood makes you bigger, doesn't it? I cannot fit into the self I was before I went there, or faced Hedrod with you. You have made me bigger, Mark, whether you meant to or no." He cinched his saddle and grimaced. "There are things I need to deal with back home. Things I must talk over with my father." He laughed, and shook his head, his eyebrows arched with that expression of wonder that Mark knew so well. "The odd thing is, now that I am grown so big, for the first time in my life I feel ready to learn what my father has to teach."

"Good! Then you can come and tell me all about Duking," Mark grinned. "I need to get some damn use out of your being Somebody's Son. You will come back to Borders, won't you?"

"I think so. Probably. I want to," Valerian said.

Old white-bearded Val dipping a black cloth in rosewa-ter. Will it really happen that way? God he'd be there, wouldn't he? He'd be there.

"For what it's worth, I think you're doing right, Val. And

I think the Val that comes back will stand a better chance wi' Lissa too."

"Perhaps," Valerian said softly. "I don't know. So many things are changing now, in all of us. Perhaps there will be something worth loving in me, anyway."

Mark grasped Val's shoulder. "There was always that." *Damn it, why can't you hug a man when you want to?* But he couldn't, not quite.

"There's summat I want you to have," he said suddenly. Quickly he took the black dagger off his belt and held it out to Val. "Here's a tool for dealing with your dad," he joked. "I had a new blade put on the haft. Just plain steel of course. Nothing—magical. . . ." The iron pommel was heavy in his hand, black as coal. He felt again its *realness:* true as something that could not be spoken, even to oneself. *Like the moment you realized that your mum was singing you to sleep so she and Dad could get at hating one another again: you knew it all your life, but hid it from yourself. That's what the dagger's like: that secret, made into a thing that's plain for all to see, who dare to look.*

What a shitty thing to give.

Valerian looked up in awe. "This would be too great a gift!"

"God no!" Mark forced a smile and tapped the sword hanging at his side. "I have one of my own now. The dagger is a spare. It . . . it's maybe a bit too grim, to give your best friend at a parting."

Valerian smiled, a small, pink, solemn, friendly smile. "I'm very good at light, Mark. It's my darkness I must explore, and this will be my candle. This is a thing of ancient power, and more than that, an emblem of the man I most admire, the friend I love the best. I will treasure it."

Their eyes met, Val's grey and honest behind his spectacles. They stood in the courtyard of Swangard Palace, too cold to be comfortable despite the sun, and they looked fully on one another, knowing that they were friends, and would always be.

A lot of water under this bridge too, Mark thought, with something like awe. He was growing older. Old enough to feel the current of what had been flowing under him, leading to his future. Old enough to look back over his shoulder, and see his past behind him, and grieve for what was gone, and honour its memory.

He felt, suddenly, how much it would hurt him if Val died; felt an echo of that pain, knowing that the Valerian he had known, fluffy and peering and hapless and altogether wonderful: this Valerian was already dying. Not physically, of course, but the man he remembered from that first night in Swangard Palace would be gone the next time they met, though his ghost would linger on in Val forever, and in their memories.

Three cheers for ghosts, Mark thought. *Three cheers for the dead.*

Of course Val would be much the same: better, even. As full of wonder and delight, with big pockets full of puzzles and fascinating stories about the lives of ants and ingenious designs for windmills that would do your washing. And they would still be friends, excellent friends. It could be even better next time.

But it would never be the same.

How much of life is like this? Mark wondered. *Is that what being grown up means? Saying goodbye as often as hello? More to wave back to with every step.* He glanced down at his hand again, that would never be a soft Court hand, and saw the fresh scar there, white no longer, but pink, like any other scar just starting to heal up.

Gravely Val belted the black dagger at his hip. Then he climbed into his saddle, pushed his spectacles firmly up his nose, and grinned at Mark. *"Adventure!"* The big bay sidled restlessly beneath him, eager to be moving in the chilly afternoon. "Goodbye, Shielder's Mark."

Mark smiled back, feeling the nip in the air, and Ashes heavy at his side. "Goodbye," he said.

Soon it was time to head back to Borders. He had plans for the Keep, for his duchy and his people. He was looking forward to being home.

Gail frowned. "Lissa, where's that brown-and-purple thing I dyed the other day—that'll be good and warm."

"I regret to tell you that a pang of conscience smote me and I burned it, Gail. It had suffered enough."

Gail scowled.

Mark looked over at Lissa, who was checking off their belongings one by one as servants packed them onto a brace of ponies. "In a world where I'm subtle and Val's brave," he said, "I want to see you giving orders, not just taking them. I'm going to make you Seneschal, Lissa. That's managing all my lands, reporting straight to me. You'll be riding out from Borders half the summer, mebbe, poking here and yon. Can you handle it . . . cousin?"

Lissa's perfect eyebrows arched a fraction of an inch. "I can indeed." Her cool blue eyes sparkled. "There will be much to do, I think: you left all in a shambles, Mark. We must first make sure of stores to see us through the spring. We need an ironmonger more, and a tapister besides, though that can wait. We should secure a weight of seed for—"

Suddenly Lissa stopped dead. "But—!" She took a deep breath. "My lord, you honour me in such an offer. But if I were to be your Seneschal, then who would attend your lady wife?"

"We can always find another lady-in-waiting," Gail said softly.

"You think it so simple! What woman could you find to scare you up a dyer in the middle of the night?" Lissa demanded. "What wench will you employ who knows a hundred ways to excuse you from a dreary dinner? Where will you meet that maid that sews as well as I a knife-sheath in a ball-gown sleeve?"

Impulsively Gail took Lissa's hands. "Nowhere, Lis. But a lady-in-waiting doesn't need to know those things; those are things only a true friend knows. And I hope we'll still be friends, even if my idiot husband gives you work equal to your genius."

"You make things happen," Mark said briskly. "That's the sort of head I need to be my Seneschal."

"Mark is right. You deserve a greater part in life than looking after a brainless royal brat," Gail said, smiling.

Lissa stopped and did not speak. She gripped Gail's hands, and then hugged her tight. A miracle rolled slowly down her cheek. "To be your friend was all the honour I ever wanted from my life."

Gail reached up with a teary smile and ruffled Lissa's hair. "Well I know that, and you know that, but try to tell my idiot husband!"

Mark chuckled. "I know squat about statecraft, Lissa: I need you more than Gail does."

"Which is saying something," Gail said, laughing and crying at once. "I don't know if I can breathe without you, or put my boots on in the morning. But I think I'd better learn."

"Well, you can ride," Mark said. "And that's all you need to know for the next week, until we get home!"

"Ride!" Gail said suspiciously. "We're not *riding* any-where."

Mark groaned. "If you really think I'm going to walk back to Borders in the middle of winter—"

"It isn't the middle of winter yet. There's barely any snow," Gail wheedled. "I love walking, Mark! Besides, by this time next year I might be pregnant, and you can't expect me to traipse all over the countryside then."

Mark looked at Gail in shock.

Sudden joy flamed in his breast, like fire bursting from blown embers. Hers was the sly, bold, laughing face he had seen in the flames. They would be friends and lovers too: they were meant to be after all.

And he would have sons, sons to take down to the river, and hold in his arms, and teach the finer points of fishing to.

"We'll walk," he gasped. "But, but what made you change your mind?"

"Might! I said I *might* be pregnant," Gail cried. She was blushing, and once again Mark had the sense of a little girl, peeping out from behind her Princess mask. Gail glanced over at Lissa. "A wise friend of mine once told me that there are only four great Adventures in life: being born, being married, being a parent, and dying. I didn't used to believe that, but now I'm coming to think it's true. About being married anyway." She scowled comically. "There's nothing so broadening as having to put up with someone else's foolishness all the time! And I looked at my sister with her new baby, and she didn't look like her life was over, and I thought, *I can do that!* I mean, what if I want to travel about and be a wife and be a mother and have a wonderful time? Who is going to stop me? I want everything, Mark: and you know I'm very good at getting what I want."

"God help us," Lissa murmured.

Gail grinned and took Mark's hand. "Have you any girls'

names you particularly care for? I feel quite certain our first child will be a girl. She'll take after me, of course."

Mark looked at her, eyes wide with alarm. *O my Lord*, he thought.

A daughter?

Sean Stewart is the author of seven novels, including *Mockingbird*, a *New York Times* Notable Book; *The Night Watch*; *Clouds End*; *Resurrection Man*, a *New York Times* Notable Book; and *Passion Play*, which was named the best science fiction novel of the year in Canada, as well as best debut mystery novel. Mr. Stewart lives with his wife and two children in Monterey, California.

Let your imagination fly with the best in fantasy

MAGIC
CARPET

BOOKS

Knight's Wyrd   (0-15-201520-5) $6.00
BY DEBRA DOYLE AND JAMES D. MACDONALD
Will Oddosson is told his wyrd—his fate—on the eve of his knighting: He will
meet Death before a year has passed. Soon he is beset by one evil beast after
another. Which will be his wyrd?

DIANE DUANE's thrilling wizardry series

So You Want to Be a Wizard   (0-15-201239-7) $6.50
Fleeing a bully, Nita discovers a manual on wizardry in her library. But magic
doesn't solve her problems—in fact, they've only just begun!

Deep Wizardry   (0-15-201240-0) $6.00
The novice wizards join a group of dolphins, whales, and one giant shark in an
ancient magical ritual—a ritual that must end with a bloody sacrifice.

High Wizardry   (0-15-201241-9) $6.00
Nita and Kit face their most terrifying challenge yet: Nita's bratty little sister,
Dairine—the newest wizard in the neighborhood!

A Wizard Abroad   (0-15-201207-9) $6.00
Nita's Irish vacation from magic turns out to be the opposite! Ireland is even more
steeped in wizardly dangers than the States. So much for a vacation abroad. . . .

ALAN GARNER's classic Alderley tales

The Weirdstone of Brisingamen   (0-15-201766-6) $6.00
All of Evil's minions are working to stop Colin and Susan from returning the
Weirdstone to its rightful owner, the wizard Cadellin, but the earth's fate
depends on them.

The Moon of Gomrath   (0-15-201796-8) $6.00

Colin and Susan's bonfire does more than warm the night—it calls forth the
Wild Hunt and launches a final desperate struggle between the children and the
forces of darkness.

Elidor   (0-15-201797-6) $6.00

BY ALAN GARNER

When the four Watson children stumble into Elidor, a world one step removed
from our own, they begin a frightening adventure that stretches their courage to
the limit. Yet far scarier is what happens when they return home....

Winner of the Carnegie Medal and the Guardian Award

The Owl Service   (0-15-201798-4) $6.00

BY ALAN GARNER

Something strange is going on in the tiny Welsh valley where Alison, Roger,
and Gwyn are vacationing.... The three teens find themselves reenacting an
ancient, tragic love story—a story that repeats itself every generation and
always ends in disaster.

Two fantasy classics by MOLLIE HUNTER

The Smartest Man in Ireland   (0-15-200993-0) $5.00

To prove his boast of being the smartest man in the land, Patrick Kentigern
Keenan tries to outwit the fairies. But wit is not much against an opponent who
has magic....

The Walking Stones   (0-15-200995-7) $5.00

A wise old man gives Donald the knowledge—and the power—to prevent
developers from destroying an ancient mystical circle of stones.

A Dark Horn Blowing   (0-15-201201-X) $6.00

BY DAHLOV IPCAR

Nora is stolen away one night and taken to Erland. There she must tend sickly
Prince Elver and avoid the eye of his father, the wicked Erl King, who would
have Nora for a wife.

The Forgotten Beasts of Eld   (0-15-200869-1) $6.00

BY PATRICIA A. MCKILLIP

Sybel's only family is the group of animals that live on Eld Mountain. She cares
nothing for humans until she is given a child to raise, changing her life utterly.

Tomorrow's Wizard   (0-15-201276-1) $6.00

BY PATRICIA MACLACHLAN

What's wrong with Tomorrow's apprentice? Can he not hear the High Wizard's
warnings? Or is it that the apprentice would rather be a human instead of a
wizard?

Are All the Giants Dead? (0-15-201523-X) $7.00
BY MARY NORTON
To stop Dulcibel from marrying a toad, James must get Jack-of-the-Beanstalk
and Jack-the-Giant-Killer to leave retirement and to kill the last of the giants.

EDITH PATTOU's epic Songs of Eirren

Hero's Song (0-15-201636-8) $6.00
The trail of his sister's kidnappers leads Collun to a giant white wurme whose
slime is acid to the touch, a wurme that Collun must kill if he is to rescue his
sister and save his world.

Fire Arrow (0-15-202264-3) $6.00
Archer Breo-Saight ("Fire Arrow") is hunting her father's murderers. Her
vendetta leads to a distant land where she finds the family she never had . . . and a
sorcerer's evil magic. To save the people she's grown to love, she must follow
her revenge to its bitter end.

MEREDITH ANN PIERCE's classic Darkangel Trilogy

The Darkangel (0-15-201768-2) $6.00
Aeriel must kill the wicked Darkangel before he finds his fourteenth bride—even
though within him is a spark of goodness that could redeem even *his* evil.

A Gathering of Gargoyles (0-15-201801-8) $6.00
Saving the darkangel Irrylath was only the beginning. Now Aeriel must confront
his mother, the dread White Witch—and her bloodthirsty vampyre sons. . . .

The Pearl of the Soul of the World (0-15-201800-X) $6.00
The stunning conclusion to the trilogy finds Aeriel at a dangerous juncture.
Irrylath has been captured and the Witch seems sure of victory—unless Aeriel
can solve the Riddle of Ravenna and unlock the magic of an iridescent pearl.

River Rats (0-15-201411-X) $6.00
BY CAROLINE STEVERMER
After a nuclear war, a group of teens steer a riverboat up and down the
Mississippi, playing rock and roll concerts and fleeing the adults who wrecked
the world in the first place.

Laughs and wonder from master wit VIVIAN VANDE VELDE

A Hidden Magic (0-15-201200-1) $5.00
Plain Princess Jennifer must rescue the vain—and cursed—prince from his own
stupidity, as well as a lisping dragon, a dim-witted giant, and a cast of crazies in
this witty fractured fairy tale.

A Well-Timed Enchantment   (0-15-201765-8) $6.00

Deanna drops her watch into a well and is magicked away to eighth-century France, where her watch, if it falls into the wrong hands, will change the world. She must find it first!

JANE YOLEN's classic Pit Dragon Trilogy

Dragon's Blood   (0-15-200866-7) $6.00

Jakkin's only hope for freedom is to kidnap and train a dragon of his own, a dragon that will grow into a champion in the vicious fighting pits of Austar IV.

Heart's Blood   (0-15-200865-9) $6.00

When his beloved vanishes, Jakkin and his dragon, Heart's Blood, become embroiled in a plot deadlier than any dragon pit match.

A Sending of Dragons   (0-15-200864-0) $6.00

On the run from government forces, Jakkin and Akki stumble upon a twisted sect of dragon worshipers.

The Transfigured Hart   (0-15-201195-1) $5.00

BY JANE YOLEN

Is Richard crazy? Or is there a unicorn hiding in the Five Mile Wood? And how will Richard and Heather protect the unicorn from the hunters who don't recognize its beauty?

Wizard's Hall   (0-15-202085-3) $6.00

BY JANE YOLEN

Poor Thornmallow. The only talent he has is for making messes of the simplest spells. But when Wizard's Hall is threatened by a fearsome beast, it is Thornmallow—using his one talent—who saves the school.

Ask for Magic Carpet Books at your local bookstore.

To order directly, call 1-800-543-1918.

Major credit cards accepted.